My Sister's Detective

by

T.J. Jones

This is a work of fiction. All the characters, events, and most of the places, are the product of the author's imagination.

My Sister's Detective

Chapter One

I was pushing forty that summer, a couple weeks out of San Diego when Maggie Jeffries came looking for me at the little airstrip where I kept my Piper. The last thing I should have spent my hard-earned money on when I finally gave up on the Navy was an airplane, but it was the first thing I wanted, so there you have it.

I was all sprawled out, lying on my back with my head stuck up under the co-pilot's instrument panel trying to reconnect a tiny wire with my ten thumbs when I saw motion and a shadow blocked some of my light. That little warning probably saved me some torn knuckles or a sore head, because I didn't jump when someone reached up and jabbed me in the ribs with a sharp finger.

"Bucky, is that you in there? The guy at the hangar said this was your airplane."

That narrowed it down, because nobody had called me Bucky since high school. I pulled myself out from under the dash of the plane, sat up and looked at her, squinting a little because the sun caught me squarely in the eyes. I didn't have a clue at first, but the voice was familiar and she was very attractive, not someone I was likely to forget.

She backed away from the wing as I stepped down onto the ground and stood there looking at me expectantly. She was all of five ten in her sandals, with chestnut hair and a healthy dose of freckles tossed across her cheeks like pepper on an egg. Her legs were nicely tanned, her cutoffs a little too short. I should have recognized her, she had the same striking blue eyes as her sister.

She looked at the Piper and made a face. "Does that thing actually fly or do you just like getting dirty?"

"Sound as the day it was built," I offered, slightly offended, and lying through my teeth.

"Aren't you supposed to know what you're doing when you work on an airplane? That looks like duct tape on the tail section. You're not getting me in that thing."

"Fine by me, I wasn't planning on giving rides today anyway. And who are you again? Nobody's called me Bucky in a lot of years."

"Maggie. Maggie Jeffries? For Christ's sake, Bucky, Angela Jeffries' little sister? I was only nine or ten when you were following her around the house like a starry-eyed puppy, but I thought you'd remember me. Davey was always giving me piggyback rides in the pool, remember? But then, you never did pay much attention to me."

"My mistake, sun was in my eyes." I extended a hand that was covered with grease. She scowled and I grabbed a rag, then failed miserably at being clever. "You grew up. And you did a really nice job of it."

"Yeah? Don't get too excited, Romeo. We figured you heard about Davey, but we didn't see you at the funeral, so we wondered."

"I was on a boat in the China Sea and couldn't get back. I sent flowers and called his mother."

"I thought Angie was going to die when she heard about it. She loved the shit out of that guy."

"Yeah, they were always really close. I felt like a third wheel sometimes."

"Still jealous? It wasn't like he was her boyfriend."

"No, of course not. I mean he was gay, so it's not like she was sleeping with him or anything."

"If you weren't always falling all over yourself trying to screw my sister, I would have guessed you and Davey had a thing back in the day. You would've had a better chance. It was sad the way Angie led you and those other idiots around by the nose. Funny how it worked out, all you chasing after her, and she ends up marrying a man too old to get it up. Davey was the only one she ever really loved, and he didn't want any."

"Charming, the way you talk about your sister," I said dryly.

She shrugged. "I never liked the way she jerked you around, that's all." She stepped back as I closed up the plane and threw my tools in the back of my old pickup.

I couldn't help myself, I had to ask. "How's Angie doing, is she okay now?"

"She's a mess, really bad, and Davey's been gone for a month. I know I shouldn't talk shit about her like I do, and I love my sister, it's just that she can be a real handful sometimes. Charlie was too old for her, but he knew how to handle her. She always listened to him for some reason. She's just really good at pushing people's buttons and getting what she wants. Sometimes she runs people over in the process."

"Yeah, I remember all too well. Is that why you're here? Is she pushing your buttons?"

"She wanted me to ask you to come by the house. She said maybe you were still mad at her from the last time you were home since you haven't called. She doesn't go out much since Charlie died and she didn't want to call you, too proud or something. I'm supposed to persuade you to come over. She said smile pretty and flirt. Not my style, but she claims you're a sucker for it."

I looked in her direction. "Not as easy as I used to be, but you could try a little sugar."

She did crack an honest smile at that, a very pretty one. "There, happy?"

"Better. You're what, thirty-two, thirty-three now? I haven't seen you in forever."

"Old enough to know better. Married and divorced already, so don't get any ideas. I'm not interested in making your day, Bucky, so talk to my face. Jeez! Did you spend too much time alone on that boat?"

All right, I probably was staring. "Give me a break. It's hard not to notice you don't look ten years old anymore. Were you this mean when you were a little kid? No wonder I didn't remember you, you were probably a brat."

"Thirty-two. I just turned thirty-two. I was kind of a brat, but you were a real dork back then. You had all that acne, and the orange hair."

"Red, it's always been red." She rolled her eyes and gave me another smile that I returned. "Okay," I admitted, "it was a little orange back then."

"Anyway, the Queen would appreciate your appearance for supper this evening."

"Wouldn't mind seeing her, but why now all of a sudden? I've been in town for a couple weeks."

"She's still wound up about Davey, like I said. She wants you to help her with something is all I know. She needs help that's for sure, but a shrink, not you. She's convinced Davey didn't kill himself."

"Rumor I heard was he got dumped. Boyfriend walked out and he couldn't take it. Hung himself in the old horse barn, didn't he?"

"Yeah. Sounded like suicide to me, but she says not. Should I tell her you're coming?"

"Are you going to be there? I mean, I was kind of hoping."

"Give it up!" She laughed. It was deep and real, not a flirty giggle. "I'm always there. Somebody has to keep an eye on her. I'm afraid she'll get drunk and overdose again. One of these times she's going to take enough."

"Wow, sorry. She must really be messed up. I'll come by, but I don't know what I can do. Like you said, I was just one of the guys chasing after her. We were all friends, but Davey was the one she was close to."

"I don't pretend to understand her, or the demons in her head. Just come tonight, okay? Dinner's at six-thirty sharp. My dad's out of town, like always, but Mom will be there. She likes you."

"She was always nice to me, even when I was just the cleaning lady's kid."

"Not everybody on the Point are snobs. Some, but not all."

"Alright, I'll try to be a little early, and I'll bring flowers."

"Screw the flowers, Bucky, just bring me some booze."

"The flowers aren't for you, Too Small, they're for your mother."

She blushed when she realized I'd remembered the old nickname. She gave me a little wave and walked off toward her car as I watched her go. Maggie Jeffries was every bit as pretty as her sister now that she'd grown up. It brought back a lot of memories.

***

I was eleven years old the first time I went to work with my mom. School was out for the summer and she didn't have a sitter. She cleaned house for several of the people who lived on Point Road, and after my father left, it was either trust me at home alone or drag me along. I sat in the car all day reading comic books and staring out at the lake, wishing I was in one of the big boats the idle rich always seemed to have tied to their docks. Eventually a couple of my mother's customers spotted me baking in the summer heat and insisted I do my reading inside, in the air conditioning.

David Templeton was one of my mother's customer's kids. He was a lonely boy a year younger than I was. We hit it off right away, and it wasn't long before I was spending most of my time at his house whenever my mom was working on the Point. I didn't know he was gay back then and I don't think he did either. We were just two awkward kids that nobody wanted on their team when it came time to choose sides. We swam in his pool and cooked hot dogs on their grill. Sometimes we rode bikes around town or swung on the big rope in the haymow of the old horse barn in the back of his parents' house.

We went to different schools, his was private, so I didn't see much of him during the school year, but we stayed friends and I spent a lot of time with him during the summers. By the time we were thirteen he'd collected a scar or two. He never talked about them, so I never asked. I figured somebody was picking on him, but I didn't know why.

I was never one of the popular kids either. At that age I was already almost six feet tall, hair the color of pumpkin, and a hundred and twenty pounds if I had a pocket full of change. I was so skinny it was a constant struggle to keep my pants up. I couldn't throw a ball or run the bases without falling down, so I got picked on my fair share. And it wasn't like in the movies, those funny movies where the bully ends up covered in piss and loses the pretty girl at the end. Most of the time it hurt. The bullies at my school kicked your ass just because they could, then the girls laughed at you because they wanted to seem cool. I survived it, eventually gained some weight and an attitude, and the bullies learned to leave me alone. I managed to avoid most of the real trouble in high school, but Davey didn't fare as well. He got beat up on a regular basis.

My Mom sat me down one day and gave me the talk. She asked me about Davey, and if I was gay. She said she'd love me anyway, which I guess was meant to be supportive. Truthfully, it had never occurred to me that she wouldn't. I explained to her that Davey and I were just friends, and that was all it would ever be. If I'd been completely honest with her, I could have said that I was relieved that Davey was gay, because it meant he wouldn't take Angela Jeffries away from me. By the eighth grade I was sure I was in love with the freckle-faced neighbor girl that lived across the road from Davey's house, and I encouraged him to invite her over as much as possible.

Angie Jeffries' hair was more blond than red, unlike her outspoken sister. She was thin and boney at thirteen, but rounding out nicely where it mattered. She had the deepest, darkest blue eyes I'd ever seen, and her lips were always painted a lurid shade of red that I couldn't stop looking at. My teenage mind spun continually with thoughts of soft kisses and moonlit walks. No sex, I was sure she was too pure for that kind of debauchery. I was going to save that for our marriage. It took a very long time for me to give up on that dream.

She and Davey were close even back then. When we played video games, Angie would always sit next to him, encircle his arm in hers and whisper secrets into his ear and laugh at some private joke, while I sat there fuming with half a hard-on wishing to Christ it was me. I knew she was the one that enjoyed making me suffer, not him. They were close and I didn't begrudge him that. But when we swam in her pool, it was always Davey that she climbed on top of and wrestled with, and always him she cuddled with under a towel to warm up. That was hard to take sometimes.

When we were sixteen, the three of us drove to Daytona one weekend after Christmas on a misguided quest for adventure. We happened onto a party at the beach, a mob of drunken college kids swilling down beer and smoking dope. I ended up getting separated from Angie and Davey and spent the best part of an hour searching the crowd for them. The moon was full and we'd been warned there was a dangerous rip tide, but I finally found them standing waist deep in the icy water, clinging to each other as the waves smashed over the top of them and tried to drag them back out into the Atlantic. They were screaming at the top of their lungs, shouting obscenities, and singing; both crying as if they'd never stop. I stood there yelling at them, scared, and mad as hell because they refused to come in, terrified that each new wave might be the one that swept them both out of my life forever. They relented finally, toweling dry and laughing at my rage. Too much weed was all they ever said.

Now Davey was gone and Angela was broken. I wasn't really surprised.

Chapter Two

I made it to the Jeffries in time to be a few minutes early, like I'd told the Brat. I thought about calling her that, especially if she insisted on calling me Bucky. My face had finally caught up with my front teeth, and most people in the Navy just called me Slater. Slater was the name on my uniform, and it didn't take long to get sick of Eric the Red. That was as bad as Bucky. When people asked, I just told them it was Slater. It sounded more like a pilot's name to me.

I said no to flowers and went with alcohol. A nice wine. I was pretty sure Maggie's Mom wasn't into Tequila shots or hard whiskey. I had to remind myself I was there to see Angela, not Maggie. I took it as a good sign, not thinking about Angie first. Maybe I wouldn't turn into that thirteen-year-old love-struck kid again when I saw her.

It had been two years, and three before that since I'd been to the Jeffries. I had a terrible weakness when it came to Angela Jeffries, a genuine incurable sickness if I'm being honest. I got it the first time I saw her, giggling and hiding behind Davey as she climbed out of the pool, all puffy eyed and hugging herself to keep warm while he introduced us. It only got worse as the years went by.

When we were kids, summers at her house were a revolving door of testosterone fueled teenagers all vying for her attentions. I had the inside track because of Davey, but it didn't make a lot of difference, she was an equal opportunity tease.

That didn't discourage me, or half a dozen other enthusiastic young boys from pursuing her. We circled her like moths drawn to the flame, unable to resist the heat of our adolescent desires. As far as I knew, no one ever managed to plunge into that fire, and most of the guys realized early on that it was never going to happen and gave up. But I was the persistent one, the unfortunate moth that refused to be swatted away; doomed to circle hopefully, forever enraptured for all of my existence.

Some days were glorious, full of shy smiles, hugs, and almost kisses. But my happiness, like hers, never lasted long. Her mood would turn suddenly and then I was just another one of the pests, an annoying inconvenience she had to swat away with a scathing look or crush with a sadistic comment. At that age I was too stupid and horny to give up, and I figured it was better to be crushed like a bug than to not be noticed at all.

Each time I visited her, I clung to the hope that things would be different, that I wouldn't turn into that hopeful teenager willing to be swatted away or crushed yet again. I stood at the front door, gathering my resolve. I was older now, worldly. I planned to be strong and resist my urges. Not be crushed.

Rosa, the housekeeper let me in. Everybody on the Point had a housekeeper, but there were very few butlers. You had to be obscenely wealthy to have a butler. Most of the people that lived on Point Road were rich, but not obscenely so. I think that's what got them out of bed every morning, trying their best to be obscenely so.

Rosa escorted me into the dining room and took my bottle of wine. Maggie wasn't in sight, but Angie and her mother were already sitting at the table and there were two empty spots. I sat down across from Angie and did my best not to look at her when her mother said hello.

"Thank you for having me, Mrs. Jeffries. Frank isn't around?"

"In Washington, I think, sucking up to some foreign dignitary. Then he flies back down to Lauderdale. He's working on some big deal, like always. Since Garret died, he has to run almost everything himself."

"Too bad about Gary. He was one of the big reasons I fell in love with flying. He used to take Davey and me up in his float plane when we were kids. I finally saved up and bought a plane of my own."

"It's a beauty too," Maggie said as she walked into the room. She paused and shook the tangled locks away from her face. She must have come

16

straight from the shower because her hair was damp and smelled of conditioner and strawberries. She tied it back with deft indifference and some sort of hairclip before taking her seat. "It looks like it runs on luck and rubber bands to me."

"Maggie, you always have to be such a smartass," Angie said, giggling.

I kept my eyes on the youngest Jeffries. "She all but begged me to take her up for a ride today."

"Right, Bucky, like I'd get in that contraption without a parachute."

"You know, most people call me Slater now, have for years."

"Really, Eric?" Angie laughed. "Are you trying to sound glamorous?" I had to look at her finally. She was still incredibly beautiful, if a little haunted looking. She had grown painfully thin and her eyes were surrounded by dark circles. But those eyes were still the same deep shade of blue and her lips clung to her alabaster skin like soft red rose petals waiting to be kissed. Damn! One look and I was right back there. Still that dumb kid, just begging to be stepped on.

Maggie snickered loudly. "Glamorous? Okay, Slater. You don't call me, Too Small, I won't call you, Bucky. Deal?" I reached out and took her hand, hoping it might make Angie just a little jealous.

Dinner was nice. Maggie teased me about my airplane and Mrs. Jeffries talked more than she normally did. She'd always been a very quiet woman without any apparent sense of humor, but she was pleasant enough and was always kind to me when I was a kid. Angie didn't say a lot, but she peeked at me occasionally over her crab and smiled shyly when our eyes met. I tried to concentrate on shredding the unlucky crustacean that had found its way to my plate, thinking all the while about how easily Angela could do that to me, metaphorically speaking.

Mrs. Jeffries had a glass of my wine, then she excused herself and disappeared into her bedroom. The big house had a bedroom on either end of the main floor, east for her, west for him. I'd never seen Angie's Mom go into her husband's bedroom, or him to hers. As far back as I could remember, they'd never shared a bedroom. The girls each had a room upstairs when they were kids, and it seemed like they did again. Rosa started clearing the table, refused Maggie's help, and we moved out onto the patio.

Angie made small talk for a while, and I avoided talking about Davey. Finally, she brought up the funeral, "I was hoping you would make it back, Eric. I know you two weren't as close as when you were kids, but he still talked about you all the time. Besides, I wanted to see you. It was really a hard time."

"Davey drove up here the day of my mother's funeral, but he had to turn right around and go back to Miami. That would have been a good time for the three of us to get together." It was a jab, but it had hurt when she didn't come to my mom's funeral.

"Charlie had just died a month before your mom, remember? I was a mess. I just couldn't face another funeral." Maggie snorted into her wine glass but didn't say anything. Angie cast a scathing look in her direction. "My sister never approved of my marriage, because of the age difference. But then, hers didn't work out that great either, did it, Maggie?"

"Richie and I were in love, at least for the first few years," the redhead replied.

"Charlie understood me, and marriage isn't always about sex. He knew what I have to deal with."

They stared at each other coldly and I broke in. "How about we all just get along? Angie, Maggie tells me you wanted to ask me for a favor of some kind. She said you don't believe Davey committed suicide?"

"It might be that he did, but it seems to me like there was more to it." I had made the mistake of sitting on the couch next to her. She reached out and rested a warm hand on my leg, well above my knee. She leaned forward and looked deep into my eyes, exuding that warmth, pulling me in. "I was hoping you could check it out, ask some questions and maybe talk to his parents for me?"

Maggie snorted again. "Jesus, Angela. Just give him some money or something, don't pretend like you're going to sleep with him. My God, Slater, you should know better by now."

"Stop it, Maggie!" Angie snapped. "Eric and I go back a long time. He's a good friend."

"Right, as long as you want something. You pull this with every guy that's ever taken a run at you. That's why you loved Davey, he actually cared about you without you having to pretend you might have sex with him."

I spoke up, bending the truth. "For what it's worth, Maggie, I care about your sister. As a friend. I gave up on us ever being more than that a long time ago." I stood up slowly. "Look, maybe you two should work this stuff out between you, then call me. I don't want to get in the middle of whatever this is. Besides, I can't imagine what good it would do to bother Davey's folks about it."

"No, please, don't go!" Angie reached out and held onto my hand as tears started tumbling from those beautiful eyes. She looked back and forth between Maggie and me. "Maggie, I'm sorry, I don't want to fight. Please, get him to stay."

Maggie looked at her sister sadly, then up at me. "Alright. I'm sorry, Slater. Can you stay, please? It's just stupid sister drama. Mom always liked you best, you got all the cute boys, that kind of crap. We fight all the time, and I get carried away sometimes."

Angela laughed and smiled at her warmly, so I sat back down. She wiped her eyes with a delicate finger and Maggie handed her a couple of tissues, then held onto her free hand.

"So why me?" I asked. "What makes you think I can figure out what happened? That's what the cops are for. They said it was a suicide, right?"

"Isn't that what you did in the Navy? I thought you were an investigator of some kind after you quit the SEALS?"

Maggie laughed. "You actually tried to be a SEAL?"

That hurt. "I was a SEAL, for a few years."

"Didn't you get your butt kicked every other day in school? I heard all the stories you and Davey told when you were around. But I was ten and didn't have boobs yet, so I was pretty much invisible as far as you were concerned."

It was actually kind of fun butting heads with her. "I get it now. You had a little girly crush on me, didn't you?"

"Oh yeah, I was into carrot-topped losers at that age. Alright, I'll give you some credit. You put on a few pounds and you must've hit the gym. You're not completely repulsive these days."

"Well, thanks, and your breasts came in nicely."

That shut her up long enough for her sister to talk. "Weren't you an MP or something? You told me you were an investigator of some sort the last

21

time you were home. Were you just trying to impress me?"

"I was an MA, kind of the same thing. I worked Naval Intelligence for the last few years. We handled some criminal cases, when our guys got involved in civilian crimes and vice versa. The last two years I worked with NCIS, as kind of a liaison, because the politicians didn't trust the Navy to investigate our own. As if everyone in Washington is so honest."

"So maybe you can ask around? I think somebody killed Davey, I really do," Angie said, tearing up. "Can you see what you can find out? His parents don't like me, because of Daddy I guess, but they'll talk to you. The police never even looked into it. You know sure as hell they just figured he was depressed; another queer kills himself. That's the way that crap always goes."

"Gay or not, people kill themselves, Angie. Usually, the simplest answer is the right one."

"But he wasn't depressed. I mean, he was always intense, but he never would have killed himself."

"And you would know," Maggie said quietly.

"Yeah, Eric, I don't know if you heard, but a couple of times I drank too much and took too many sleeping pills. Honestly, it was an accident. I was too drunk or too tired to remember taking them. But hanging yourself is different. Once you kick that chair over, there's no coming back. Davey didn't have that in him. If it was that bad, he would have called me."

"If it wasn't suicide, then what? Why would anybody kill him?"

"I don't know, but he said something that started me wondering the last time he was home."

"Like what?"

"He told me to go away, move. He said take Mom and Maggie, sell the house and leave. He said he didn't think it was safe here."

"And your Dad? What about him?"

"Davey didn't like Daddy much. You remember what it was like when we were kids. Daddy is old school, and you know how he can be. He pretended Davey didn't exist because he was gay. Anyway, Davey said that about us moving one night when we were both shitfaced, about a month before he died."

"Maybe you get shitfaced more than you should, Angie," I offered. Maggie nodded her agreement.

Angie glared at her sister again. "You drink as much I do."

"No, not really. A cold beer now and then is one thing. I don't use Crown to wash down sleeping pills."

Angie ignored the comment. "What do you think, Eric? Can you at least ask around a little bit? Everybody said he got dumped and that's why he did it, but he wasn't even seeing anyone. Ask his friends, nobody believed he would kill himself. If you don't find anything, I'll give it up." She choked up. "Maybe he did, maybe I missed something." She was sobbing suddenly and collapsed into my arms, shaking and rambling incoherently as Maggie looked on glumly. I sat there and held her, overwhelmed by the smell of her hair and the depth of her grief.

I left half an hour later after agreeing to see what I could find out. Beautiful as Angela Jeffries still was, I didn't feel thirteen anymore. I just felt sad.

Chapter Three

What all the locals call Point Road doesn't follow anyone's definition of a point. It roughly parallels the Saint John's River on the south end of Jacksonville. A normal city and we would have been a good distance out in the suburbs, but Jacksonville covers a lot of ground and collects a lot of taxes from the residents along that shoreline. The neighborhood that we considered the Point ran for several miles and is crowded with houses that regular people call estates. Davey and I tried to calculate the number of millionaires that inhabited that stretch of road when we were kids on our bikes. We counted over a hundred, then gave up.

The millionaires weren't all on the water. Some of the older estates were tucked back into the woods on the other side of Point Road with barns and fields that had once been full of tobacco and cotton. They had long winding driveways with Live Oak trees dripping moss that squeezed moisture from the air and stayed wet and acrid even when it hadn't rained in a week, which was hardly ever.

The Templeton's driveway was a quarter mile long, bordered by a half high rock wall on both sides that had been built with slave labor. Tough to grow tobacco or cotton in rock. First you had to dig all the rocks out, then you had to put them somewhere. Might as well build a wall. Every plantation had a wall, but nobody called them plantations anymore.

I called Edith Templeton to ask if it was alright to go over and pay my respects, since I was an asshole and had missed the funeral. I didn't put it to her quite like that, but that's how I felt. Mrs. Templeton had always been the best of the people my mother worked for, and the most cheerful. Not so now. She answered the door herself, shorter, bent, and a lot older than I remembered. Her smile was gone and she looked haggard, wrinkles and lines tracing a roadmap of despair across her face. Finding your son dangling by his neck in the barn can do that to you.

"Eric, it's so nice to see you again." She leaned into a hug, the top of her head well below my chin and kind of snuggled against me. I just stood there, awkward like, and squeezed her as hard as I dared. She finally backed away, her eyes a little wet. "David always said you were his best friend, because you didn't pay any mind to him liking boys, you know."

"He was a great guy. I didn't get to see a lot of him the last few years. He was always working or I was. I'm really, really sorry I couldn't get back here for the funeral."

"It's okay. I got your flowers and card. You being good to him when he was alive was more important than anything you could do after."

"How are you doing? And Edward?"

"He took it hard, of course. He and David had made their peace finally. Eddy has always been the macho shithead type, excuse my French, bit of a redneck I guess you could say. But they were in a good place the last few years."

"That's a great thing, right? Mr. Templeton was a lot of help when my Mom died, getting the house off the market right away. She figured she'd need the money for doctor bills, but the cancer took her really fast."

"He was glad to do it, Eric. He wasn't about to hold you to a real estate contract your mother signed. Most of his deals are commercial anyway. I was glad you decided to keep it and come back here." She pulled the refrigerator open and poured us both a glass of sweet tea.

"Where's Claire? You're not in this big old house alone, are you?" I asked.

"She has the day off, went to see her sister up on the north end. Much as Eddy's gone, I'd be a crazy person if she wasn't here. Cookies?" She put a small plate in front of me. I bit into one and she sat down across from me, watching me solemnly. Finally, she said what was on her mind. "Angela Jeffries called me this morning."

I played dumb. "Yeah? What did she have to say?"

"Sounded half-drunk. Nine-thirty in the morning is pretty early to be tipping it."

"I know she's had a hard time with Davey's passing, but I'm not sure she needs an excuse to hit the bottle, if what Maggie says is true."

"She rambled on about how she liked me and everything, and about how we shouldn't be feuding just because her Daddy and Eddy don't get along."

"Yeah?" I chewed on my cookie, trying for thoughtful. "Well, that makes sense."

"I never had a problem with her or Maggie. Maggie's a spitfire, and she has a lot more gumption than her sister. Who the hell knows about their mother? Possibly the most boring woman I've ever met."

I couldn't help snickering. "She was always nice to Davey and me when we hung around over there. Angie was here quite a bit, too, as I remember."

"Like I said, there was never any feud as far as I was concerned. Eddy and Frank had their share of trouble, but that was because of business. Angie just likes drama. It was always that way with her and David. He was as bad as she is, always making a big deal out of nothing. Maybe that's why he did it, I don't know."

"Hell of a thing. Never thought he'd...you know."

"You can say it, kill himself. Angie doesn't think he did, right? Did she send you?"

"She kind of twisted my arm, asked me to look into it."

Edith shook her head and chuckled a little, which was nice to hear. "If that girl said shit, you'd ask her how much and what color. Still crazy about her after all this time?"

"Crazy is a good word, considering. But I couldn't say no. She has the idea maybe I can find something out if it wasn't a suicide. I was an investigator in the Navy, but I doubt I can come up with anything if the cops didn't. I wanted to come anyway, just to see how you were doing."

"If I were you, I'd forget about Angie Jeffries. Maggie's the one you ought to have your eye on."

I squirmed and may have blushed a little. "Yeah, she's nice, and normal, far as I can tell. But really, is there any doubt in your mind that Davey killed himself? If this is too hard for you, I'll forget the whole thing."

"Nobody wants to think they missed the signs. But he worked in Miami, Eric. He wasn't here that often, and when he was, he seemed fine. Stressed a little, maybe. He said work was running him ragged. He was always a moody kid, but never actually depressed. Everybody has ups and downs, but as far as any signs of real depression, I don't think so. He was perfectly comfortable with his sexuality. I'm sure it wasn't about that."

I thought she might get emotional, but she held it together better than I would've in her place. One thing was bothering me. "Why the barn? Why would he do it there when he had to know you would be the one who found him? He absolutely worshipped you."

That was too much; she grabbed a napkin and wiped away some stray tears. "Thank you for saying that, Eric. We were always very close. Yeah, if there is one thing that would make me wonder if Angie's right, it's that. It sounds macabre, but he was just too considerate to do that to me. Even if something snapped, I think he would have found another place, just so he wouldn't hurt me. I really believe that."

"Did the cops find anything out of the ordinary?"

"How could they, they weren't here long enough. They didn't investigate anything, said it was obvious. And Eddy didn't help matters any, he went right along with them. He was more worried about people talking, than Davey being dead."

"I'm sorry to ask you this, but can you tell me any of the details?"

"I was the one that found him, I can tell you all the details." She took a breath. "He said he had a meeting in town and drove off. Then later on, an hour, maybe an hour and a half, he drove through the yard and back out to the barn. I didn't think much about it at first, but then it got dark and he never came back, so I walked out there. It was raining like crazy and I didn't think to grab a coat. His car was sitting there running with the lights on and I found him in one of the old horse stalls. There are those railings that hold up the big doors and there's an old table and four chairs in the tack room, for when the workers used to take their breaks. Of course, there haven't been horses for years and years, or workers, but the damn chairs were still there.

"I guess the haying rope was too stiff, because he used his belt. It must not have been long enough, because he kind of looped it over the railing, tied it together with twine-string and used the buckle as a noose. One of the old chairs was lying there on its back." Her voice broke and she dropped her face into her hands for a moment, then mopped at her eyes with a tissue.

I reached out and covered her hand with mine. "I'm so sorry, Edith, the last thing I want is to bring it all back. Would it be okay if I walk out there?"

"Do you think there's any chance that it wasn't suicide?"

"I think it's like we said, no matter how messed up he was he wouldn't have done it here where it was you that might find him. And Angie said some things that make me wonder. Let me go look. He worked in Miami, but how often did he come home?"

"Once every couple of months, sometimes a little longer. His room is just like he left it. I locked the door and I haven't been in there since. You should take a look up there too if you think it will

31

help. Maybe you could throw his stuff in some boxes for me?"

"Let me walk down to the barn, then I'll see what's in his room and box it up for you. Are you sure this is all okay, me snooping around?"

"Eric, you were one of his closest friends. He didn't keep much stuff here, but I don't know that I'll ever have the strength to dig through it, and it would be just as hard for Claire. You'd be doing me a favor."

***

The walk to the barn was slightly less than the length of the driveway. The barn was in remarkably good condition considering that it was seldom used for anything. A vintage Ford tractor and a small hay wagon sat building rust near the horse stalls. I took the time to look things over pretty carefully. There were marks on the back of the hay wagon, like someone may have climbed up on it and judged the distance to the railings. The hitch pin that held it to the tractor had fresh scratches on it, visible through the rust. Someone might have unhooked the wagon at some point and stood on it, but after a month, anyone could have made those marks. I walked around scratching my head for a while. The four chairs and table were still there, miscellaneous hand tools, and the heavy rope we had swung on as kids, too heavy to tie into a noose.

I finally had a thought and pulled my belt off. The railings that held the stall doors that Davey had supposedly used to tie his belt to were pretty high up, probably nine feet. I pulled the closest chair over from the break room and climbed up on it. It was short and wobbly.

The gangly thirteen-year-old that Davey Templeton had welcomed into his home had grown some. I was on the high side of six three now in my socks, about six inches taller than Davey had been. I double checked my measurement and subtracted a couple of inches because I was a little thick around the middle, then made a noose with my belt and looped it around my neck. I stood up and lifted the remainder of the belt up. It was two inches short of reaching the rail. I took the belt off my neck and flipped the end over the railing, trying to imagine how Davey could have secured it. Even standing on my toes, I couldn't quite reach the rail, and securing the belt with twine would have been almost impossible for someone five eight. There was an outside chance that he had used the wagon when he tied the belt to the rail, moved it back, then climbed up on the back of a chair, balanced somehow, and more or less jumped through the noose. Good way to kill yourself, even if you weren't trying. The wagon would have been high enough to get the belt around his neck, but Edith had said he had used a chair.

The chairs were old. There hadn't been horses in that barn since before Davey was born and the chairs were at least that old. They had rounded backs with spindles smaller than my little finger, several of which were missing. They didn't look strong enough to support the weight of an adult, and I couldn't imagine balancing on the back of one long enough to slip a noose around your own neck. I inspected the top of the chair backs of the three chairs still in the break room and didn't find any marks on them.

Finally, I stood on the chair I had retrieved, jumped up and grabbed the door rail, then put one foot on the rounded back. I eased some of my weight onto the chair back, a small percentage of my two hundred and forty odd pounds and it collapsed, crumbling so easily that I nearly joined the shards of spindles as they fell to the floor. Even if you had the balance of a gymnast, it would have been impossible for a person to stand on the back of one of those chairs.

All things considered, he might have managed it, but there were sure easier ways to kill yourself. It wasn't much, but it was enough to get me wondering.

***

I didn't explain my weak theory to Edith. She handed me a couple of cardboard boxes and opened Davey's room for me, then fled down the stairs without a glance. She was right, there wasn't much in there. He had a few shirts hanging in the closet, clean, and the pockets were empty. Two pairs of dress pants, same thing. I pulled the blankets off the bed, flipped the mattress over and looked under the box spring and found nothing. There was an end table and I found a few business cards lying there and an old medical alert bracelet. Davey had a rare blood type and was HIV positive, which I already knew. I dropped everything into my pocket and kept looking.

The dresser had a few socks in it and a couple more cards. I pocketed them with the others. I pulled out each drawer and checked under the bottoms. When I took the lowest drawer out, I saw the corner of something white and the carpet below, so I tipped the dresser down and lifted it to the side. There were two envelopes. The first one had five wraps of hundred-dollar bills, and the other held a small notebook with several pages of writing inside and a few more cards. I pushed the second envelope into my pocket, threw all of the clothes and laundry into one of the boxes, and tossed the money on top of it. I carried the whole works down the stairs to Edith.

"I found a few cards and stuff that I'll keep and take a closer look at." I tried to be vague, but not lie outright. "There's a couple changes of clothes and he had this money stashed. Looks like five thousand dollars, emergency cash maybe. I shut the door, but I didn't lock it."

"That's fine, Eric, I'll vacuum up in there so Claire doesn't have to. She loved him so much, it was really hard on her, too. It's time we accept the fact that he's gone."

"Yeah, me too. I have to say, things don't quite add up. If you're alright with it, I'll make some phone calls and talk to some of his other friends. It might even be worth a quick trip to Miami to talk to the people he worked with."

"You really think there's a chance that it was foul play?"

"Probably not, but a couple things don't seem right. What about his cell phone?"

"Eddy threw it away." She looked down at the table, fidgeting with her boney fingers. "He said there were pictures of men, inappropriate texts. He didn't handle it well. I should have made him give it to me or dug it out of the garbage. I wasn't thinking clearly at the time."

"Understandable. What about his laptop, or his computer at work? Davey told me he was in advertising or represented people somehow?"

"He was an agent of some sort, like a talent scout from what I could get out of him. They represented people for television and theater, commercials too, so maybe that was the advertising part. He didn't like to talk about work, said it stressed him out. I called his office and they acted very odd. They said his computer was company property and I couldn't have it. I thought I might be able to find some of his friends that way. Nobody from Miami came to the funeral, not even his roommate."

"Roommate?" I didn't need to ask the obvious question.

"Sam something. David swore they were just friends, and that's what Sam said when I called him about David hanging himself. He was upset, but not like a person in a relationship would be. I don't think they would have lied; there was no reason to lie to me. I have Sam's number, and the address of the apartment if you decide to look into it for me."

"If it would help you to get some closure, of course I'll dig into it. Are you really sure you want me to?"

"Davey's lifestyle was different from what we're used to around here, but he was my son. No matter what you find, if what happened wasn't what it looked like, I have to know that. Here, take this." She handed me the money.

"No, I can't. I'm doing it for you, and for Davey."

"I've actually been thinking about hiring a private detective. I would think having known Davey would be helpful. Investigators get paid, Eric, and if you go to Miami, that costs money. I insist."

"But Angie's the one who asked me to look into it, and I'm not a real detective."

"If you think it might have been foul play, I want to know what happened. You already know more than the cops. They didn't investigate at all, so as of now you're a real detective, my detective. Please?"

I took the money.

***

When I pulled out of the driveway and glanced to my left, I spotted a jogger coming down the side of the road, running at a pretty good pace. She looked familiar. I dropped the window down and Maggie Jeffries slowed and walked up, breathing easily.

"Didn't take you long." She half smiled, pulling on her ankle and flexing her leg.

"What do you mean?"

"Angie asked you to talk to Davey's parents, and here you are. Good boy."

It was too close to the truth. "You are a brat, like I said. Did it occur to you that maybe I'd like to know if what happened was really a suicide too?"

"How's Davey's Mom doing? Angie makes out like we have this big feud going, but it's all in her head. I talk to Edith all the time. I see her on the road sometimes when I'm running."

"You're not breathing very hard. Run the last hundred yards just to impress me?"

"Right, Slater, that's my goal." Definite sarcasm. "I was cooling down, that was three quarter speed. I go ten miles every day."

"Well, it's working, you look like you're in good shape, really nice shape." I knew that was a stupid thing to say as soon as it left my mouth.

"A lot of women consider that harassment these days, but I'm guessing that's how you dorks flirt. You should come running with me. Maybe you can lose that spare tire."

Now I was a fat dork. "Hey, be nice, I'm almost forty. It's harder to keep it off at my age."

"Start coming to my classes. I teach four hours a day at the Athletic center, I could have you whipped into shape in no time."

"You have a job?"

"Not much of one, but I don't have rent or any expenses since I'm living with the folks again. Richie bought me out of our house. I got my car and some traveling money in the divorce. Richie got a pregnant, twenty-something girlfriend, and a new life."

"Wow, too much information."

"So, what's the deal, any chance Davey didn't hang himself?"

"Unlikely, but less so than I thought. I have a few leads I'm going to check out."

"Now you're Sherlock Holmes?" She laughed lightly. "Are you going to use this as an excuse to start hanging around Angie again? Your obsession with my sister is borderline creepy."

"You really are jealous, aren't you?" I was kidding, but it brought some color to her cheeks and made her freckles pop. I laid it on. "I knew you had a little girly crush on me."

"You're a dreamer." She rested a hand on the pickup and leaned closer, suddenly serious. "But really, Eric...Slater, Angie's messed up right now, even more so than usual. She's not dealing with anything well. I wasn't kidding about her needing a shrink."

"And I was serious about just being her friend. I'll admit, sometimes I act like that lovesick kid around her, but old habits die hard."

"Just try and keep it in your pants, all right?"

"If only there was some other attractive woman around here who could help me take my mind off her." I smiled slyly. "Want to go up in the Piper this afternoon, maybe get a couple drinks after?"

She pushed away from the truck, laughing, but I could see she was thinking about it. "I'd need to have more than a couple or I'd never get in that pile of scrap metal."

"I'll consider that a maybe."

"Yeah, maybe. How about just one drink, and we can catch up. I'm free tonight. You can tell me about these big leads you have."

"Hey, I'm a real detective now, I even got a retainer." I lifted the envelope with the hundreds in it. "Not taking another dime of Edith's money, but it's enough for gas and a motel in Miami."

"What's in Miami?"

"Davey's life for the most part. Edith had me clean out his room and there are a couple things I found that look interesting. I'm going to look through it this afternoon and see if there's anything sketchy. What time should I pick you up?"

"I'll meet you. I'm working at the Athletic Center until eight. How about Bayside? I can walk over there. Say eight-thirty?"

"Okay, it's a date." I grinned and put the pickup in gear.

"Not a date, just a drink," She called out as I drove away.

Chapter Four

The house my mother left me was nothing spectacular, but it was comfortable. Hard to say how many toilets she scrubbed and beds she changed to pay the mortgage on that place after my Dad ran off with some waitress. Once I moved up in the ranks, I was able to help her and lighten the load, but years of stress and cigarettes took their toll. The cancer caught up with her at the tender age of fifty-eight, a year before I retired from the Navy. The three-bedroom rambler was tucked behind the Wal-Mart on a side street a mile and a half from the opulence of Point Road. Not a Porsche or a Maserati in sight.

The best thing about the location was the fact that it was a short drive, fifteen minutes by bicycle, from the small airport where I kept my airplane. As a kid, when I wasn't at the Point occasionally snagging rides with Angie's uncle, I spent a lot of time at the airfield. Youthful enthusiasm goes a long way with some people, or dogged persistence if that's what it takes. By the time I was fourteen I was a regular, and by sixteen I had half a dozen locals that would let me tag along when they were going up. Inevitably, they let me take the controls, and I got a lot of free flying lessons. I was hooked.

Flying jets for the Navy was a job reserved for the officers, which meant a college degree or the Naval Academy. Let's just say my grades weren't good enough and leave it at that. But most of the bases had flying clubs, and I had my pilot's license by the time I was twenty. The clubs were affordable, and some of the planes were acrobatic, which was an extra level of excitement. Planes like that were beyond my budget when I mustered out, and not very practical. The old Piper was enough airplane for now.

I'd spent most of the last month working on the house, fixing what needed fixing and making it my own. I hadn't even thought about a job, and I didn't have a clue of what I wanted to do. I always figured life has a way of opening up for you if you let it, like driving down a winding road without knowing where it goes. Sometimes it's good to just put your foot down and go without looking at a map. That was the thing about the Navy, there was always a map. The direction you went was predetermined for you. I was looking forward to not knowing what was around the next corner. For now, trying to figure out what had happened to Davey Templeton would keep me busy for a while.

Being a mile and a half from Angela Jeffries had been hard, after I came home. Those blue eyes kept popping into my head unbidden. I was too stubborn to call her, and she hadn't bothered calling me. She never did, unless she wanted something, like Maggie had said. That had always defined our relationship. More often than not I was an annoyance to her.

I'd gone to see her when I was home for my mother's funeral, which she hadn't attended. She was borderline surly, half-drunk as was her habit, and unapologetic about not making it to the funeral. I walked out of that big house angry and promised myself that I was done with her for good. But here we were again, she whistled and I came running. She hadn't even bothered to call me herself.

Sending Maggie was a typical Angie move, it saved her from any personal discomfort. Not that I minded. Angie had been right. A big smile from Maggie had been enough to entice me back into the Jeffries' household. It was something I hoped to see on a regular basis. And there was Davey. Murder seemed unlikely, but not beyond the realm of possibility.

Since I had three bedrooms, I had remodeled a little and turned the smallest one into my office. Can't say that I needed an office, but it seemed like a waste of space otherwise, and it was a place to put my newly purchased desk and computer. Not all of my career had been spent on a ship, but enough of it to really appreciate the space and solitude of my own house.

Being single meant no strings, and no reason they couldn't assign me on board when it suited them. Some of the shipboard assignments were voluntary, some not. But being deployed meant more money and looked good when it came time for promotions. That was more important when I was younger. There was a time when I thought I'd stay in and maybe do thirty, but after my mom passed away, I decided it was time to put down roots somewhere, and maybe look for someone to have a life with.

I had a month of my time left when I got the last letter from Davey. He never called and refused to text. He said he liked the time it took to write things down, the thought it took, and the fact that he could always throw a letter away if he said too much. I should have realized it was a cry for help, but I was too self-involved and interested in what he had to say about Angie to read between the lines.

The letter was in the top drawer of my desk, sandwiched between my discharge and my mother's will. I pulled it out and unfolded it slowly. His handwriting always made me smile. Each letter was perfectly formed and eloquent, like calligraphy or a page of ancient script back when writing was an art practiced by patient old men with quills. I started to read, resting my hand on the desk to stop it from shaking.

"Hey there, Sailor! Too gay? Lol. Been a long time since we talked, but you know I prefer writing things down. Miami sucks right now, hot as hell, and work is kicking my ass. I'm in over my head, and I don't know how it all ended up like this. I keep

trying to make the clients happy, but it's always about the money. Anything for a buck, right? You say that too many times and pretty soon they own your soul. Wow, I'm dramatic!

Angie says hello. I came home for the weekend and we cried on each other's shoulder the whole time and talked about a lot of things. I swear, that girl has more drama in her life than I do. Her Dad is home right now, and that always makes her crazy, that love, hate thing, I guess. I know all about father issues! Things are really hard right now, but I'm trying to make them right. I'd give anything to just be a kid again, hanging out with you and Angie, swinging on that rope in the old horse barn. Remember how you always said you wished you were rich like us? We didn't realize it at the time, but of the three of us, you were the lucky one.

Better sign off, I just wanted to drop a line to say I love you, man. We'll have a beer and catch up next time you're in town. Your friend always, David.

P.S. Angie didn't really say Hi, I just knew that's what you'd want to hear."

I realized suddenly that my eyes were wet. I wasn't generally a crier, I was too practical for that. Crying wouldn't bring the dead back to life or stop the cancer from stealing your mother away before her time. But at the moment I didn't seem able to stop myself, and I didn't try. Davey deserved a few of my tears.

He had known that I wasn't the least bit interested in guys, what with fawning over Angela non-stop, but one drunken teenage night he had tried to kiss me. I pulled away and laughed it off, and when he sobered up he was horribly embarrassed, and laughed about it too. He knew I was a one-woman man, and not about to give up on Angie Jeffries.

I hadn't shared the fact that I heard from Davey a short while before the supposed suicide with Angie or Maggie, and I didn't know if I would. Other than sounding stressed, there was nothing in the letter that indicated Davey was depressed enough to kill himself and no reason to tell Davey's mother about it either, at least not yet.

I put the letter away and laid out everything I had taken from Davey's room on my desk. There were a dozen cards and I separated the ones I found hidden under the dresser, presuming they had some special significance. The notebook was confusing, even in Davey's perfect handwriting. Letters and numbers, broken into groups of five or six at a time with headings. There were arrows pointing back and forth, and page numbers. Some of the first pages were referenced on later pages, almost like footnotes. The only thing I saw that made any sense were some of the letters, capitalized, referencing what I took to be cities. NY,

LA, CX, all fairly obvious. STL had me stumped, but it could be Seattle. There were nine headings in all, with more abbreviations following, and numbers that seemed random, three and four digits. A few of the items were circled, but there didn't seem to be any correlation between those that were numbered and those that were not. On the back page, separate from the other notes, there was a list of women's names, seven in all. A couple sounded Asian, and two were Latina, but no notations, just their names.

Four of the cards were from clubs in Miami Beach with a few notes on the back; celebrity sightings, age of the clientele, and a couple of phone numbers with names. Possible talent? There were a few of his own cards with his name and number of the outfit he worked for.

The five cards I found in the notebook weren't any more enlightening. All five were from other talent agencies, affiliates, but none that were in Miami. One was from LA, which wasn't a surprising place to have a talent agency. The other four were from points scattered across the globe: Minneapolis, Buenos Aires, Dubai, and Singapore. All huge cities, with the exception of Minneapolis, all known as affluent and progressive, given their locations in the world. I knew very little about any of them. Really, I knew very little about any exotic places. I had joined the Navy to see the world, but most of the time it was from the deck of an aircraft carrier.

Each card had a name and a contact number for that individual as well as the number of the agency. It didn't make sense to hide them, since a quick Google search identified them as all part of the same franchise. International Talent. Maybe the names were the important part, but why hide them with the notebook? I decided I would let Maggie see the lists and the cards. A fresh set of eyes might be all it took, and it was possible she knew things about Davey's business that I didn't. Edith had described her as having a lot of gumption. She had that, and a whole lot more.

***

Bayside was a private club on the water that anyone who was anyone on Point Road frequented. I wasn't sure I could even get in, much less just plop down at the bar and wait for Maggie to show up. I decided to go early and drove to the Saint John's Athletic Center. Bayside was visible from there, across a road and a couple hundred yards to the south, perched on hurricane posts out over the water. The parking lot was already full of Bentleys and Cadillacs, and I knew my ratty old pickup would stand out, maybe even get towed. I parked in the lot of the workout place, figuring we could walk over to Bayside together.

It dawned on me that I hadn't even asked what it was that Maggie taught. Yoga maybe, or Pilates? I figured every other person in Florida was into one of those, at least the ones that were still spry enough to walk. I walked in and went to the front desk. The woman sitting there looked like she belonged at the gym, tanned and muscular, not a day less than seventy years old.

"I'm meeting Maggie Jeffries here, and I'm kind of early. Can I just hang around and wait for her?"

"You can wait for me, Sweetie, I'm done at ten." She flashed me a nice smile.

I blushed and may have stuttered. "Probably couldn't keep up with you, and I don't imagine I better stand Maggie up."

"No, probably you better not." She chuckled. "Go down the hall there to the left, all the way to the back. There's a viewing area, kind of above the gym where the parents sit. There are half a dozen Moms and Dads back there. Can't miss it, all the way to the back."

I glanced at my watch, seven-forty, which meant twenty minutes of watching over-privileged children doing stretching exercises just because their parents wanted an excuse to get them out of the house. I followed the hall and went through an open door into what was more or less a small theater, elevated and separated from the gym half a story below by a large pane of glass. Quite an expense, just so the kids weren't interrupted by unruly parents. As a kid at public school, I'd seen fist fights break out between overly involved parents more than once. Of course, that was Soccer and this was Yoga. No chance of a fight here. Only it wasn't Yoga.

The kids were fourteen to seventeen, some of the boys as tall as me and in a whole lot better shape. There were probably twenty of them, girls and boys, and they were all focused on Maggie like she was the Dalai Lama dispensing ancient wisdom. It turned out she was just showing some fourteen-year-old girl how to kick her would be attacker in the nuts.

I'm not a fan of Karate. Pepper spray or a whistle always seemed like a better option if you were a woman, but I've been told that's sexist. I tend to put my foot in my mouth when it comes to that sort of thing, but I'm working on it. That said, Maggie looked pretty damn cute in her little white Karate outfit.

I watched the rest of the class, and had to admit, I was impressed. The couple sitting next to me had a daughter out on the floor wearing a white belt. A beginner, I was told. Derrick Lane was the son of an investment banker, studious looking, with a plump, pretty blond wife that was enthusiastic about Karate and Maggie in particular. She talked my ear off for a while, then started trying to pick my brain.

"Did you know that Maggie went to Japan for a year to get her last two certifications?"

"I'm an old family friend, just reconnected. Most of what I remember about Maggie, she was a ten-year old tomboy with a face full of freckles and a habit of showing up when I didn't want her to."

"I suppose you used to date Angie, and Maggie kept getting in the way?"

"Date would be an exaggeration, but I tried a lot," I said.

"That poor girl, she's been through so much." Her husband poked her and gave her a black look. She laughed, eyes wide. "Not because you tried to date her, that's not what I meant. I just heard she took the thing with David Templeton killing himself really hard." Her husband leaned over and muttered something into her ear.

"Did you know Davey?" I asked. "He was one of my best friends when I was a kid."

"No, we just hear things. Everybody on the Point loves to gossip. Were you and David really close?"

I wanted to make her ask, just for being so damn nosy. "Yes, we were close. He was a very sweet guy."

Her husband poked her with his elbow again and she went back to talking about Maggie. "Anyway, Maggie is like a third degree black-belt or something. She teaches the kids how to defend themselves if they have to, but she teaches them how to stay out of situations where they would need to, too. The Club is lucky to have her, and we are, as parents."

"Sounds like it. She looks like she really knows what she's doing." Maggie was demonstrating a takedown on a tall teenager who seemed to be enjoying himself. Sometimes gossip is based in fact, and the blond woman wanted to talk, so like an idiot, I encouraged her. "Angie isn't quite as levelheaded as her sister, I guess."

"Oh, I know. Angela was in the hospital at one point for quite a while, some sort of a breakdown."

"You mean after Davey died?"

"Then too? Not surprised. No, I was talking about a year ago, right before Maggie moved back here. That's why Maggie came back, you know, to take care of Angela. Up and left her husband and just came running back because her sister needed her."

"Wow, that's a good sister, right?" I sure as hell wasn't going to volunteer anything different.

"I'm really surprised Maggie turned out as good as she did, what with their Dad being such an asshole." She gave her husband a quick look. I suspected he had pinched her. "Well, he is an ass, from what I hear. He spends all his time down south chasing women half his age, then comes home and ignores his poor wife, and does God knows what else. I've always heard he's a philandering pig and bereft of common decency."

"Enough, Stacey!" Derrick finally said something. "You're just repeating gossip, and it's never about something good. Practice is over, we need to get going." We all stood up as the kids started filing out of the gym and he extended a hand. "It was great to meet you, Mr. Slater."

"You too, Derrick, Stacey." I tried to slip away.

"So, are you and Maggie dating now, Mr. Slater?"

I had to laugh; she had no filter. I gave her something. "Kind of like her sister, I'm trying a lot." She nodded and started to ask me another question but I turned and bolted for the lobby.

***

Maggie came out half an hour later, wearing a dress and heels, with her hair all piled on top of her head. I suddenly felt very under-dressed. I had thrown on a decent shirt and long pants instead of my usual shorts. It was as accommodating as I wanted to be for the wealthy snobs of Point Road. She bit back a smile, and I knew I'd screwed up.

"What? This is dressed up for me. Are they going to make me wear a house jacket that's been God knows where and smells like God knows who?"

"No, forget the Club. We'll take my car and run to the Players. It's a sports bar. Not as quiet, but who needs that, right?" She reached up and pulled at whatever it was that held her hair in place. Her chestnut locks tumbled free and fell halfway down her back. She tipped her head back and shook the snarls out, combing it with her fingers. I swear to Christ my heart stopped a couple of times.

The old hardbody behind the desk smiled knowingly and gave me a wink. "You two have fun, see you tomorrow, Maggie."

Maggie's car was a convertible, but it had rained so the top was up. She threw her gym bag in the back and we drove north a couple miles to the sports bar. It was a little noisy, but we found a table in the back. The waiter brought us menus and we both got a beer. He insisted on listing off all the craft beer options, but she went with what was on tap. I was liking her more by the minute.

"I'm starving, were you planning to eat?" She flipped open the menu and started looking.

"Yeah, and now I can have a burger instead of whatever it is you rich people eat at that club."

She laughed. "Stop acting underprivileged. I'm having a burger too. Rich people are no different than us, they just bitch about different things."

"Us? I was including you with the rich people."

"I'm doing okay, but just because I have a free place to live. I think my dad is hanging on by his teeth, but Angie is loaded. Charlie left her a pile when he died. So, if your plan is to date a rich girl, you should go after my sister again, because I'm not it." I sat there grinning, looking down at my menu. She arched a brow. "What? What did I say?"

"You said this was a date."

"I said if you want to date a rich girl, go somewhere else. I'm not admitting to anything." She was grinning and her face was red, which I took to be a good sign. We both studied the menu for a couple of minutes, then she started in on me. "If you're having a burger, you might want to pass on the fries."

"What are you saying? Are you implying I'm fat?"

"You aren't skinny. A private detective needs to keep in shape so you can chase after the bad guys. You need to come to my adult class, lose some weight, and learn some moves."

"I know moves. We had a lot of training when I was an MA. Granted, I could drop ten pounds, or maybe fifteen. Are you volunteering to be my personal trainer?"

"If you came to my classes, you'd slim down in a hurry. Or come running with me. No mercy though, you'd have to keep up. Probably have to be running, because this round of classes are almost over. It'll be a month before we start again."

"When you said you taught at the Club, I imagined something different."

"Careful. You're going to tell me you thought I taught Yoga or dance? Both are hard as hell by the way, so there's not much you can say that won't get you in trouble at this point."

I exaggerated a sigh. "It's difficult being a man in the twenty-first century. You can't say anything without offending somebody, and for sure nothing that might get you laid."

"Digging a deeper hole," she commented.

"I'm kidding, kind of. But really, sometimes it's hard to know what not to say. I don't have any time for guys being inappropriate, grabbing girls and stuff, but I don't think I should get in trouble for telling you, you look nice."

"Not likely I'd get mad if you told me that."

"How about, you smell really nice?"

"That's always good to hear. Nobody wants to smell bad."

"How about, I like the way you look and the way you smell, and I would like to take you back to my house and see what else I like about you."

She grinned back at me. "That's pushing it. You forgot to say please."

"Would that work?"

"Not one chance in hell, Sailor." She laughed. "Tell me about Davey. You were going to share those big leads with me."

"Not a good place for that, too noisy and dark. Davey hid some things in his room, some cash, a few business cards, and a notebook he had scribbled in. Weird notes. I couldn't really decipher them. But he went to the trouble of hiding them, so maybe they're important. I was hoping you might get something from them, but we can look at them next time I'm at your house."

"I can stop over at your place. I don't want to get Angie going about this any more than she already is."

"If you come over, I'll be a perfect gentleman. I don't need to get my ass kicked by a pretty girl. Sorry, was that sexist?" She gave me a pass on that one. "How'd you turn into Bruce Lee anyway?"

"It started as exercise, but Richie and I weren't getting along so it got to be therapy after a while. It's really self-empowering, and it helped me keep my head on straight. I got kind of obsessed though, even went to Japan for a couple months."

"Stacey, one of your student's mom. She said it was a year. She's quite a gabber."

"Yeah, I'll say. She tends to exaggerate everything she talks about, just to make it more interesting. By now everybody at Bayside figures you and I are doing it out behind the Club."

"Interesting concept, but I know what you mean. She likes to gossip. She really wanted to talk about Angie. She mentioned Angie had been in treatment or had a breakdown of some sort?"

"I came back from Japan early, to help my mom deal with her. You know she's bipolar, right? Angie, not my mom."

"I didn't, but that explains a whole bunch of things. I always thought it was just teenage hormones, because she couldn't seem to decide if she loved or hated me from one day to the next."

"She's that way with everybody. My Dad has never been diagnosed, but I swear he's the same way. That was part of why I got married so young, to get away from their craziness. Everybody thinks my mom is antisocial, but she's just made herself numb to all the crap she's had to put up with over the years. Like I said, I love my sister, but she's a handful. My Dad, he's never around, and I can't remember a time when he was. Angie talks about the trips we all took, but I don't remember any of that. Angie and Dad were always close. Me, not so much."

"Sorry. I was around a lot, but when you're a teenager you don't notice stuff."

"You were pretty busy, my sister's pussy and all."

"Wow. A person would think you're the sailor."

"Sexist again, Slater. I can cuss if I want. But you're right, I shouldn't be mean. You were a teenager, that's what teenage boys think about. For the record, I did have a bit of a girly crush on you back then." The waiter saved her from some teasing when he finally showed up to take our order.

"So, did Davey commit suicide?" She asked as we waited for our food. "What's the plan from here?"

I told her about the high railing and the broken chair. She pointed out the fact that Davey was fifty pounds lighter than me, so I had set myself up for that. "Still, there's enough to make me wonder. The hidden notes, the fact that he went to a meeting that night, the warning to Angie. Edith said he drove through the yard back to the barn, but who knows? Maybe the people who killed him were driving. It's possible he was already dead. Nobody checked for extra footprints in the barn or in the yard. The cops didn't investigate at all, nothing. Edith said it was pouring that night. She ended up wet and miserable, walking to the barn, then found her only kid hanging there dead!"

"Take it easy." Maggie reached out to cover my hand, stroking it gently with a thumb.

I realized suddenly I had raised my voice and people were staring, "I'm sorry. Davey's dying got to me more than I thought."

"I get that. He was a wonderful guy, and a big part of all our lives. We'll figure out what happened."

"We?"

"Yeah. I want to help. What's our next move?"

"Probably Miami. I'll have to go down there and talk to his roommate, go to the agency he worked at, maybe hit some of the clubs he went to."

"You walk into a gay bar alone and you're going to learn all about sexual harassment. You're like man candy. I'll have to go with you just for backup."

"You think I'm man candy?"

"Don't start! It's for the investigation, and it's Miami. Did you ever learn Spanish?"

"Are you kidding? English is hard enough. How about you?"

"Si Amigo. Hablo espanol con fluidez."

"That sounds like it could be Spanish."

"It is, trust me. My classes are done Thursday of this week. I should stop over tomorrow and look at that notebook."

"I'll text you my address."

"I know where your house is, Slater, I had a bicycle."

It took me a minute. "You mean you rode your bicycle all the way to my house? When you were ten?"

She squirmed uncomfortably in her chair and the freckles stood out again. "Yeah, girly crush, what can I say."

"You are never, ever, going to hear the end of that." The waiter came back with our food so I had to stop laughing to feed my face, but I kept giving Maggie an occasional look. She kept her face buried in her food.

Miami was going to be interesting.

Chapter Five

My crush on Angela Jeffries had not always been unrequited, or at least my desire to take her to bed hadn't been. The year I turned thirty I came back to Point Road for three weeks. I'd been saving up my leave to do some work on my mother's house. She was still healthy back then, optimistic because her little cleaning business was doing well, and she had a boyfriend.

By that time of her life, cleaning whole houses by herself was getting to be too much for my mother and she had hired a couple of younger women to help her. The younger of the two was single and attractive. Hot, is what she was, and very friendly. Her name was Juanita Perez, and she was indirectly responsible for the one and only time I had sex with Angela Jeffries.

Every Tuesday afternoon my mother and her crew cleaned the Jeffries' home. During my leave that summer, when I wasn't working on my mom's roof, I was usually at Angie's trying as always to coax a smile out of her. It rained that day, so I went to Point Road and parked on Angie's couch. For whatever reason, and her being bipolar explains a lot, she was in a really good mood that day. When my mom came with her crew to clean, Angie pulled me out onto the covered porch and sat beside me on the small couch that looked out at the pool.

Sitting there doing nothing, I felt guilty, like I was one of the rich kids and was too self-entitled to help my mother if she needed it. "Angie, I better go in and see if my mom needs any help, okay?"

She glared at me. "You just want to go hang out with the good-looking Mexican girl."

Angela Jeffries jealous? It didn't seem possible, but I took advantage. "She is pretty, isn't she? Juanita, I think that's her name, and she's really nice too."

"What, I'm not nice? I put up with you all those years when no other girls would even look at you. That was nice wasn't it?"

"Honestly, I always figured that was just because Davey and I were friends."

"Maybe I was just biding my time. Now we're grown up, and consenting adults. You actually got pretty damn good looking since school." We were sitting on the couch with our feet resting on the coffee table, kind of sprawled out. Angie suddenly rolled over on top of me and started kissing me, grinding against me and sliding a hand to my belt. Things were getting pretty heated when I heard the glass slider open and Juanita's soft voice. In her defense, the back of the couch blocked her view of what we were doing.

"Ah, Eric, your mother asked me to come get you. She needs a hand?"

Angela leapt off the couch. She would have started screaming, but I got up quickly and stood between her and Juanita, partially to prevent a scene, and partially to hide my erection. Juanita spun and fled into the house, undoubtedly sure she was about to be fired. Angie stepped back and gave me a black look. "Go home, Eric. If you play your cards right, maybe you'll get to screw the help." She ran up the stairs to her bedroom and locked the door. No amount of begging would get her to talk to me. I finally went home, embarrassed and crushed yet again by Angela's ever-changing moods.

I was working on the roof the next morning, replacing the last of hail-damaged shingles when Angie pulled up in the driveway and walked up to the house. It had rained again early, but now it was heating up, lifting a small cloud of steam around me as I moved shingles around. I looked down at her quizzically as the sun beat down on us both; the dorky redheaded teenager grown into a man, and the blond-haired love of his childhood. She looked incredible that morning, all smiles, wind-swept hair, and flashing blue eyes. She was wearing a blue skirt and a white blouse a size too small. It was open halfway down the front and she had nothing under it. Even from the roof I could see her nipples clearly and the outline of her full breasts pushing against the sheer fabric.

She smiled up at me like the previous afternoon had never happened. "I saw your mother's van pull in next door to my house about half an hour ago, so I knew you'd be here alone. Are you going to come down here and fuck me, or did I waste a trip?"

I about broke my neck getting off that roof. I knew it was because of Juanita. Angie didn't really want me, she just wanted to be sure nobody else had me. I didn't care. I had built it up in my head to be this magical moment. I wanted to make love, not just screw her. But if I'm being honest, sometimes the distinction is difficult.

It was hot and crazy, but not passionate the way I hoped for. It was sex, and as satisfying as that can be, I think we both wanted it to be something more. It wasn't. I guess I was expecting the earth to move and my life to change, but that didn't happen.

I can't say if it was me not living up to her expectations, or the fact that she knew she hadn't lived up to mine, but it turned awkward pretty quickly. I tried to hold her, planning to reassure her that the next time would be better and that we just needed time to learn each other's rhythms, but before my breathing had slowed and my heart rate settled into a normal pace she was up and pulling her skirt on. I could hear her sobs as she ran for the door, half dressed, tugging her shirt around her as she jumped into her car and sped out of the driveway.

I didn't see her again the rest of the time I was on leave. She wouldn't answer my calls, and Rosa had instructions to not let me in. Eventually she texted me and said it had been a mistake, but that she hoped we could stay friends. It reset the relationship we had always had. I was the moth again, and she was the flame.

By the time I returned to Point Road again, she had married Charlie.

***

Maggie knocked on my door the morning after our night out. I offered her a sugary donut and got a dirty look for my efforts. "Slater, you can't eat that crap and get in shape. I ran my ten miles this morning, where were you?"

"We left my pickup over at the club, remember?"

"I switched to water. You're the one who drank too much beer. It's only two miles over there, so if you jogged it, brought your truck back here, then ran over to meet me and finished the last half of my workout with me. All that poison would be out of your system by now."

"Or I'd be dead from a heart attack. I know that's your secret plan."

"I have plans for you, but not that. Seriously, if we're going to work together, you need to be able to keep up."

"Work together? Keep up? What is it we're working on?"

"Figuring out what happened to Davey, of course. I'm going to have to go to Miami with you. You really need to learn some Spanish."

"Settle down, you have way too much energy. Eat a donut and screw up your metabolism like the rest of the human race." She grabbed a donut and bit into it. Soon she had a very cute powdered sugar mustache. I handed her a napkin and motioned to the general area of the problem. "What about your job, and Angie?"

"Classes end Thursday, but what about Angie? Are you afraid she'll get jealous?"

"She couldn't care less, I'm sure. Nothing to be jealous of anyway, unless your plan includes something fun. I'm up for it, if you are."

"Down boy," she cautioned. "The state Angie is in, she might be weird about it. Still, we better fill her in, and let her know you think it's worth checking into. If she offers to pay you, take it, she has money coming out of her ass."

I raised a brow. "I really don't get you sometimes. You don't seem very compassionate where she's concerned."

She shrugged. "I love her like crazy, Slater, of course I do. But I've spent so many years watching her be like she is, so beautiful and warm one minute, then cold and mean five minutes later. It's hard, and it's hard not to get numb to it. I've tried to convince her to see a shrink, really get some therapy, and she won't do it. I got her to go years ago, when I was living in Charleston and couldn't be around to watch out for her. She went long enough to get a prescription for anti-depressants, but she ended up refusing to take them. She self-medicates with booze and sleeping pills. I don't know what to do anymore to help her, or why she's like she is sometimes."

"People like me, enablers, I think they call them."

"It's more than that, something deeper. Some basic unhappiness. But like I said, she is really good at getting people to do what she wants. I'm as guilty of it as anyone. I can't help it, she's my sister, and I do love her."

I had sense enough to keep my mouth shut for once. "So, we go to Miami, two rooms? I should book something."

"One room, two beds, Slater." She broke into a welcome smile. "No funny business either. Girly crush or not, my divorce kicked my ass. I'm off men for the foreseeable future."

"Never occurred to me," I lied. "I'll grab that notebook. There are some cards too, clubs he frequented, I think. He hid a few of them, and some were just lying around." I retrieved the small notebook and the cards from my office and put them down in front of her on the kitchen table.

"I'm no detective, Slater," she said, opening the notebook.

"Maybe not, but you might see something I haven't, and you talked to him more in the last few years."

"So, it looks like he was keeping track of some sort of shipments, right? See the lines and arrows? When each shipment reached its final destination, he circled it. Like this one, it started in Seattle, came to Miami, then went to SP. What's SP?"

"Sao Paulo? Yeah, kind of what I thought too." It wasn't, but I didn't want to admit it. "What was he moving around? Drugs?"

"Maybe. Do you think Davey would get involved with something like that? And why would drugs go to three or four locations? It's definitely a distribution network of some sort. What are the numbers? Quantities?"

"You're pretty good at this," I admitted.

"Why write this down and hide it in his childhood bedroom if it's something legit?"

"Look at the last page, just a list of seven women."

"Well, we know he wasn't dating them. Maybe they were his mules. But if he was shipping drugs, what point would there be in keeping a written record and identifying his accomplices? And what about the dates?"

"Dates? I thought those were page numbers."

"Why would he number pages when they're attached to the notebook? And they start at 09, not 01. Davey didn't move to Miami until 2008. I think it's a record of transfers for each year, two pages each, then four pages for the last two. Business was booming, whatever it was."

"Obviously." I shrugged.

"Slater, is that what you got out of it, or am I wrong?"

"Honestly, I didn't have a clue. You're as smart as you are beautiful."

She smiled shyly and looked up at me, suddenly warm and close. "Thanks, that was only slightly sexist. You think I'm beautiful?"

"Of course, really beautiful." We stared at each other like idiots, but I let the moment slip away.

She looked back down at the notebook, laughing. "But not as beautiful as Angie, right?"

As if on cue, her phone rang and I saw the caller ID, Angela. I gave her some privacy, used the bathroom, then went to the bedroom I called my office. I read a couple emails and the news until she came looking for me.

"You're invited to supper tonight. Angie wants to know what you're planning, as far as investigating this thing with Davey. She knows you talked to Edith, and she knows we went out to eat last night. I'll bet Stacey Lane was on the phone five minutes after class. Angie was in bed by the time I got home and I went running before she got up."

"Is this the way it's going to be? Are you two going to fight over me all the time?"

"You wish," she scoffed. "I have to say, there's enough of you for two women."

"Isn't that politically incorrect? You're fat shaming me, and it's hurtful." She didn't seem at all sorry. "Are you going to tell her that you're going to Miami with me? I can't see her being jealous, it isn't like she wants anything to do with me, romantically speaking."

"But she's like that, like a little kid that doesn't want a toy until somebody else has it, then it's their favorite and they can't live without it. My Dad is exactly the same way."

"I feel so used," I mocked. "But seriously, I don't know if we should tell her you're going along. What if she decides she wants to come along too. It's not a vacation or just for fun. And if someone actually did kill Davey, they might not like us poking around. There's an outside chance it could be dangerous."

"You don't care if I'm in danger, but you don't want Angela to get hurt?"

I knew better than to take that seriously, so I messed with her. "I can't protect you both, watching out for one woman will be hard enough."

"You ass!" She spotted my smirk and stopped her rant, but gave me a backhanded slap on the shoulder. "Trust me, I can take care of myself."

"No doubt. I saw you at the gym. Should we take the Piper down there?"

"It's only six hours, we can take my car. If we took your crop-duster, we would just have to rent something when we got there, if we got there."

"I'm starting to think you're scared of flying, or is it just my flying?"

She shrugged and glanced out the window, "Nice day, want to go up? Really, I love flying. I used to go with my Uncle Gary once in a while when I was little."

"Yeah, we could run out to the coast and see if there are any sharks circling the beaches. You'd be surprised how many times I've seen some big ones close to shore."

"They say there's getting to be more every year. You going to let me fly that thing?"

"Now I'm the one that's scared. We'll see."

***

The Piper fired up on the first turn and I showed Maggie how to do the preflight while it warmed up. My plane was a four-seat Arrow. A very common, hence affordable utility plane that is easy to fly. The model I'd bought included retractable landing gear to increase airspeed. It was a perfect trainer, and I had already taken more than one budding pilot up since I'd been home, paying it forward.

We flew south to avoid the congestion of Jacksonville proper and the extra traffic around the Naval base. I put the plane in a slow climb then turned east. Once we were comfortably high, I eased back on the throttle and leveled off. The coastline came up quickly and we followed it south for fifteen minutes.

"Want to take the controls for a while?" I asked.

I was surprised when she frowned and shook her head. "My Uncle Gary ended up yelling at me every time I tried."

"How old were you?"

"Twelve, maybe thirteen."

"Just try it okay? We're a mile up so you can't do anything that I can't correct before we hit the water."

She did a couple of slow turns while I explained the rudder operation and showed her how everything worked in unison. She nodded but seemed to be unsure of herself, concentrating. She started making slow sweeping turns and I let her have the controls, watching her enjoy the feel of the airplane.

After a couple of minutes, she reached out suddenly and added power, climbed into a tight turn, then rocked sharply back in the other direction and put us into a spiraling dive. She all but put the Piper on its back more than once, all while making tight, balanced turns. No skidding or slipping. Then she dove again, dropped a thousand feet, and pulled up on a heading for home, flying straight and level. I'd been had. She gave me back the controls and laughed when I glared at her.

She was still amused with herself when we climbed out of the Piper. I have to admit, I was pouting. I had really wanted to teach her to fly. She helped me with the moorings and it was clear she was familiar with the process. She didn't say anything until we got in her car and headed back to my house.

"Come on, Slater, don't be mad at me. I had to mess with you a little. My uncle did take me flying when I was thirteen, and he did yell at me. But it worked out for the best. Like I said, Dad's like Angie. He barely knew I existed until he heard about Gary letting me fly his floatplane, then he insisted that I learn to fly his Mooney. It was pretty much the only thing we ever did together. Angie was always his perfect daughter and I was just the tag along. But I got to know my Dad a little bit, because of flying. I never got my license, but I used to fly back and forth to Miami when he had to go down on business."

"Does he still have that plane? Mooneys are nice rides, not that there's anything wrong with my Piper."

"No, he sold it a few years ago. When Uncle Gary went down in his float plane, that was it. There wasn't enough of him to bury after the

74

alligators finished. I like your Piper, Slater, duct tape and all."

"Not duct tape, you do know that?" She continued kidding me until she pulled into my driveway. I sat in the car for a couple minutes, picking her brain about her dad's airplane, then reached for the door handle.

"What time should I come over tonight? Six-thirty sharp, like last time? Do I dress for dinner, or do you have a house jacket?" She laughed lightly, and turned toward me, smiling and close. I didn't move, but suddenly she leaned across and put her hand around the back of my head, pulling my face against hers as she kissed me. Her lips were full and soft and her tongue barely touched mine, hinting of better things to come. My blood boiled and I slid my hand around her neck, trying to gently deepen the kiss. It didn't last nearly long enough.

She pulled away, smiling warmly. "That was for Too Small, the little girl that always wanted to kiss you. And I'm sorry about tricking you. Maybe you can help me get my pilot's license?"

"I will help you do anything you want," I said enthusiastically. "Want to come in for a while? You can make fun of my airplane some more."

"I better not, Slater. I promised myself no men for a while because of the divorce, and then I went ahead and kissed you anyway. I have no willpower."

"Willpower is highly overrated," I said. "I break promises to myself daily. That's why I'm fat."

"And we're going to work on that. Just friends for now, okay?"

"That sounds doable, but it's undefined. How about now, any change?"

She laughed and pushed me away again. "Still too soon. I'll be sure and drop a hint when I'm ready. Dinner is at six-thirty, now get out of my car."

I climbed out and waved, grinning like an idiot. It wasn't like being that horny teenage kid again. This was much better.

Chapter Six

I had just dressed after a shower when my phone rang. Edith Templeton. She sounded upset and possibly a little drunk.

"Eric, I've been thinking about everything we talked about, about things with David. There is something I didn't tell you, something that's probably important. I just didn't want to tell you about it because it makes David look bad."

"Are you alright?"

"I'm fine. Eddy and I had a big argument. He doesn't think we should be digging into David's death. He says he killed himself because he was gay, and we just need to put it behind us. That's bullshit. He wasn't ashamed of being gay, and if he killed himself, that wasn't why. Besides, losing a child isn't something you ever put behind you, it's there every day." Her voice dropped and I heard her crying. "It's the first thing I think about in the morning, and the last thing at night."

"I'm really sorry, Edith. I'm planning to go to Miami and talk to some of the people that knew him, see if anyone might have any idea, one way or the other." I avoided saying the words. "What was it you wanted to tell me?"

"I should have said something before, but it's not easy to talk about. It's a money thing. David had some money in his bank account, quite a lot of money. He always talked like he was pinching pennies and he said he had that roommate because he couldn't afford to live alone."

"Buying or renting are both expensive in Miami, at least down where his place was. I could see him needing to split the rent."

"He had a little less than three million dollars in the bank."

"Holy crap. How could he have that kind of money? Maybe people on the Point don't think that's a lot, but to me it's a fortune. Not the kind of money you make working eight to five. Was he a really good investor?"

"I have his bank statements, several years of them. He paid enough taxes to stay out of trouble, but a lot of the deposits weren't checks, they were cash or cashier checks. And there were cash withdrawals too, twenty thousand dollars at a time. Our lawyer says it looks really shady, like it had to be drug money. He's worried the bank might have reported it as suspicious, said the IRS might come after us and want the money back. We were his only beneficiary, and of course we had Federal estate tax on it, but so far no one from the government has knocked on my door. Davey was supposed to have to worry about our estate, not the other way around."

"I'll need to see those bank statements. Honestly, it does sound like drug money to me."

"I made copies of everything, because I don't trust my husband. I was so damn mad when Eddy tossed David's cellphone, I just wanted to beat him. I should have been able to see what was on that phone, who Davey's friends were, everything. I don't care if some of it was pornographic, I'm a big girl. It was a record of his life."

"Eddy is old school, he probably thought he was protecting you."

"Eddy thinks I'm clueless about money and everything. I guess he thinks he's taking care of me, shielding me from what David might have been doing. But he was my son too, I have a right to know what was going on, even if he was dealing dope."

"Absolutely. I'll tell you anything I find out Edith, even if it isn't what you want to hear."

"I know you think you have to do this for David, but you charge me whatever it takes, Eric. I want to know what happened to my son, no matter what it costs. If Eddy can't get on board with that, he can go live in one of his listings, because he won't be living here."

***

The more I learned, the less sure I was that Davey had committed suicide. There were suddenly about three million more reasons why someone might have killed him. His dad had to be considered a suspect, much as I hated to even think it. Father issues, Davey had said in the letter. I knew Eddy Templeton could be hard to get along with at times. Angie claimed that he and her father had nearly come to blows more than once.

Eddy had always struggled with his son's sexuality, but it was a big leap to think he might kill him over it, or for any amount of money. Still, why was he so adamant that no one look into it? And destroying his cell phone was really stupid, unless of course he had reasons other than a few dirty pictures. Without a court order there was no getting to cell phone records, and since it had long since been ruled a suicide, an official investigation seemed unlikely no matter what I found. And, a conspiracy with the local police also seemed improbable. Undoubtedly just a bunch of "good ole boys" that thought they were helping out a father ashamed of his son. Davey deserved better than that.

I made it to the Jeffries' right on time, but dinner had been delayed. Frank Jeffries had flown in and would be joining us. His plane was on the ground and he was on his way. Rosa explained the situation to me and led me out to the porch.

Angela was euphoric, possibly manic, I realized, knowing what I now knew. She was dressed for dinner, wearing a lowcut gown and jewelry, her blond locks curled softly to frame her face. To say she was beautiful was an understatement. I tried to fight the impulse, but when she rushed into my arms, I was helpless.

"Eric, I am so happy! Daddy's going to be home in a little while. I haven't seen him in two months. Wow, you look so handsome, why did I ever let you get away." She was all over me, holding my hands and smiling up at me, then suddenly sliding close and pulling me into a long, painfully passionate kiss. I finally pushed her away, just a little too late.

Maggie coughed softly and walked into the room, just about the time Angie's lips left mine. That teenager in me thought having two sisters fight over me might be exciting. Maggie didn't find it amusing, at all.

"Well, Slater, there you are again. Nice, Angela."

"Oh, Maggie, don't be silly, I'm not going to steal your new boyfriend."

"Don't worry, he's still all yours as far as I'm concerned."

I stepped away from Angela as fast as I could, but she continued clinging to my hand and smiling at me like I was her date to the prom and about to take her virginity. It didn't help that I was five shades of red and mumbling instead of talking. I finally got a sentence out, "I thought we were going to talk about Davey."

"See Maggie? He can't wait to take you to Miami. She told me you two are going away together. You'll have an adventure! Are you going to bang her, Eric? Slater, I forgot, I'm supposed to call you Slater now. That does sound a lot sexier.

81

Let's be honest, Slater, my sister needs a really good screwing. She's much too serious." Angie was grinning and rocking from one foot to the other. I was amazed I hadn't seen it before, the bipolar thing. Maybe Maggie would understand and give me a pass.

Instead, she gave me another dark look. "Don't worry Angie, Slater still has a thing for you. I wouldn't dream of getting between you two."

"Davey, let's talk about Davey." I stared at Maggie, hoping for some understanding, but she avoided eye contact. Angela pulled me over to the small couch and sat down next to me. Maggie sat in the small recliner across the table from us. I decided to ignore the drama and try to act professional, as if I were a real detective.

"I am beginning to think that there is a possibility that Davey didn't kill himself, Angie. Did Maggie explain the notebook to you?"

"A little, but I'm going to leave it up to you." She pulled an envelope from her handbag and handed it to me. "Ten thousand to get you started. When you need more, just say so."

"Angie, no. Edith already gave me some money."

"I don't care, you'll need it. You may be down there for a while. Hire anyone you need to and bribe whoever you see fit, just find out who killed Davey! I loved him so much." She teared up and leaned into me suddenly with her head against my shoulder, making a small whimpering sound. Then, just as suddenly, she leapt up and bolted from the room, crying and wailing loudly as she ran up the open stairs.

I sat there shocked, looking across the table at Maggie. I finally asked what I thought was the obvious question. "Is she going to be alright? She won't hurt herself, will she?"

"No, not when she's like this. She gets so wound up she can't control her emotions. She'll crash, sooner or later. You should spend some time with her then, maybe you'd get over your obsession."

"She kissed me, Maggie. It was nothing."

"Yeah? You should have seen the way you were looking at her before you knew I was in the room. It didn't look like nothing to me."

"I like you a lot, you know that. The thing with Angie, that was a long time ago."

"I'm not interested right now, I told you that," she replied coldly.

"Alright, can we at least be civil to each other?"

"I have to smile for you again? I'll smile when I damn well feel like it."

"I hope you feel like it pretty soon," I tried. She did stop glaring, so that was nice.

***

83

Frank Jeffries was a big man, tall as me and a lot heavier. Maggie had made it sound like he was having financial trouble, but he didn't act like a man having any trouble at all. He was as confident as he had always been and by confident I mean arrogant.

I could remember him being mad at us as kids, chasing Davey and I and whatever other unlucky suitors Angela had that day out of the pool and off the premises. He had an ugly temper at times. There were occasions when he seemed friendly, but they were rare. I hadn't seen him in a dozen years, and now he acted surprised that I was there.

We all sat down at the table and waited for Angela to come down from her room. Frank sat at the end of the table opposite his wife, then looked over at me.

"Eric, right? Sorry to hear about your mother. She was a good woman."

"Thank you, I sure liked her."

"Well, of course you did." He sounded angry, like he thought I was being glib. He looked at me coldly, then turned his head toward the stairs and bellowed at his daughter. "Angela, get your ass down here."

"She's upset again, about David," his wife said. "She's wound up tonight, Dear, so go easy on her."

"You still in the Navy?" He didn't acknowledge Mrs. Jeffries, but turned his attention back to me. "You must have close to twenty in by now, right?"

"Just hung it up. Twenty years and a couple days seemed like enough."

"What are you going to do now? You're still young enough to start something new."

"Not real sure. I've been fixing up the house my mom left me. I was thinking about maybe buying another one, fix it up and sell it. Keep flipping them." Honestly, the idea came to me mid-sentence, but it sounded pretty good. For some reason a small part of me wanted his approval, and it was something to say.

"There's money in that. Maybe hire some help and really go after it. I could line you up with some financing for something like that."

"It's a thought, that's for sure." Something to say again. I was sure dealing with Frank Jeffries meant a lot of strings, and I wasn't really interested.

"Eric has an airplane, Daddy," Angela said as she walked in and settled into a chair.

"Yeah? What kind?" he asked, suddenly interested.

"It's a Piper, an Arrow. Landing gear and the constant speed prop, but nothing fancy."

"Yeah, nothing special about those. Is it the turbo?"

I was a little deflated and had to admit it wasn't.

Maggie came to my defense. "I went up with him and flew it a little. I've never been in a Piper before. It isn't as fast as the Mooney, but it has plenty of zip, and it's more stable. Not squirrely at all."

"Yeah? You're an expert pilot now?" He glanced in her direction.

"Nice to see you too, Dad." Maggie got up and walked into the kitchen to help Rosa. Angela was seated next to her father. She had returned to her previous giddiness.

"Daddy, how are things going down south? Mom said you went to Washington again. Do you have another big money deal going? Are you still working with Uncle Gary? The last time we talked, you said you were."

"Angela, what is wrong with you? Gary's been dead for four years. You're babbling. Stop it!" he snapped suddenly. "You really need to take your medication. Jesus, Maggie, aren't you helping her at all?"

"Daddy, don't be mad, please." Angela teared up. She glanced at me apologetically, then put an elegant hand on her father's forearm. "I hate the medicine, it makes me feel numb all over. It isn't Maggie's fault."

He drew a deep breath, like life and having a bipolar daughter was slowly killing him. At that moment, I would have volunteered to help.

"What kind of financing do you think I could get?" I tried to steer the conversation away from Angie as Maggie returned with Rosa and the food.

"What kind of rate do they offer for short term construction?"

"Daddy!" Angela interrupted suddenly, still brimming with energy. "Did you know Eric was an investigator in the Navy? He and Maggie are going down to Miami to see if they can find out what happened to Davey."

"Jesus Christ!" he erupted. "David Templeton killed himself, Angie, what is there to find out?"

I wasn't sure if the question was for me or his daughter, but I wanted to give him the answer most likely to get us through the rest of supper peacefully. "I'm just going down to tie up some loose ends for Edith. Probably talk to his roommate and maybe go by where he worked. Very likely, it's just a case of suicide."

"And why are you involved?" He had turned to Maggie.

"Slater doesn't speak Spanish, plus it'll be nice to get out of here for a couple days."

"I just know Davey didn't kill himself, I just know it," Angie said to no one in particular.

Frank was quiet for a moment, then he looked coldly at his younger daughter. "You're not going, Miami is a dangerous place."

Maggie didn't raise her voice but looked him in the eye. "Pretty sure I am going, Dad. I'm thirty-two years old, I'll do whatever I want."

"Bullshit! You're living under my roof. You'll do what I tell you to do."

I really didn't want to be in the middle of a domestic, but another part of me wanted to punch the old prick. I took a deep breath and put in my two cents. "I've spent some time in Miami, Mr. Jeffries. I'll watch out for her." Every time I opened my mouth, I put my foot in it.

Maggie glared, again. "You're not helping, Slater. I'm a big girl and I don't need watching out for. I will go where I want and when I want, with or without either of your permission or help."

Frank Jeffries was incensed. "I said you can't go, and that's the end of it! Rita, talk some sense into your daughter. Angie, Davey hung himself because he was screwed up. I don't know if he couldn't handle being queer or what it was about, but he's dead and that's that. Eric, you are not going to drag my daughter off to Miami, is that clear?"

"No disrespect, Sir, but I'm going down there, and if Maggie wants to ride along, she's welcome to come with me."

Surprisingly, he didn't throw me out of the house this time, but it was a quiet, tense supper. I was pretty sure there was no chance in hell that he planned to help me line up financing to start buying spec houses. The more I thought about it, the more I liked the idea, but I sure didn't want Frank Jeffries as a partner. I stayed for dessert, then Maggie walked me out.

"Wow, sorry about all that," she said, standing by my car. "He gets like that sometimes. He hates it when Angie is all worked up, it sets him off."

"Are you still planning on going to Miami with me? Maybe it's not worth the hassle."

"And let him win after that scene? No damn way. He can throw me out for all I care. I'll come sleep on your couch."

"If I'd thought that was on the table, I would have tried harder to piss him off. My couch is lumpy, but my bed is very comfortable."

"You're still on my shit-list, Slater." She laughed. "I catch you making out with my sister and I'm supposed to come jump in bed with you? Not one chance in hell."

"That's fair, I guess. Want to go down Thursday night after your last class, or Friday morning?"

"I'll let you decide. How long will we be gone? I hate leaving Angela for more than a couple days. Mom can't watch her all the time, and my dad is worse than useless. He riles her up more than anybody."

"We need to get there early enough on Friday to talk to the people he worked with, then maybe go see his roommate. I'm going to do some looking online and see what some of those clubs are about."

"I can imagine what they're about. See you tomorrow, Slater."

***

Judging by their websites, the clubs whose cards Davey had weren't what Maggie or I would have expected. They were mostly upscale dance clubs in high end neighborhoods, catering to the young, rich, and straight crowd. One of the cards on his nightstand had been from a club that targeted gay men, but that was the only one. Maybe the individual contacts were the important thing. Maybe I would have to talk to them.

It was nearly midnight when my phone rang. I didn't recognize the number, but it was the right area code, so I answered it. I could barely hear the caller.

"Eric? Are you there?" It was Rita Jefferies.

"Yeah, I'm here, Rita. Sorry about making Frank mad tonight. It sure wasn't my intention."

"It doesn't matter. He's always mad."

I waited, but she didn't continue. "It's almost midnight, Rita, what can I do for you?"

"I have to ask you," she rasped, then paused so long I thought one of our phones had dropped the call. "I have to ask you to drop this thing with Davey. I know you're going to go to Miami and ask around, but I hope that after that, you can let it go."

"Why would I do that, and why would you want me to? You always liked Davey. Don't you want to know what happened to him?"

"Of course, if that's all there was to it. I can't explain. I'm looking out for my family, Eric. That's all it is. I think the poor kid just killed himself."

"I'm sorry, Rita, but Davey was like my brother when I was a kid, and his mother is broken-hearted. If Davey didn't really hang himself, if someone murdered him, I have to find that out if I can. If not for Edith, then for me. And for Angela. Maybe knowing that will help her."

"But he's gone. What good will it do?"

"Knowing the truth is always important, Rita, and Davey deserves that."

"Alright, I was afraid I was wasting my breath." There was anger in her tone. "Can I at least ask you to not mention this phone call to either of the girls?"

"I won't. It would help to know why you thought it necessary to call me in the first place."

"I can't explain." That was it, she ended the call without the benefit of a goodbye.

I stayed awake for an hour, staring at the dimly lit ceiling in my bedroom. There was a whole lot more to the story of Davey's death than a belt and the horse barn, and the Jeffries were smack in the middle of it. Considering how I'd left things with Frank, I really didn't want to go back to the Jeffries' anytime soon, but I needed to talk to Angela. I was sure she knew a lot more than she was saying.

Chapter Seven

Maggie Jeffries loped out of her driveway at seven o'clock in the morning and turned east. She barely cracked a smile when I fell in beside her, just picked up the pace a little. It was already warm and sticky, and I was out of shape. I made it about two miles, then all but collapsed on the side of the road. Maggie walked back to me, looking pretty smug.

"Too fast, Slater? I can slow down for you, or pick you up on the way back if you'd rather."

"I can make it," I panted. "Maybe just a little slower. It's my first time out, so you can't expect me to run full bore right away."

"That wasn't full out. You can set the pace, but I want to see you sweating. The idea is to get exercise, not just go for a nature walk." She reached a hand out and pulled me to my feet. I started trudging toward the rising sun, worked out the kinks, and managed to keep up with the pretty redhead when she took over the lead. We must have reached the five-mile mark, because she stopped for a minute and started stretching. She eyed me as I sat down again. I moaned and stood up.

"You're going to get cramps if you don't keep moving around. Did you really want some exercise, or is there an ulterior motive behind this sudden interest in running."

"A little bit of both. I've got to get serious about getting in shape. You watch, in two months I'll be back to my fighting weight." We started back down the road, jogging at a comfortable pace for talking.

She glanced over at me. "Ever been in a real fight, other than when the jocks used to pick on you in school?"

"Lots, unfortunately. Some of it was sanctioned boxing in the Navy, some of it was busting heads when drunken sailors didn't come along peacefully."

"Okay, so I shamed you into getting into shape. What else is going on."

"I need to know what Angie knows about Davey. There are things she's not telling us, or has she been talking to you?"

"She never talks to me, just at me. She had Davey growing up, and I was too little to ever really connect with her. She's a mess right now, Slater, and Dad being home only makes it worse. Hard to say how she'll wake up. She does have stretches when she is okay, not the crazy highs and lows. But my dad will have a fit if he finds out you're pumping her for information."

"I got a letter from Davey about a month before he died. He said he was up here and that he and Angie cried on each other's shoulders. It sounded like it might have been important to him, and he might have shared some secrets with her."

"They always had secrets, as far back as I can remember."

"Yeah, I remember that too. But maybe he told her something that would help us now."

"What you're saying is, can I bring her to your house?"

"That might be better." Frank wasn't the only Jeffries I was worried about eavesdropping. "She might be able to tell us things that would be useful when we go to Miami."

"Okay, I'll try. If she crashes, she'll lock herself in her room and there'll be no getting her out of the house. She barely goes anywhere as it is."

"Your Dad made it pretty clear he doesn't want me around, so if you can get her to come over, that would be better."

"Sure you want me to come along?" She glanced over with just a trace of a smile framing her freckles.

I wasn't sure she was kidding, so I did. "You really need to stop crushing on me." She laughed and started running faster. She was a quarter mile ahead of me when she waved and trotted off down her driveway.

***

I went back to my house and started planning the finer points of our trip to Miami. Davey's apartment was on Collins in South Beach, so it wasn't surprising that he needed a roommate. If you wanted to be right in the middle of the action in Miami Beach, that was the place to be. Spring break, miles of white beaches, nightlife, prostitution, drugs; whatever your preference, you could find it on South Beach if you had enough cash. Like Davey said, it was all about the money.

I never did make it to the beach for spring break. My spring break was spent at the Great Lakes Recruit Training Center, compliments of the US Navy. Not a bikini in sight. Maggie talked like she had spent plenty of time in Miami, so I was hoping she could play tour guide to some degree. If what I'd heard from friends over the years was true, Frank was right, it could be a dangerous place. But that was true of any big city. Miami was no worse than most.

Finding a place to stay had been easier than I expected. It was still hot as hell in Miami, and the kids were back in school, so hotel rooms were plentiful. Still, I didn't want to blow Edith's money on a fancy hotel when the Holiday Inn in Miami proper would do. I'd decided to use the five grand she gave me first, then move on to Angie's money if it was necessary. I had no idea what I should be charging for my time, not to mention what my new sidekick would want to be paid for her time and the use of her car. Neither of us was busy, and the main thing was to find out what happened to

Davey. It was something we could talk about on the drive down there.

I googled the hotel and Davey's apartment building, then took a look at the location of Davey's office. It wasn't what I expected. Kind of a seedy looking two story with a pawn shop on the main floor. Most of the clubs I had cards for were in Miami Beach. I found some videos of each on You-tube, all filled with over-indulging, scantily clad young men and women having the time of their lives. Talking to someone who might have known Davey, or what he was up to would be difficult in that setting.

I was deep in thought when someone rapped on my front door. I looked at my phone, thinking I might have missed a text from Maggie, then walked to the door. Probably a Jehovah's Witness or someone getting a jump on the election.

The man standing at my front door was wearing a tan suit and a comically small straw Fedora with a black band. He swept it from his head and tucked it under an arm, revealing half a head of hair that was plastered straight back onto his scalp. He carried a small, soft-sided briefcase under his arm and looked every bit like one of those televangelists you see on cable at three o'clock in the morning, warning about the second coming and advising you to send him money. Since he wasn't carrying a bible, I decided to risk it.

"Can I help you?" I pulled the interior door open but didn't unlatch the screen.

"Mr. Slater? I'm hoping I can help you. I'd like to sit down with you and discuss a business opportunity, a very good business opportunity."

I was glad I hadn't let him in, guys like that are hard to get rid of once they make it past the front door. I shook my head vigorously. "Not buying anything today, but thanks." I started to push the door shut.

"But, Frank Jeffries sent me!"

I opened the door halfway again. "And why is that?"

"Might I come in and talk? He called me first thing this morning, and he was very persistent. When Frank calls me with an idea, I listen."

Intrigued, I unlatched the screen door. "Alright, I'm not sure if I want what your selling, but you can sit down and have a cup of coffee."

"Black would be fine." He dropped his hat on the kitchen table and extended a hand. "James Kennedy, in charge of building acquisitions and land consultation. Our group has done a lot of work with Frank, and he has a reputation for making good things happen."

"I'll bet. Good things?" If he caught the sarcasm, he ignored it. I poured him the last of my morning coffee and sat down across from him.

He looked down at the cup and blew at it, but never picked it up. "I took the liberty of looking at the outside of your place. Very nice, very nice. New stucco?" He jumped up suddenly and walked stiff-legged over to the kitchen sink and ran his hand around the edge of it, then put his head down next to the dark granite and slid his fingertips across the surface, apparently looking for ripples.

"So smooth." He closed his eyes and smiled, still stroking the granite. It was a little creepy. "Did you install the new kitchen cabinets, and the granite? Granite really adds to the value of a home. Nice touch, very nice touch." He scurried back to the table, opened his briefcase and started throwing things out on the table, spreading out some pictures and what could have been contracts. He kept rocking back and forth and talking to himself as I reached out and pulled his coffee out of harm's way.

"Thanks. Now what is this about?"

"Property in this area has rebounded nicely after the recession and now's the time to get into the market. This is a really great deal for you. I have several properties I know you'll find interesting."

"Like I said, what are you talking about? I am perfectly happy living right here, and I have no intention of selling. If you're looking for a listing, I'm not your guy."

"Oh, no, that's not it. I only meant that you seem very good at what you do."

"What I do?"

"Yes, remodeling, of course. Mr. Jeffries insisted that I come here today and show you a few of the houses we want you to work on. We want you to start right away. Right away. Our company, along with Mr. Jeffries, owns dozens of lower-end homes in the area, all snapped up during the recession and still in need of repair. We have the option of hiring an established contractor, but if you were co-owner, you could make the repairs yourself and avoid a lot of the expense."

"I'm sure you've heard the expression that if something sounds too good to be true it usually is, right, Mr. Kennedy? This sounds like one of those times."

He bounced his head quickly, doing an excellent impression of a balding, middle aged bobblehead. "I understand what you're saying, but the timing is really fortunate, and Frank Jeffries' optimism about the project is a huge bonus."

"His optimism? How about his money? Is that part of the deal?"

"No, not directly." Kennedy struggled a little, trying to frame it right and catch his breath. "But we work with him a lot, and he is a valued client. When he suggests a project, we pay attention. He has the Midas touch. You're very lucky, it's really a good deal."

"So, I'd be part owner?"

"Absolutely. Our company would sell you each house on contract, with no money down. After you complete the remodel, we would handle the sale, recoup the price of the house and split the profits with you. And of course, pay you for labor and whatever improvements you saw fit to make."

"Once again, sounds too good. What's the catch?"

"No catch whatsoever. We move these older homes without any overhead, you make a nice profit on each one, plus your labor. You can't lose. Really a great deal."

"Yeah, it's a great deal, you said that. What does Frank get out of this?"

"A few of the older homes are his, so he would benefit as well. That's what we do for him, property management."

"How about you leave me one of your proposals. I'll look it over, maybe have my lawyer take a look at it. I'm tied up for a while, but maybe the first of November or so, I could get going on a project."

"Oh, yikes. Yikes! That could be a problem. Yeah, that's going to be a problem." He bobbled his head again. It was beginning to make sense to me, but I had to hear it. Kennedy shook his head and looked upset, then took another breath and made a visible effort to talk slower, like I might have missed what a wonderful opportunity he was offering me.

"That's what I was saying, about the fortunate timing. Our company has given me until the end of this month to get things moving on these properties or they're going to liquidate for whatever they can get out of them. If I don't show some progress on at least a couple of these houses, a signed contract, and the start of some work, I don't think I can convince them to hold onto them."

There it was, Frank Jeffries pulling strings and throwing his weight around. His way to keep me out of the way, maybe even a subtle bribe. If I was pounding nails and hanging sheetrock, I wouldn't have time to play detective and drag his daughter off to Miami.

"Sorry, Mr. Kennedy, but I have other obligations. If the deal is still available in a couple months, we'll talk."

"This could turn into a very lucrative business for you, Mr. Slater. My company has a lot of contacts around here, we could get you a lot of work."

"I'd appreciate that, but that can happen in November just as well as now."

"But all these houses, they'll probably be gone. Think about it, please. It's too good a deal to pass up."

He was entirely too desperate. His company would turn a profit either way, if in fact there was such a company, not just Frank Jeffries trying to run my life. I had tried to be cordial. "Leave me your card and I'll think about it, best I can do." I stood up, grabbed his coffee cup and emptied it in the sink.

"It's a really good deal," he mumbled again as he stuffed his papers back in his briefcase and tried to coax the Fedora into place on his head. "I really think you should reconsider. I'm afraid you may regret this." I let him out and had shut the door before it dawned on me that what he said could have been considered a threat. Lucky for James Kennedy it hadn't occurred to me sooner.

***

Angela Jeffries knocked on my door just after lunch. She was wearing dark sunglasses with yellow rims, a floppy white hat, and a pair of shorts the color of lemons. Her paisley shirt hung open revealing a yellow bikini top and the three strands of pearls that were nestled comfortably between her ample breasts. Maggie stood behind her, looking slightly less like a sixties' movie star, but every bit as beautiful as her sister. I stood aside and let them come in, giving Maggie the slightest wink.

"You two look lovely today. Thanks for coming over, Angela."

"I love the new countertop. I haven't been in here for years." She pulled her sunglasses off and bit her lip, looking petulant. "Sorry about that time, Slater."

"Water under an old bridge. Hey, you called me Slater. Thank you."

"Eric Slater, Private Eye!" She mocked as she framed an invisible movie screen with her hands. "I'll play the helpless damsel in distress, and Maggie can be your trusty, if slightly inept sidekick. Coming to theaters near you!"

Maggie had to get in the act. "Wrong. I'm the lead. Slater's the bumbling gumshoe that I am continually saving. The Chubby Gumshoe. Now that's a movie I'd go to."

"My whole body hurts from trying to keep up with you this morning, so be nice. But thanks, Angela, I don't think your dad would be happy if he knew you were here."

"No, so we just won't tell him," she said with a grin. "What do you have planned as far as the trip to South Beach?"

"I've never been there, so I'm hoping you two can help me. We're staying in Miami and I thought we could take a cab over to Davey's office first thing Friday morning. Then we can go to Miami Beach and talk to his roommate and hoof it from there. The apartment is just a block off Collins on the opposite side of Ocean Drive. Two of the clubs he had cards for are walking distance from there. I'm not sure how to play it, just wander in and start asking the bartenders if anyone knows him, or sit down with some management before they open. If he was dealing drugs, maybe they were selling for him." I stopped talking, but not soon enough.

"Why in the world would you think he was selling drugs?" Angie asked quickly.

I didn't want to give too much away, but I suspected she might already know about the money. "I guess he had a lot of cash, coming and going. Did he ever say anything to you, about having a lot of money?"

"He told me once that he helped people, like a charity or something. That's why he was always broke."

"Nothing else? I got a letter from him and he said the last time he was home you two had a heart to heart."

"Yeah, kind of," she said cautiously. "Mostly it was just about me, being dramatic."

"Not you?" For whatever reason, Maggie had to get into it. Angela took the ribbing well, which surprised me.

"I was all wound up, like I get when I have my mood swings, and I was mad at Daddy. Davey always said we cried on each other's shoulders, but mostly it was just me crying on his. He did say that things were really bad at work because some big boss had been in town with a client from overseas, and things didn't go like they were supposed to. It was kind of weird."

"Weird how?"

"It seemed like he took it very personally, he was close to crying." She pursed her lips, like she was thinking. I caught myself staring at those pearls, and looked away quickly. Angela continued. "I think maybe he liked the guy or had some kind of a relationship with him. He didn't say it exactly, but I just got that feeling, that the man was really important to him."

"Slater knows all about being obsessed with someone," Maggie said dryly.

Angie glanced between us and I deflected. "Yeah, I used to have this little girl that was always riding past my house on her bicycle. Too Small, somebody."

Angela laughed loudly. "God, I can't believe you used to do that, Maggie. Mom actually had to take her bike away to keep her at home."

Maggie turned several shades of scarlet. "Enough about me when I was ten. Slater, I take it you want to go down Thursday night? Did you plan to walk?"

"They make bicycles for two people." Angela giggled, refusing to give it up.

"Alright, let's give Maggie a break. Anything else about Davey? I thought this agency was just local at first, but it seems more like a franchise. Did he say where this big boss was from, or where the important client might have been located?"

"Dubai. I remember that because I was impressed that he had a client that far away. He said the guy was really mad and making all kinds of threats."

"Dubai, huh?" Maggie put in. "Pretty big reach for a talent agency."

"Good question to ask the people he worked with, if they'll talk to us."

They stayed for another hour, and it was nice. They were acting like sisters, sisters that cared about each other; laughing and joking and taking turns picking on me. We talked about Davey some and about Miami, then they got in Maggie's convertible and went home.

I'll admit, I was a little obsessed. Sisters will do that to you.

Chapter Eight

If there is one thing that defines the quintessential American dream for me, it's driving down the Florida coast in a convertible with the top down, the sun shining, and a beautiful woman beside you. In my teenage fantasies, I was driving, and the woman was Maggie Jeffries' sister. But this was pretty damn close. It was about as perfect as an aging ex-sailor turned private investigator could hope for.

The funny thing was that I was beginning to think of myself as a detective. Not the Chubby Gumshoe a certain redhead had started calling me, more a worn but still serviceable version of the guys on television that always cracked the case without ever firing a shot. I even had the sometimes comical, good looking side kick. The fact that I had yet to solve anything at all didn't fit into the fantasy, but I was working on it, and the sidekick.

"What are you staring at, Slater? Do I have something on my face?" Maggie moved the mirror and peered at her own reflection.

"Your face is about as perfect as it can get," I said.

"Have you been drinking, or are you trying to soften me up for the motel tonight? I told you, no fooling around. I'm only here because I know you need help with your Spanish."

"Not just my Spanish. You're good at this detective stuff. You figured out Davey's little map thing like it was nothing. I'd have got it, I was close." She knew that was a lie. "Besides, I need more than just your mind. Some of these clubs are hard to get into. Looking like you do, we'll both be able to walk right in."

"I'm leaving you at the door, just to get even for the whole bicycle thing."

"You do realize I'm not obsessed with Angela? I'm over that."

She looked over at me. "I saw you staring at her when we were at your house."

"I stare at you all the time too. It's a guy thing. We're biologically programmed to look. If a guy doesn't look at you or Angie, he's gay, I guarantee it."

"You really are a sexist ass, you know that?"

"Biology, like I said." We drove along in silence for a while, then I said what was on my mind. "I hope what Davey was doing...I hope it wasn't something too awful."

"Nothing good about dealing drugs, Slater. How much money did Davey have hidden away? You said a lot, but you weren't specific."

"Three million dollars, give or take a few bucks."

"Wow, that is a lot, even for a drug dealer."

"Yeah, he must have been really good at it, or he was holding all that money for his boss. Maybe he was keeping it for the big boss that Angie talked about."

"If that was the case, it would kind of eliminate whoever that is as a suspect, right? Didn't you say Davey's parents were the only ones with access to that account? Hard to get your money back from Eddy and Edith."

"Unless Eddy was in on it."

"No way, Slater. Nobody is going to kill their own kid, not even for that kind of money."

"Maybe it was an accident, or maybe this boss of Davey's flipped out. It's just a theory, I have a lot of them."

"Maybe Davey got that money legitimately."

"Edith said he wouldn't take a dime from Eddy or her when he moved out. That was back when Eddy was still being a dick about Davey being gay."

"But Edith told me they were alright the last few years."

"She didn't tell me about the money at first. She said it was because it made Davey look like a drug dealer, but I wonder if she thinks maybe Eddy is involved somehow, too."

"I don't know about you, but I'm starting to think Davey didn't kill himself."

"Yeah, I know what you mean. Same time, it would have to have been someone who knew that old barn was out back of the house."

"True, probably not a random drug dealer from Dubai," she mused.

"Somebody he knew, because he told his mother about the meeting. Unfortunately, it was most likely somebody from the Point."

"Where are we headed first?"

"I think we should go to his old office, maybe just walk in cold. If we call ahead, they'll have a chance to think about it and give us a canned answer. It isn't likely they're going to tell us anything, but maybe if we surprise them, we'll get some honest reaction. I called Davey's roommate and he said he would be home until early afternoon. He's got a few things he couldn't send to Edith, so maybe we'll get lucky."

"Long drive, but what a night."

The sun was settling in the west, while off Maggie's left shoulder a full moon was dragging itself out of the Atlantic. The water and the fading sunlight distorted the size and color, creating the illusion of a giant golden orb covering half the skyline. I was torn, between staring at the moon and watching the soft shadows play across Maggie's cheekbones. She finally pulled her eyes away from the scene, and glanced over at me. "Beautiful, isn't it?"

"It sure as hell is," I said. I think she knew what I meant.

**

The hotel was awkward. The two beds weren't very far apart and neither was very big. As a joke, I suggested we push them together, but that didn't happen. I wore a pair of boxers to bed. I didn't make a spectacle of it, just slipped under the covers on my side of the room after pulling the rest of my clothes off.

Maggie must have packed with the shared room in mind. She wore a pair of flannels that left everything to the imagination. It had been a long drive and I was beat.

"Night, Maggie, thanks for coming along."

"It's better than being around Dad and Angie. I hate the way he treats her."

"Didn't work on you, I noticed."

"Angie always tries so hard to please him. I don't get it."

"You two are very different, and I mean that as a compliment."

"And yet she is the one you're obsessed with."

"Jealous? Or was that the hint?"

"Not a hint, Slater, go to sleep." She was only quiet for a moment. "Slater?"

"Yeah?"

"You didn't deny it this time, about being obsessed with Angie."

I rolled over and could see the trace of a smile on her face. "Can't deny I was, but things change. I'd really like a normal relationship with someone that knows what they want."

She was quiet again for half a minute. "I thought I had that, but it all went to hell. I wouldn't want to go through that again anytime soon."

"I'm not going anywhere, anytime soon, just so you know."

"Is that a hint?" She chuckled.

"I don't hint. I'm here when you're ready." I couldn't say it any plainer.

"Thanks, Slater. I'm glad I came down here with you. Goodnight."

"Yeah, goodnight."

* * *

We slept in the next morning, and by the time we had breakfast and both showered, it was ten o'clock. I dressed in my normal Florida attire: shorts, a golf shirt, and sandals. Maggie put in a little more effort.

She wore shorts that were a hot orange color with short platform shoes and a tank top that tied in the front and accented her taut stomach and revealed plenty of cleavage. Maggie wasn't thin like her sister, and I'm not saying that's a bad thing. All that training and working out had paid off. Her legs rippled with muscle when she walked across the room. I had to say something.

"Good God, every guy in Miami is going to want to be me. Nice!"

"Sexist again, Slater," She commented, but she was smiling and her cheeks colored.

"Screw being politically correct, you look hot."

"Thank you. Unfortunate as it sometimes is, you attract more flies with honey. Actually, I think Angie told me that one time."

"She would know," I said off-hand. Wrong thing to say, the smile disappeared. I covered as best I could. "They opened at nine, we better get going."

We took Maggie's car since Davey's office was close and parking looked feasible. The building looked better than what I'd seen online, as did the neighborhood. There were several businesses sharing the space. The main floor was occupied by a pawn shop and a bail bondsman, but there was a sign indicating that Miami Talent and Model Management was on the second floor. There was a small lobby of sorts with an elevator and a set of stairs. Maggie ignored the elevator and we climbed the stairs to a landing. A small sign indicated a lawyers' office on one side, and by default we opened the door with an opaque glass window that was across the hall. We walked in carefully, not completely sure we were in the right spot.

A woman about Maggie's age sat behind a desk, snapping her gum and studying a computer screen. She glanced at us and pointed at a row of chairs along the wall. "Be with you in a minute. Andy, I mean Mr. Gleason, is with a client right now. They had an appointment." She appraised Maggie top to bottom and smiled. "He's got a meeting downtown, but he's going to want to talk to you."

"But, we're not..." Maggie started. I grabbed her elbow and steered her over to the chairs.

After we sat down, I leaned in and whispered to her. "She thinks you're looking for a gig, just play along. The flies and honey thing." There were two offices in the small space and Davey's name was still on the second door. The stenciling proclaimed he was the manager and head of talent acquisitions.

Ten minutes later the first door opened and a red-headed boy in need of a front tooth and a comb burst out of the office. A disgruntled looking woman steered him past us and out the door without saying a word. A squat middle-aged man with a cheesy mustache and terrible pit stains stepped through the open door. He tipped his head in our direction. "Susy?"

"Walk-ins. I thought you'd want to talk to them."

Mr. Gleason looked at us and like Susy, gave Maggie the up and down, then walked across the room with his hand out. We both stood up and shook hands. He looked at her again, piece by piece, without any attempt at discretion.

"You're a very attractive girl, and very well proportioned. A little older than the girls we usually get in here, but some clients are looking for that. Mister Slater, are you Maggie's representation?"

"No, ah, she's my fiancée."

Maggie spoke up. "I saw your sign, and honestly I always thought it would be fun to maybe talk to someone in the business. I'm not expecting much, but maybe I could pick up a few bucks? I see girls at the boat shows just standing around and handing out cards. I could do that. And I can sing reasonably well. I know I'm too old, but I figured I'd give it a shot if you're interested."

"You're very pretty. Do you have any glam shots?" Maggie shrugged and looked disappointed. Pit-stains frowned and shook his head. "In order to sign you, and so we can promote you properly, we need pictures."

"Well, this was kind of spur of the moment. Sorry, maybe I'll have to come back."

I went along. "Yeah, Mags, let's just come back."

Pit-stains spoke up. "I'd hate to see you have to do that. You look great just the way you are, and we have a little studio in the back. I get people in here all the time, like the woman that just left, sure little Tommy is going to be a movie star. Sometimes I take shots just to make them happy. I could put a small portfolio together for you pretty quickly. Of course, there's a fee."

"What do you think, Hon?" Maggie looked at me and took my hand.

"Anything you want, Sugs." I grinned at her. "Anything to keep my girl happy."

"You're the sweetest!" She smiled and dug a nail into my wrist.

"You can pay Susy, Mister Slater. It'll only take a few minutes, half hour tops. I would ask that you wait out here. I need Maggie to concentrate on what I'm asking for. Susy, you remember how to do that, right?" The receptionist nodded.

"God, I feel like an actual model," Maggie gushed. "This is going to be so cool." Andy opened his office door and followed her in. I hoped he would behave himself, for his sake.

"It'll be five hundred for the pictures," Susy said.

I stood up and peeled off the cash, then looked around the office. "We should have known to bring pictures. It wasn't really random, us coming in here."

"Yeah? A lot of girls have to work up the nerve, figure they aren't pretty enough. Your fiancée is a knockout, she'll do fine."

"That's not what I meant. I brought her in here because one of your agents suggested it, but he never said anything about needing pictures. We ran into him in a club over at the Beach and he told Maggie she should be modeling. I thought at first he was trying to hit on her, but I got the impression he was gay, so I figured maybe he wasn't just feeding her a line. I have his card." I fumbled for one of Davey's cards, but it wasn't necessary.

Susy turned ashen. "Davey. That was Davey Templeton." She pointed at the office door with his name on it. "Davey killed himself about a month ago. He was such a good guy, and we got really close in the short amount of time I worked with him. I loved that man." She tipped her head in the direction of Andy's office. "That asshole wouldn't even give me the day off to go to the funeral."

"Oh God, I'm sorry. It was about a month ago when he and I talked. It must have been right before it happened. He didn't seem like the type, but I guess you never know."

"I still can't believe it. You saw him in one of the clubs at South Beach?" I nodded and she got suddenly curious. "Was he alone the night you talked to him, or with another guy?"

"Alone, I think. I guess I don't remember. Why?" It seemed like an odd question.

"I think he was hanging out with some creep. I always wondered if that was why he killed himself. He had bruises."

"Being gay, people can be assholes."

"Yeah, but it happened too often. Davey was a great guy. If somebody was mean to him and he killed himself because of it, I'd like to give him a good swift kick where it counts, if you get my drift."

117

"Sure, but I don't remember him being with anyone."

She glanced at the office door. "He was talking about quitting. He said he needed to be at home. I know he had family up north he was worried about. I wish he had gone." She seemed lost in thought for a moment and I was afraid she might cry, then she came back to me. "So, your fiancée never thought about modeling before?"

"We come from a small town. She's never had the chance to talk to a real talent scout before. Do you just represent people in Miami?"

"No, we have other branches, even a couple overseas. That's why Andy didn't like Davey, he got to travel and Andy didn't. But we have branches in New York, LA, Seattle, and Minneapolis. We get girls down from up north a lot, wanting to get out of the cold, I guess. A lot of those girls end up at the strip clubs."

"No way. You represent strippers?"

"Sometimes we send them to the clubs if they're interested and we get a fee. Money's money, right? High class stuff, no hookers or anything."

"If that's what your guy has in mind for Maggie, he's not going to be happy. She won't go for that. She's more likely to give him that swift kick you were talking about."

"It's part of the business. David was always careful that the girls were legal and weren't being forced into it. I know for a fact he gave some of them money out of his own pocket to go home when things got too tough for them. Like I said, he was a great guy."

"Is it normal for modeling agencies to get involved with strippers and that kind of stuff?"

"I haven't been doing this long enough to say, but who knows what's normal anymore? It's all about the money."

"Yeah, not the first time I've heard that."

I wanted to keep it going, but the phone rang so I sat back down. After the phone call Susy disappeared into the bathroom and came out red-eyed and sniffling. I smiled sympathetically and sat reading an old magazine for another ten minutes. Maggie came out followed by Andy. He was smiling, but seemed a little more restrained than before. He shook my hand again. "You have my number, Maggie, and I have yours. Let's stay in touch. I'll give you a call if something you might be interested in comes up."

We went down the stairs and into the street before she said anything. "Andy was an interesting guy, if you're interested in disgusting scumbags that keep trying to touch your ass. He said I could to go to work tomorrow if I was willing to take my clothes off."

"No deal though?"

"Bite me, Slater," she growled. "Did my complete humiliation accomplish anything? Did you get anything out of the receptionist?"

"Davey was a great guy as far as she was concerned. She seemed really upset that he had killed himself. She said he traveled a lot and she thought he was in an abusive relationship. She said he showed up with bruises."

"Well, that's a lot, isn't it? Maybe his roommate can fill in the gaps. Angie swears there was no boyfriend, but maybe he didn't want to tell her if things were that bad."

"Or she didn't want to tell us."

"Yeah, she always stuck up for him. But I have to believe she'd tell us about that if she knew. It wouldn't be the first time some psycho guy killed his lover."

I jumped on that. "A lot of psycho women have done the same thing."

"I'll admit, that's true. At the moment, I can see how that might happen."

***

Parking is a nightmare at South Beach. It wasn't worth the hassle of worrying about Maggie's car being vandalized while we were out clubbing, so we took a cab.

Davey's apartment was on the fifteenth floor of a luxury apartment building, tall enough to see the beach and have an ocean view even though it was four blocks away. Location, location is what they say, and it would have been hard to find a better one. Prime real estate, and undoubtedly an expensive place to live. They even had a doorman. He eyed us uneasily and pushed a button on his desk phone, then opened the elevator for us, saying Mr. Chopra was expecting us.

There were only two apartments on the fifteenth floor. A window in the small hallway beside the elevator looked south and east. The building was situated so that none of the large hotels down on Ocean blocked the view and I could see the beach and the windswept Atlantic beyond. From that distance the throng of people already filling up the bright white sand looked like so many ants scurrying around on spilled sugar, all hurrying to claim the sweetest spot. September was still blistering hot at this latitude, and the beaches would be full by early afternoon.

The door swung open before we knocked and a stunning girl in her mid-twenties stepped out of the apartment, smiled at us shyly, and walked over to the elevator. Her hair and skin were dark and she had a red dot on her forehead which I happen to know is called a Bindi. That's the sum total of my knowledge of Indian culture, and I may have been staring.

"Slater." Maggie poked me with her elbow.

The young Indian man who held out his hand was as attractive as his friend, in a guy way. Maggie shook his hand. "Hi, Samath is it? I'm Maggie Jeffries and this is Eric Slater."

"Call me Sam, and no, Deepak is no relation. I get asked that a lot, but it's a fairly common name where I come from. Come in, please. You were friends with Davey I gathered from our conversation? I spoke with his mother and she said I should give you the rest of his belongings. Sit, please. Would you like some coffee or tea?"

"Coffee would be great. Incredible view." The big curtains were pulled back and a large expanse of South Beach was visible.

"Davey loved to look out at the ocean and watch the sunrise. It breaks my heart every time I think about him being gone."

Maggie and I sat on the big leather couch and looked around at the enormous room while Sam busied himself pouring coffee. He put our cups down then grabbed his own tea and settled onto a cushion on the floor, sitting cross legged, a position that would have crippled me for a good twenty minutes. Sam looked considerably younger than me, not normally someone who could afford such an extravagant place.

"I hope that you won't be offended, but like I said on the phone, we aren't convinced that Davey killed himself. I don't mean to pry into your business, but I'm trying to get a sense of what was going on in his life."

"Feel free to ask me anything you wish, Mister Slater. I was as surprised as anyone that Davey would kill himself. We had a complex relationship, but I will tell you what I can."

"Complex, in what way? You and Davey, were you just roommates, friends, more?"

"I am heterosexual in my proclivities, mostly. Davey and I started out as more than friends, but it was casual and it didn't amount to anything. Curiosity on my part. But we remained friends, and this place is huge. He needed a place close in and wanted to get away from a difficult situation in a hurry."

"Difficult, in what way? A jilted ex could be motivation for murder."

"I don't think it was a romantic relationship, but somebody with a lot of money, and some kind of a hold over him. One time he came home with a shiner, but he kept going back to see the guy. It was like he couldn't stop."

"We all know people like that," Maggie agreed.

"Could he have been being blackmailed somehow?" I asked.

"I haven't a clue. I think he got beat up more than once by whoever it was. When I asked him about it, he said it was just a part of some game. I got the sense that it wasn't sexual, but like I said, he refused to tell me about it. He was about as normal as anybody I ever knew, romantically speaking. Whatever was going on, he was hurting, and he didn't seem to be enjoying it. He certainly never struck me as a masochist."

"So maybe this person had something on him?"

"I don't know. Davey told me one time that in a past life he had done some things he wasn't proud of, and that he owed a penance. Of course, he was always kidding me about the past life thing."

"We've all done things we aren't proud of." I nodded, then asked the big question. "What about drugs? Was Davey doing drugs, or could he have been selling them? Looking at this place, I'm guessing his half of the rent took a big bite out of his checkbook."

"He smoked a little pot from time to time, but nothing else. He was hard core about taking care of himself and staying in shape. As for rent, he never paid a dime. I wouldn't let him. I come from a very wealthy family and this place is all paid for by my grandfather's estate, as is my allowance."

"Wow, generous of you."

"I also work with my father's firm here in town and draw a nice salary from that. I'm spoiled and privileged, so why not give back when I can? David's mother was under the impression that we were splitting the rent too, and I never told her any different. She didn't seem convinced that our relationship was platonic, but it was. He was a great guy and a friend.

"But you're sure, no drugs."

"Sure as I can be. We both had busy lives." He stood up suddenly, as if reminded of his busy life, and disappeared into one of the other rooms. He reappeared shortly with a small stack of papers and a handgun, complete with a shoulder holster and a box of shells. He put it down carefully on the coffee table, being sure the muzzle was aimed away from us. "It's empty, but I'm not a fan of guns. Davey had a permit to carry."

"Kind of odd, knowing Davey." Maggie slid the handgun out of its holster and inspected it. "Glock 19, decent gun, small enough to hide."

"Why am I not surprised that you know that?" I asked. "But I agree, I never thought Davey would be a guy to carry. I guess there's a lot we didn't know about him."

"It was back on the top shelf of his closet with those old bank statements. I missed it the first time through. His mother told me to just keep the gun, but I would never use it and probably wind-up shooting myself in the foot. You should take it with you." He paused and looked down. "I should have come to the funeral, but I hate them, and it would have been no help to his parents. His father was sure he was lying about our living arrangement."

"Eddy needed to accept his son for what he was, which was a great guy." It was a touchy

125

subject for me and I stood up and extended my hand. "I didn't make it to the funeral either, so don't feel bad. We'd better go. It looks like you have things to do. Is it alright if we call you if we need to?"

"Absolutely, whatever I can do. I hope it isn't the case, but if someone killed Davey, I will pray that you catch the bastard and he becomes a cockroach in the next life."

***

"Good guy," I said as we rode the elevator down to street level.

"Yeah, cute too. We keep hearing about this mysterious man that Davey was involved with, maybe boyfriend, maybe abuser. Soon as we sit somewhere, I'll call Angie and see if she's holding out on us. Close as they were, you'd think he would have said something to her about this guy. She needs to tell us everything if she expects us to figure this out."

"Okay, Nancy Drew, hungry yet?"

"A little. Maybe some steamed crab? There are plenty of outdoor places."

"Let's walk down to Billy's. That's one of the bars that he had a card for. It's only six blocks from here, south on Collins. It's early, maybe it isn't packed and we can talk to someone who knew Davey. I don't think we should make too big a deal out of it, just act like we're his old friends, not like we're investigating in any official capacity."

"We are his old friends, and we have no official capacity."

I nodded. "Good point, but you do have that Glock in your bag now. Don't accidently shoot anybody."

"I have a permit to carry, Slater. Besides, you'd be my most likely target, and it wouldn't be an accident." She flashed me a grin.

As soon as we hit Collins the pedestrian traffic tripled. There were a fair number of panhandlers and people doing various forms of street art, from a guy with cornrows playing Bob Marley beside an open guitar case, to some clown pretending to be a Mime, apparently just for the fun of it. I tossed a five in Marley's guitar case, and Maggie grabbed my elbow and pulled me away.

"Slater, this is Miami. Everybody is running a scam of some kind and they all want your cash, so don't flash it around."

"What? That guy was really good, he even looked like Marley."

"Just pay attention, that's all I'm saying."

Billy's was a big, high-end place, three levels with a bar that wrapped half way around the big dance floor in the middle. My guess was that by eight o'clock that evening there would be a line and you would need to look rich, famous, or both to get in the door. It was empty save for a few couples eating lunch at the tables. We slid onto barstools near the door to the kitchen.

"What'll it be folks, pick your poison." The bartender was a jovial looking guy with a white shirt, black vest and a shiny head. Another pair of bartenders were chatting to each other nearby, one a big man with an enormous belly and the other a small slender woman.

"Couple of cold beers, tap is fine." Maggie ordered for us.

"Light beer for me." I winked at her. "Want to split an order of onion rings?"

"Alright. I usually avoid the deep-fried stuff, but we are kind of on vacation. Onion rings it is."

"I didn't think you'd go for it, but it sounds good to me." We started drinking our beers, watching the big screen television, and eating a few peanuts. The woman who was bartending wandered over, checked out Maggie's earrings and started making girl talk. Our timing was perfect. The shift had just started and there weren't enough customers yet to keep everyone busy. Another hour and the place would be bustling.

It seemed like a good time to jump in. The bald guy walked back over and I caught his eye. "Do you happen to know a guy by the name of David Templeton? I went to high school with him up in Jacksonville. Another guy I know from home said he bumped into him in here and he's a talent scout or something? My girl here can sing like Carrie Underwood and I wouldn't mind finding him."

"Yeah? Sorry, but you're going to have to find another agent. Templeton's dead. Killed himself about a month ago I heard."

"Good riddance, if you ask me." The third bartender walked up. He had a bushy beard and several missing teeth.

"I didn't know him very well in school, but I know he was gay. Is that why you weren't a fan?" I asked the guy.

"He was a frigging perv. Talent scout? From what I heard the talent he liked was all pretty damn young, and it wasn't their singing he was after."

The woman bartender scowled at him. "Jesus, Ricky, why do you keep harping on that old rumor. Davey was a nice guy. He was lonely, that's why he came in here all the time. He was gay, so you figure he had to be perving on kids. Look in the police blotter, Dipshit, most of the pedophiles in there look a lot more like you than Davey Templeton."

"You women, you're always sticking up for the queers," Toothless muttered, and tossed a peanut between his four brown teeth.

"I'm not a woman, and I liked Davey just fine," I said.

"Yeah, whatever. Damn liberals, country's gone straight to hell." Ricky grumbled and walked away.

"So anyway, Davey killed himself? We already lost a lot of people from my senior class. The next reunion is getting smaller in a hurry."

"I was really surprised when I heard about it." The woman nodded, leaning against her side of the bar.

"No truth to that rumor then? It wasn't a guilt suicide?"

She frowned at me. "Davey came in once a week or so, he'd sit at the bar and bullshit, just like you're doing. I don't know how the rumor got started about him pimping kids, probably just because he worked for that talent agency. I've been here six years, and some of the guys were saying that way back then. Bunch of morons. Just people looking for something lousy to say."

"But he was dealing drugs, that's what that friend of mine said."

"I thought you were a friend of Davey's?" She pushed away from her spot at the bar.

"I knew him, like I said, we were in the same class. Don't get mad at me, I'm just saying what I heard." I was curious how far she would go to defend him.

"Now you sound like the rest of them, just spreading shit you heard second-hand. Like I said, Davey was a good guy, period. I have work to do in the back." She turned and slammed through the double doors into the kitchen.

Maggie shook her head. "Nice move, Slater, you have all the bartenders mad at us. Hard to say what she's doing to our onion rings back there."

"Well, I had to ask. Obviously, she was a Davey fan, and the fat guy wasn't. But just because he wasn't peddling drugs in here, doesn't mean he wasn't selling them somewhere else. It still comes down to all that money in his bank account."

"We have to consider the idea that maybe it belonged to the mysterious boyfriend. If Davey hid it in his account the guy would really have to trust him, or figure Davey was too scared of him to try to run with it."

"What if he threatened Davey's family? The woman at the agency said Davey was planning to quit because he wanted to go home to take care of family," I said.

"And he told Angie we should all move away. Did he figure this guy might go after us too, just because we were close to him?"

"Threatening to hurt his Mom would be about the worst thing you could do to Davey, and he would have done anything to protect Angie and you." The first bartender brought our onion rings, and I pushed a couple of them in my mouth. "Eat up. We need to hit the next place before it gets crowded."

***

The next place I had a card for was on a side street and it wasn't nearly as nice. Not really nice at all. It was dark and smelled of stale beer. The bartender waited on us but didn't bother making conversation. I asked him and one of the waitresses about Davey and just got blank looks. But, after we sat for another ten minutes, one of the girls came up to us and nodded her head.

"My boss was wondering if he could have a word with you, in the back."

We followed the girl down a short, even darker hallway into a small office that reeked of sweat and cheap cigars. There was a dim fluorescent on the ceiling and a single light bulb hanging over a cluttered desk. The stout, puffy man behind the desk stared at us coldly through tiny slits that passed for eyes and motioned at a pair of chairs. There were no introductions and the waitress turned and hurried back to the front. He picked up his smoldering cigar and pointed it at us like an extra finger.

"Heard you're asking about David Templeton. What do you know about that piece of shit?"

I frowned at him. "What do you know? I'm investigating his death."

"You the cops? You don't look like cops." He glanced at Maggie. "You sure as hell don't look like a cop."

I made a move as if to pull out my wallet. "His mother hired me to look into his death, I'm a licensed private investigator," I lied.

He waved a chubby hand. "A little piece of paper doesn't mean crap to me." He picked up his cigar again and took a puff, then sat peering at us through the haze. "I ran Templeton out of here about a year ago. If you talked to anyone else in South Beach, you must have heard the rumors that he was pimping young girls. Mostly runaways and refugees, some migrant kids that came into the country without their folks. He was sending them all over, some of them overseas. Selling kids! Damn piece of shit, like I said."

I shrugged. "We heard that rumor. Any facts, or are you just repeating gossip?"

"Absolute fact. I'd heard it before, and I figured it was bullshit too, just people talking, because he liked guys. Haters gonna' hate, you know?" Another big puff, then he inhaled and told his story.

"About a year ago I hired a young Latino girl to wash dishes. She'd been a street walker, drug addict, you name it, but I gave her a chance. I brought her in off the street and she ended up being a damn good worker, still here to this day. Anyway, one afternoon right after she started, she's bussing dishes and she sees Davey Templeton come into the bar. She runs in the back room screaming and yelling that he's the devil, or works

133

for the devil, and that if he recognizes her, she's as good as dead."

"Why would she think that?"

"That's when she told me what happened to her. And this is firsthand, not a Goddamn rumor. She said she met Templeton when she was fourteen years old, fresh off the boat that brought her here from Honduras. He promised her the moon and lined her up with some big shot that claimed he would make her a star. This big shot told her she was beautiful, really special, all the things they tell desperate young girls until they get their hooks into them. She called him Diablo de pelo blanco."

"The white-haired Devil," Maggie translated.

"I guess. I don't speak Spanish very well, but I heard that phrase enough times to figure out what she meant."

"How long ago was it that she met Davey?" I asked.

"Four years, give or take. Anyway, this white-haired Devil was a real sicko. He locked her in a cage and shot her full of drugs, beat her up and screwed her until he got tired of it, then put her out on the street. She had no idea who he was or where he lived, just woke up starving and homeless, in bad need of a fix. You can imagine what happened next. Pimp came along, gave her some drugs and a hot meal. Pretty soon she's just another hooker turning tricks to stay alive."

"Doesn't sound like the Davey Templeton I know. He wouldn't be a part of anything like that."

"Yeah? He used to be a regular in here and I thought he was okay, but when I jumped his ass about what the girl said, the look on his face told me everything I needed to know. He's lucky I'm not a violent guy. I did mention the fact that I'd see him dead if he ever came in my bar again. It could be someone overheard that, so don't go thinking it was me that killed him."

"Supposedly he committed suicide. His being murdered, is that just another rumor?"

"Word around on the Beach is that somebody helped with that suicide, and it doesn't hurt my feelings a bit. That Diablo Blanco asshole would be my guess."

"White haired, you said de pelo, with white hair," Maggie corrected him.

"Far as my dishwasher's concerned he's the God damn Devil, and he's a white man, so close enough."

"Why did you call us back here? My name's Slater, and this is Maggie." I extended a hand that he ignored. "If you hate Davey so much, why talk to us?"

He took another long pull on his cigar. "Carson, but don't get the idea we're friends now. Somebody comes around asking about a guy that's been murdered, I want to know why. I've had my share of trouble with the cops and I don't need more."

"What about this girl? Any chance we could talk to her?" Maggie asked.

"Her English isn't great and she's still scared this Diablo guy is going to come after her. Last thing I'd want is for her to run and end up on the streets again. I know this place may seem like a dump compared to some of those up the street, but I'm a loyal guy and I take care of my people."

"We just need more information about this Diablo, if she can remember," I put in. "Like you said, it seems possible he killed Davey, and that's what we're trying to find out. I'd like to know how much Davey did and how involved he was with her kidnapping, or whatever it was."

"Whatever? Did you hear what I just told you? It was a God-damn kidnapping, torture and rape to boot. Don't defend that son of a bitch to me."

I tried to backtrack. "Sorry, Mr. Carson. This just doesn't sound like the kid I grew up with. Can you talk to your dishwasher, see if she'd be willing to talk to us? If what I find out ends up starting a police investigation, this could all get really messy. Better for both of us if I can sort out your end of it now, instead of having the cops sort it out later."

Carson shook his head. "God, I hate private investigators. You're always threatening to go to the real cops. Give me a card, I'll talk to her and see what she says." I had cards, but of course they didn't mention the fact that I was a private investigator.

Maggie pulled a card out of her bag quickly. "Have this woman call me directly. I speak fluent Spanish, and talking to another woman might be easier for her."

He studied her card. "No promises, but I'll tell her you're going to get this White Devil put in jail. She doesn't want anything to do with the law. I happen to know she's still undocumented."

"Then be sure and explain that we aren't real cops. We really need to talk to her." I stood up and held out my hand. Carson ignored it again.

"You get your business with my dishwasher wrapped up, Mr. Slater, then I don't ever want to see your face in here again, ever, is that clear?"

"Crystal clear. Get her to talk to us and you'll be rid of us for good." We didn't slow down at the bar to finish our drinks, we just kept on walking.

***

"What do you think?" I asked Maggie, knowing she would confirm what I feared.

"Pretty compelling story. What if the notebook we have isn't about dealing drugs?"

"Yeah, I was afraid you'd say that. Maybe he was moving people around. Maybe he was moving kids around, Maggie. Selling young girls for sex, just to put a small fortune in the bank."

"We don't know that yet, Slater. Maybe there's more to it. So far, this woman, the rumors, they happened years ago. But the notebook looks like business was better than ever the last couple years. That doesn't make sense."

"Maybe he just got better at hiding it, and brought kids in from other places, like Minneapolis and Buenos Aires. Look on the internet, those are two of the worst places for kids getting dragged into prostitution. Shit, Maggie, I can't believe he could be that guy. I don't want to believe it."

She pulled me close as we walked and put her head on my shoulder. "Let's give it a rest. Let's just walk and play tourist and not think about it for a while. We can walk down to the beach and watch the moon come up later."

"Sounds like a good place to get mugged," I said glumly.

She laughed. "I'm not worried, I have a big strong man to protect me."

"I know sarcasm when I hear it. You're a black belt, and you have the gun."

The afternoon was hot, even for Miami, and we took our time walking down Collins then strolled over to Ocean Drive, people watching and taking in all the activity. The street was full of high-end vehicles, and I could have spent the rest of the day just looking at the Lamborghinis, Porsches and Ferraris on slow parade, picking their way through the mob of people. And it was a mob. We walked along the edge of the street, dodging the street artists and panhandlers. The noise was continual and I didn't hear the rush of feet behind me until it was too late.

A high-pitched female scream alerted me, and I spun around as a tiny Latino girl wearing just a string bikini came running across the street, heading straight at me. Another woman, a little older and considerably larger was right behind her, screaming in a mixture of English and Spanish, the gist of which was that she was going to kill the bitch. The first girl ran around me and circled my waist with an arm, then hid behind me, all the while screaming at the top of her lungs.

"Help me, help me, Senor, she is going to kill me!"

The second woman was very substantial, wearing shorts and a tank top that revealed entirely too much. At least I didn't see a knife or a gun. She plowed into me like a jiggly freight train, all chubby legs and arms and ample breasts. I tried to step back and just get the hell out of the way. The girl behind me was screaming bloody murder and the chunky one in front had clenched her fists and was swinging wildly, trying to reach the little one. The big girl missed her intended target but managed a blow that landed on the end of my nose. I grabbed at her, and she and I and the little one all went down in a big pile.

My nose hurt and I was getting mad. I pushed the hefty one off me and started trying to get up. I was afraid the big one would keep trying to beat the hell out of the younger girl, but as soon as she got to her feet she turned and bolted, running as fast as she could down the street and into the crowd. Figuring on a thank you, at least, I turned to help the smaller girl up. She was already on her feet too, but she didn't run in the opposite direction like you would expect. Instead, she took off after the older gal that had just been trying to kill her. She only made it half a dozen steps.

Maggie stepped forward and clotheslined her like Steve Austin closing out a cage match on pay per view, except there wasn't anything fake about it. By the time I got the rest of the way to my feet she had the pretty Latino by a thumb and was twisting her hand back while she pushed a knee into her neck. With her free hand she reached into the front of the girl's bikini bottoms and came out of there with my billfold. She turned and tossed it to me. "I told you, Slater, this is Miami!"

The girl on the ground was screaming bloody murder and Maggie stood up and stepped away from her. The first girl, the big tough looking one, came running back and stood over the small Latino, also screaming and swearing loudly in Spanish. I think. Then she lowered her head and stepped toward Maggie, her meaty fists clenched.

Maggie, somehow shoeless now, crouched into a fighting stance. I have to say, she looked pretty damned intimidating. She didn't yell, but we all heard her. "Take your game somewhere else bitches, or you're not going to like what happens next."

I believed her. It took the chunky woman a few seconds, but I think she believed her too. She pulled her accomplice up and they turned and disappeared into the crowd. A small group of drunken college boys had gathered and they booed loudly, disappointed that the chick fight had ended so quickly. I grinned at the young guys as I stuck my billfold into the front pocket of my shorts, then stood by humbly as Maggie slipped her short heels back on.

"Holy Shit, you were awesome!" I said, laughing. "That was the coolest thing I've ever seen. None of the girls, I mean, nobody I knew in my squadron could have done that. How'd you know she had my billfold?"

"For an ex-cop, even a military one, you're pretty easy, Slater. Nothing distracts a guy faster than a girl fight, but I knew they were playing you. The little one tripped you on purpose, that's why you went down. I hope I didn't hurt her, but I wasn't about to let her get away with our lunch money."

"I thought the big one was going to go after you. You could have taken her, right?"

"Isn't that why I have a big strong man along, to protect me?"

Definitely sarcasm.

***

The revelation about Davey really threw me and I wasn't in the mood to go to another club to hear a story of more atrocities he might have been involved in. Once we had cleared the worst of the crowd, I made a suggestion. "How would you feel about forgetting the investigation for the rest of the night? I say we go to one of the clubs and see how these spoiled twenty-somethings party, maybe even dance a little."

Maggie knitted a brow. "You just want to get me drunk."

"I just want to get me drunk. Mostly I want to have fun and not think about what Davey might have done."

"Yeah, I get that. I'll be your wingman. One of us needs to stay sober."

"You're the best-looking wingman I've ever had." She surprised me and slipped her hand into mine and gave it a squeeze.

"Just don't get too drunk, I don't want to have to drag you up to bed tonight."

"Don't worry, I'm not going to drink that much."

Chapter Nine

A single ray of sunlight tunneled its way around or through the curtains of the motel room the next morning, searched the room for a victim, then decided to pierce my eyelids with its mind-numbing brilliance. My head really hurt. I glanced at my watch, six-fifty. No point in moving yet.

I didn't move, just lay there trying to piece together the events of the previous evening. There had been dancing, and a lot of drinking. Maybe a fight? I ran my hand across my face quickly. My nose was a little tender, but that was from the altercation with the pickpockets. Other than that, I couldn't locate any tender spots that might have indicated damage. Way, way too much to drink, that was for sure.

There had been some sort of an argument. I was sure I remembered being escorted out of the bar, and maybe throwing a punch? Then there was a lot of laughing in the cab. It came back slowly. There had been laughing in the cab...and kissing. More kissing in the elevator, and even more in the bed? I turned my head slightly. Maggie was lying on the pillow next to me, snoring softly. We must have pushed the beds together at some point, and most of the blankets were gone, just an undersized bedspread that covered both of us. One long shapely leg had found its way on top of the covers, and it wasn't mine.

Cautiously I lifted my side of the blankets to verify that I was still wearing underwear. I was, and I wasn't sure how I felt about that. Relieved, I guess. It would have been really unfortunate to not remember something like that. I closed my eyes for a minute, searching my brain for any particulars. Maggie's breathing changed and I opened my eyes again. She was smiling at me, so that was a good sign.

"Morning," I mumbled. "Crazy night, huh?" It was a fair assumption.

"Morning, Slater. You were absolutely magnificent last night." She gave me a coy look, and I almost fell for it.

I called her bluff. "Don't even go there. I was drunk, but I would remember that."

She rolled out of bed laughing. "Damn, I had you going for a minute there."

"I am wondering why the beds are pushed together, and why you're wearing my shirt instead of those God-awful pajamas."

"I may have had too much to drink, too. I think we both had intentions, but luckily we fell asleep before we could follow through."

"Damn. It's still early."

Either she didn't get what I was saying or chose to ignore me. "Time for a workout before we go talk to that dishwasher. She called me last night, remember?"

"No, I sure don't. I remember some kind of fight. I think."

"Not much of a fight. Remember the bartender from Billy's Bar, the guy with no teeth? He showed up because his shift ended early and he probably can't drink where he works. Anyway, he came over and got in your face right away, started badmouthing Davey again. No pushing or shoving, you just wound up and drilled him. Took all of thirty seconds and you were helped out the door by two really big bouncers. Last count, we're not allowed in three of the bars on Collins and we've only been here one day. Impressive, Slater."

"Well tough, he needed an attitude adjustment, the stupid redneck. As a rule, I don't hit people unless I absolutely have to. You were my wingman, you were supposed to keep me out of trouble."

"I kept you out of jail. Actually, Ricky probably did, because he came running out looking for you and the bouncers ended up having to jump on him. We made a run for it."

"Damn, I missed all the good stuff."

"Getting shitfaced to the point where you don't remember anything isn't okay, Slater," Maggie said, suddenly serious. "It's fun to party, and we all get carried away from time to time, but I hope this isn't a frequent thing for you."

"Speaking of getting carried away, tell me again why you're wearing my shirt?"

145

"I keep forgetting that I'm off men."

"Couldn't you just be on me, once in a while?" It was a cheesy pun and she threw a pillow.

"Are you coming down to the gym with me? You can sweat that poison out, shower, breakfast, and we're back on the case. You need to get a license." I stared at her, confused. "A license to be a private investigator? Sooner or later, someone will want to see it for real."

"I need to get a contracting license. Then I can start remodeling houses and have a real job."

"Investigating is a real job, and you'll be helping people. I'd get one, but I don't have any experience. All that training you had in the military, you can probably just write the State of Florida a check and we'll be good to go."

"We'll be good to go? If we figure out what happened to Davey, I'll be happy to retire from investigating. I'm going to start pounding nails, remodeling houses, and flipping them."

"We'll see." She laughed, disappeared into the bathroom and came out a minute later in sweats. "Come on, Slater. A good workout and a hot shower and you'll feel like a new man."

Not a new man, but better. After breakfast I reminded Maggie that she had planned to call her sister and pick her brain about what she knew about Davey's boyfriend situation. While she did that, I pulled out the small stack of papers Sam had found in Davey's bedroom. They were all bank

146

statements going back several years and I skimmed through them quickly then folded them up and stuffed them into my suitcase.

Maggie had gone out on the balcony to make her call. I couldn't hear much, but from her tone I suspected that it hadn't gone well. She pulled the slider shut a little too forcefully and looked at me glumly.

"Well, she's back down. She didn't answer at first, I had to call twice. She said she didn't know anything about any boyfriend and then started crying. She sounded bad."

"You worried about her?"

"All I do is worry about her, Slater. I think she could be alright if she'd take her meds, but she won't. I don't want to go to another funeral."

"We should talk to that dishwasher and then head back tonight. I don't know what else we can find out by being down here. If the dishwasher's story is as bad as it sounds, maybe it'd be better to just go home anyway. I can make phone calls and get Davey's bank records from Edith. I can always come back down here if I need to."

"I hate to come all this way and have to run home just because she's crashing. She's the one that started us looking in the first place. I think we should go to the gay bar before we leave, talk to some of the people that might have been his friends. Whatever this gal says, it was years ago.

We need to figure out if Davey was depressed. Seems like he had plenty of reason to be."

"Angie was right, not a suicide," I said. "If I was taking bets, my money would be on this white-haired Devil. There's got to be something that will tie him and Davey together if they had something going on for that long. Of course, we have no way of knowing if the perv that caged up that girl years ago is the same guy that was knocking Davey around recently."

"People that level of crazy, it's about control, not the sex. I'm betting it's the same guy. We better get going. I texted her and told her we're on our way. She lives north, off 95 a few blocks. Nothing like South Beach up there, it's a bad neighborhood. She said her boyfriend is not thrilled about her talking to us, but she wants to. She's hoping we can put old Blanco in jail. It sounded like her guy would just as soon take care of it himself."

"Understandable, but then he goes to jail for a long time, which is the wrong outcome. Should one of us be carrying Davey's Glock?"

"Should you be, you mean?" Maggie asked. "I can shoot, but I imagine you carried in the service. Can you hit what you're shooting at if we get in trouble?"

"One of the few things I'm really good at, that, and flying."

"You're not a bad kisser, for what that's worth," she said.

"Wish I could remember that. Next time I'll make sure I'm sober."

She raised a brow. "You're presuming there will be a next time."

"Fingers crossed. At the risk of sounding sexist again, I still think you should have the gun. I'd rather take a beating if we get in a bad spot than have something happen to you. Kung-Fu aside, somebody tries anything, shoot them. In this state you're allowed."

"I'm not going to shoot anybody unless I have to, but I get your point. Thanks, Slater, you're my hero."

***

The neighborhood was pretty rough. There was street-gang graffiti everywhere, a couple of burned out cars sitting in yards, and several houses with no windows. We found the address and pulled up to the curb. A stocky dark-skinned man in his late twenties strode up to the car before we had made a complete stop. He was flanked by two other men that could have been his brothers.

"Rosie don't want to talk to you, she changed her mind," he said loudly.

"All we want is to find the man that mistreated her, put him in jail." I nodded to the other two men and tried a smile.

Maggie shut the car off and turned in the seat, facing the men. "I just talked to her last night about all this, and she was adamant that she wanted to tell us what happened to her. She understands that it's important, so what happened to her doesn't happen to someone else."

"I said you need to go, we don't need your stinking help. You'll have the cops down on us. I'm telling you, get the hell out of here!" He stepped forward, and the other two men moved forward too, spreading out a little. Wisely, Maggie started the car.

The screen door of the house banged open suddenly and a small Hispanic woman came running across the yard barefoot, waving her arms and yelling Spanish obscenities that even I understood. She walked up and stood directly between our car and the three men, pointing and arguing with the stocky man who I presumed was her boyfriend. Finally, she stepped forward and pushed him back repeatedly, yelling and pointing at an old Pontiac across the street. After another minute of verbal abuse the poor guy shrugged, gave me a dark look, and stomped off across the street with the other two. They climbed in the car and drove off as the small woman watched from the curb, her hands on her hips.

She nodded to us. "He is a good man, he just wishes to protect me."

Rosie was a pretty woman that looked much older than her nineteen years. It had undoubtedly not been an easy life. The house she shared with her boyfriend was badly in need of paint and the screen door was peppered with holes. A small air conditioner hung from one of the windows, rattling noisily as if it were about to grind to a stop at any minute, and a Dodge pickup sat in the front yard with two flat tires. From across the street, a radio blared out what I thought to be Cuban hip-hop.

She stood aside as we walked into the kitchen and waved us to a pair of chairs. She pulled open the refrigerator and without asking set a pair of Arnie Palmers in front of us, then pulled a stool over from the counter and perched on it between us. She spun the top off a bottle of water and held it up. "Agua? Is the Arnie okay?"

"This is fine," Maggie said quickly. "Hablas ingles en absoluto?"

"Si, my English is good. I am learning. Mi novio, my man, he wishes I don't talk to you."

We had agreed Maggie would do the talking, because she understood Spanish, and being a woman, Rosie might be more comfortable. But I had a sudden thought. "Rosie, is that short for Rosalyn?"

"Si, yes. Rosalyn Cabello."

I nodded. It was the first of the names on Davey's list of seven women in the back of the notebook.

It wasn't lost on Maggie, but she didn't miss a beat. "We really appreciate you doing this. We aren't cops, or even fake cops. We're just trying to understand how our friend was involved in what happened to you."

"Senor David? I am happy he is dead!" she snapped, with sudden anger. "Now he cannot go to the Diablo Blanco that put me in that juala, and tell him where I am!"

"He put you in a cell?" Maggie asked. "Can you describe him, this Diablo?"

"Very big, tall and heavy with hair like an old man, white. And when he grew angry, when I did not do what he wanted, his face would grow very red and dark. I have dreams of him, his face so dark with anger that his eyebrows, they looked even more white. Like a ghost or a demon. And his eyes! The true Devil himself could not have more terrible eyes."

"His eyes, what color were they?"

"Blue, but not like yours, almost white."

"And he locked you up in his house? Could you see outside?"

"House? Not his house. In a cage I said. I was his animal, a dog to him. Two weeks, three weeks maybe, I cannot say. I was in a dark room, a basement with no windows. He kept me locked in that cage with a bucket to relieve myself, a gallon jug of water and a little food when it suited him. He started with the needle right away. By the end of a week I needed it and he made me beg for it. He loved that I cried, that I needed the drugs. Sometimes he chained me to a wall, sometimes to the bed. Always he hit me if I cried out. He was an animal. A beast! A terrible beast."

"Take your time, I know this is hard." Maggie reached out, but the woman pulled her hand away, as if the touch of flesh on flesh would heighten the terrible memory. She wasn't crying, but she had started shaking violently.

"When I could not please him enough, when my young flesh was not to his liking no matter what degrading things he did to me, he would hit me anyway. He hit me again and again, until my nose was broken and I shit blood. I would love to know where he is, to find him. Manny and his compadres, they would skin him like a goat and I would listen to him scream the way I did. Then I would slit his throat."

"We want him to pay for what he did to you, but legally, through the justice system." I made the mistake of talking. The young woman stared at me like I was crazy.

"And what justice is there for me, Mr. Slater? You know that I am an illegal. Your police would send me back to Honduras and this man would not be in jail long. Do they beat rich Americans when they are in jail the way I was beaten? Do they rape them in the way I was raped? That would be just a little of the justice I want. Mostly, I just want him dead."

"Rosalyn, we can't take back what happened to you. God, I am so sorry." This time she let Maggie take her hand and hold onto it. "And Davey, did he know about any of this?"

"Of course, he knew," she snapped. "It was him that took me from the Contrabandistas. He bought me from them after my uncle had already paid to have me smuggled here. David told me he had paid for me and that I must go with him, that it was the way of this country. I was fourteen, I didn't know any better. He took me to that Devil, the Diablo Blanco."

"But, Davey, are you sure he knew how you were treated?" I couldn't just sit there, I had to ask.

"The man with the white hair, he hit David too, when he tried to make him stop. He laughed and hit him and made him watch."

"My God," Maggie choked out. "He forced Davey to watch?"

"Yes. And he brought another man I could not see. The other man, he took me too."

"Oh, Jesus. No wonder you want to skin the bastard," Maggie said, tears creeping down her cheeks. I was nearly there, so enraged and sickened by what I had just heard that I couldn't breathe. I really thought I was going to be sick and I stepped toward the door. The feeling passed, and I turned back toward the two women.

154

Rosalyn wasn't done yet. "Again, one more time David Templeton watched what happened to me while he cowered in a corner. Maybe he couldn't stop it, but where were the police then? Why didn't he go to them? Why couldn't he have stopped it?" She was sobbing suddenly and Maggie pulled her into a hug, looking as miserable as I felt. Finally, Rosalyn picked her head up again and looked at me. "God may punish me, Mister Slater, but I will never forgive Templeton for not helping me. I am glad he is dead."

I stood there looking down at her. "If we find this white-haired Diablo, so help me, I will skin him for you."

In that moment, I think I could have done it. It was becoming clear to me that I was naïve when it came to what people were capable of, even a person as gentle as Davey Templeton. What kind of person had he become?

***

"No, Slater, we're not doing that! One more place, we'll go in and talk to the bartenders, like we did at Billy's."

"If we left now, we could be back before dark. I feel sick. That girl had no reason to lie to us, and it was pretty obvious she wasn't. How could anyone do that?"

"Davey, or the Diablo Blanco?"

"Either one! What kind of a monster is that guy? And how could Davey go along with it? Even if he had something on Davey, or he was blackmailing him, or threatening him somehow. How could he see that and not go to the police? Why didn't he just come home and ask for help?"

"Maybe the guy was threatening his Mom. We can't give up now. It's pretty clear Davey must have finally ended it, or stood up to this Diablo and the guy killed him."

"Maybe, or Rosalyn's boyfriend tracked him down somehow. He looked like he would have been more than happy to skin me, much less the Diablo. Davey had a meeting that night and he drove into Jacksonville. If the guy was that dangerous and Davey had ended it, why would he meet him? Was it someone else entirely?"

"We can make a lot of guesses or we can do what we came here for, to ask questions and find out everything we can. It's early. We'll go to the gay bar, hopefully talk to someone who knew him, then come back here and check out if it's not too late. Worst case we'll stay the night and go home first thing in the morning."

I would have been fine with checking out of the hotel right then and driving north, but I gave in. Everything pointed to Davey being a guy I didn't know, a person capable of things I couldn't imagine or forgive, but Maggie kept insisting that there might be more to the story.

*****

It was early afternoon and the bar was nearly empty. Just one bartender. I could see a cook cleaning the grill back in the kitchen. There were half a dozen guys and a couple of women sitting at tables watching a baseball game on a big screen television. It was a small place, more like your local corner bar than the nightclubs we had been to on the Beach. It didn't look like a gay bar to me, but I had nothing to compare it to.

Maggie ordered herself a beer and made a beeline for the bathroom. I pulled up a stool and ordered a beer too, then picked up the menu the bartender had dropped in front of me. I caught movement to my left and turned. One of the women who'd been sitting at a table made herself at home on the stool next to me and smiled. She was tall, blond, and good looking. If it hadn't been for the fact that Maggie was with me, I would have thought she was a hooker looking for a date. That, and the Adam's apple.

"Hello there," the blonde purred in a voice an octave too low. "Is that your girlfriend that just ran off to the bathroom?"

"Yeah, sure is, fiancée actually," I said quickly.

"You're cute. What brings you in here, curiosity?" she asked casually.

I shook my head violently. "We just wanted a burger. I'm straight. Really straight. Don't take this the wrong way, but as long as you're already sitting here, can I buy you a beer?"

"Yeah, that would be nice." She, or he, sighed and scooted closer to the bar and took the beer the bartender opened as Maggie came back from the bathroom.

She grinned at me and winked. "Don't let me interrupt anything."

"Funny." I laughed a little too loudly. I extended my hand and made the introductions. "I'm Slater, this is Maggie, my fiancée."

Thankfully, Maggie played along. "Pleased to meet you, Jeannie is it?"

"It's Jeannie when I'm dressed like this." That cleared things up for me, mostly. Being politically correct was never one of my strong suits, and when it came to cross-dressing, I was flummoxed. I didn't want to say the wrong thing and hurt the guy's feelings, but at least now I was confident it was a guy.

Maggie was enjoying my discomfort, but she bailed me out. "Come in here a lot, Jeannie?"

"Most days. I don't usually dress up, but it's fun sometimes, arousing."

"We never do anything fun like that." She laughed at me and bumped my arm. "Slater's an old stick in the mud, a real stuffed shirt." Maggie took the direct approach. "We're kind of making the rounds to some of the bars, trying to find anybody who knew an old friend of ours. A guy by the name of Davey Templeton."

"Why would you be doing that?" Jeannie asked, suddenly wary. "Sweet, sweet man. Let him rest in peace."

"You knew him?"

"Of course, we were good friends. Everybody in here knew Davey, he was a regular. Hard to believe someone killed him, but that happens a lot to our people, or maybe his past caught up to him."

"Suicide we were told, but maybe not," I said. "We heard he was mixed up with some nasty people a few years ago."

"I guess. Boy like Davey, he was too nice for his own good. Joe, tell these folks what a great guy Davey was."

The bartender nodded and put in his two cents. "Great guy, wouldn't hurt a soul, no matter what anybody says."

"What did they say?" Maggie asked quickly.

"There were stories." Jeannie peered at us cautiously. "How is it that you know Davey and why all the questions about him?"

"We're old friends from Jacksonville." For whatever reason I trusted Jeannie, and leveled with him. "We grew up with him, good friends since we were kids. Honestly, the cops at home said suicide, but we don't think he killed himself and we're trying to figure out who did."

The bartender looked curiously at Maggie. "Are you Angela? I thought you were a blond."

"No, I'm Angela's sister, Maggie. Did Davey mention us?"

"He talked about a girl named Angela all the time, about how gorgeous and messed up she was."

Maggie shrugged and looked at me. "Of course, Angela. Me, he never even mentioned."

"What do you guys think happened to Davey? His past caught up to him, what does that mean?" I asked.

"A few years ago. he had a sugar daddy, a really bad guy. Davey was one of those obsessive-compulsive types, you know?" Jeannie peered at me with an eyebrow raised.

I shrugged. "Nope. Stuffed shirt, what she said."

"Some people have addictive personalities, and some people like to be dominated. My therapist talks about it all the time. Once they get into that kind of a relationship it gets to be like a drug, they actually crave the abuse. It's not a gay thing necessarily, I know a lot of women and some straight men who love to be treated like crap. Some people, and I think Davey was one of them, they take it to the next level, a dangerous level sometimes."

"We heard that back in the day Davey did some things, some bad things," Maggie said soberly. "Maybe he was manipulated, or forced. Maybe he just wasn't strong enough to say no to this guy. Is that what you mean?"

"Something like that. I don't know for sure, but we all heard the rumors. Bad isn't the word for that guy. Twisted. He liked young stuff, younger the better."

"Davey wouldn't have been okay with that."

"You know how it is with rumors, nobody talks about the good stuff. Rumor was this guy was back in Davey's life lately, trying to drag him back in. Davey was better than that, always doing good things for people. He'd give you his last dollar if you needed it." Jeannie looked around. "We're like family in here, Mr. Slater, even more so now after Orlando. I don't care what people say about him, Davey was a great person."

"But he never told you who this guy was?"

"He never told me his name, just said he knew him because of work. I think that's how the rumors got started that Davey was peddling kids. Working for a talent agency, Davey saw a lot of young, good looking people. I mean, that's kind of the idea, that's what people want to see on their screens, right? But the guy that had his hooks into him, I'm guessing he was a serious pedophile. Davey may have sent kids to him without knowing what was going on."

"Why would Davey be with a guy like that?"

"Like I said, he always seemed to look for that, somebody domineering."

"Was he still dating this guy when he died?"

Jeannie gave me an odd look. "No, no, darling, not dating. It wasn't like that."

"Now I'm lost. I thought he had a thing for this guy, and that's why he went along with him. You said he was his Sugar Daddy."

"Yeah, the dude had a ton of money. But when I said this perv liked young stuff, what I meant was young girls. I'm sure it wasn't sexual between them, just some kind of control issue. I know Davey and his father weren't close, I just figured it was Davey having daddy issues, like we all do. He would have told me if the guy was a lover. We always gossiped about the people we were sleeping with."

"I thought maybe it was just casual sex."

"Queer folk are no different than straight people, Mr. Slater, most of us are looking for true love just like you and Maggie here. Congrats by the way."

"The wedding isn't until next June," Maggie chimed in, grinning from ear to ear. "I can't believe this big lug finally pinned me down."

I raised my beer and toasted her. "Yeah, I find that hard to believe myself."

***

I felt better after talking with Jeannie, or whatever his name was. Despite my misgivings about amateur psychology, it did seem possible that Davey had been controlled to some degree. Maybe he had been forced into kidnapping Rosalyn somehow, and maybe it was like Maggie said, maybe he just wasn't strong enough to deny the guy what he wanted. Maybe he'd been brainwashed and forced into it, kind of like Stockholm syndrome. I wanted very badly to believe that, because any other explanation was too painful to imagine. Maggie agreed.

"Let's go home and regroup, Slater. We can go over all the paperwork, look through the bank records, and maybe come up with a name. I'm afraid for Angie. My Mom can't watch her all the time and my Dad's back at work already. He comes home long enough to make everybody miserable, then off he goes again."

I spoke without thinking. "I really don't think I want him for a partner."

"Why would he be your partner, in what?"

"Remodeling houses. He sent some real estate guy over to talk about flipping houses. I got the impression your Dad would be involved. Actually, I know he would be involved. But they wanted me to start right away, which just sounded like another way of saying, don't take my daughter to Miami."

"I won't let him run my life so he tries to run yours. What a dick."

"Not how I'd put it, but I'm going to look for my own financing and buy my own run-down shacks to fix up."

"You're going to be too busy being a private eye to be pounding nails."

"Investigator. Private eye sounds cheesy. I need a real job, Maggie. I'd starve to death if I had to depend on solving crimes for a living. Look at this case. So far all we've accomplished is to figure out that my best friend from childhood may have been a hideous douchebag. Not a roaring success. And neither one of the two women that hired me are going to be happy to hear it."

"But we're pretty sure he was murdered, right? That's not nothing, it's a really good start. Now all we have to do is pin it on the guy that did it. We'll figure it out."

"It's always we, with you. Am I supposed to be paying you?"

"We're partners. We split whatever we make!" She grinned at me as we pulled into the hotel's parking ramp.

"Half of nothing is nothing, you do know that?"

"But I get to have all this fun with you, Slater." We both got out of Maggie's convertible and I walked around the back side, headed for the service door to the hotel.

Parking ramps are like a big room that you've just moved all the furniture out of, an echo chamber where noise becomes amplified. I heard the squeal of tires and the sudden roar of an engine behind me sounded especially loud. Maggie yelled and I spun around in time to see a large black truck cornering around a cement barrier. The vehicle didn't slow down, but instead accelerated and headed straight at me. Maggie was already close to the exit near another cement stanchion, but I was in the open, an easy target. I had just a second and I spun around and jumped onto the trunk of Maggie's convertible, then dove from there onto the roof of a Suburban that was parked next to it.

As I landed on the roof of the SUV, I heard a rending crash and felt the vehicle move under me from the impact of Maggie's car sliding against it. I managed to twist around as the truck, its windows tinted and impossible to see through, backed up and then slammed forward again, finishing the job of crushing the side of Maggie's once beautiful BMW. The truck had a sizeable homemade grill guard and the collision barely scratched it. Whoever it was backed up and stopped for a moment as the driver gunned the motor a time or two, considering his options. There was no doubt it was not an accident.

Maggie stepped out suddenly from behind the Suburban with the Glock leveled at the pickup. The driver cranked the wheel and hit the gas, spun sideways, and raced off down the exit ramp. There was no license plate, and the best I could do was guess at the year of the Dodge Ram.

I climbed down from the top of the Suburban as Maggie slid the gun into her bag.

"You alright?" she asked.

I was shaking at little, but I didn't admit to it. "Yeah, I'm good. You?"

"I'm fine. I didn't know you could move that fast, Slater. Good thing, at least you're okay. My car didn't come out of it so great." We stood there surveying the damage to her car for a minute then Maggie looked at me again. "Think I can put this in the expense report?"

It was funny in a sad way, but at least neither one of us had been hurt, or worse. Was the intention to kill me, or just scare us? Immediately I thought of Rosalyn's boyfriend and the ugly look he'd sent me just hours ago. Maybe him, maybe not. Someone sure didn't like us poking around.

Chapter Ten

Everybody knows that when you're a kid, things are a lot simpler. When I was thirteen or fourteen my biggest challenges were avoiding Tommy Ackerman after History class so he couldn't slap me on the side of the head with his notebook, and not getting caught looking at Angie Jeffries' cleavage. I knew my best friend was gay, but the subject never came up and except for an occasional dirty look from the guy at the gas station when we rode our bikes up there to buy a soda, most people didn't seem to know or care. Maybe Mel, the gas station guy didn't care either. Maybe he just thought we were trying to steal candy from the rack when he wasn't looking.

But as I got older, I started seeing that it wasn't easy for Davey. We were friends, but we didn't go to the same school, so during the year I didn't see a lot of him, but I know he took a lot of abuse. There's a certain percentage of the population that are always going to hate anyone different than they are and use it for an excuse to do rotten things. Haters gonna' hate. Even Carson, the cigar chomping bar owner that was still on my list of suspects had heard that song. Had the cumulative effect of all that hate built up in Davey until he thought that was just the way the world worked and was something everyone did? Did he really think that what the White Devil had done to him and Rosalyn was even close to normal or acceptable?

Bottom line, I was feeling guilty that I hadn't done a better job of staying in touch with him and done more to help him through those high school years. By the time junior year came around I had filled out considerably, started lifting weights, and grew to my full height. Tommy Ackerman showed up at Angela's for a pool party one day and called Davey a faggot. I knocked him in the pool and dared him to try and climb out. Angie's Mom finally had to come out and pull me away so Tommy could go home. I couldn't help wishing I had been around a few more times like that when Davey really needed me. Maybe things would have been different for him.

"What are you thinking about?" Maggie asked. We were on the way home in the rental car. It was late, but Maggie wanted to get home to look in on Angela.

"Just years ago, how much easier it was back then, hanging around with Angie and Davey, not a care in the world."

"I was there too, remember?"

"You were ten, inappropriate if I would have acknowledged your existence."

"Well, you didn't, so no worries. Just a lot of miles on my bicycle for no good reason." That made me laugh, which was nice. She continued. "But I think you're just remembering all the good stuff. I remember a lot of fighting, mostly Mom and Dad, but you were there a lot of the times. And Angela, she had all those teenage hormones, plus nobody had figured out she was bipolar yet. It didn't bother you a lot, but I remember more than once Davey getting scared and running out of the house, just running all the way home without even taking his bicycle. I used to push it home for him sometimes before I was tall enough to reach the pedals and then I'd have to walk back."

"See? You were a little kid and you knew what he was going through. I should have helped him more and been a better friend."

"It's called being a teenager, Slater. Granted, I have no idea what he went through either. Did it set him up for what happened later? Maybe. Bottom line we still don't know exactly what all is going on here. Maybe what happened to Rosalyn didn't go down like she remembers. Maybe she was too drugged up to remember it right, or dreamed parts of it. I'm not making excuses for him, or saying that she's lying, but maybe the truth is in the middle somewhere."

"But what she said, and the way she said it, at the very least she was telling us what she thinks she remembers. I had to believe her. It was just too painful a story not to be real."

"Nothing in my experiences with Davey would ever make me think that he was capable of what she says he did, and most of the people we talked to agree. Not saying she's lying, just saying there might be more to it."

"I need a break. Tomorrow I'm sleeping late, then I'll go get copies of those bank statements from Edith and look through them, compare everything."

"What did you find in the papers you got from Sam?"

"I didn't see anything interesting, just more bank statements. Okay if I sleep? Wake me up if you see any big black trucks trying to run us into the swamp, okay?"

***

It turned out getting licensed as a private investigator was easier than being a licensed contractor. My experience in the Navy counted for a lot. There was an examination that I could study for online, an association I could join, and of course a hefty licensing fee. There was an apprentice program, but a couple phone calls took care of that. Normally you would expect to get paid a little something as an apprentice, but in my case the money was going the other way and there was no actual work involved. A bit unethical, but I was sure I knew as much as most of the retired cops already doing the job.

That wasn't true of pounding nails. I knew just enough to be dangerous. Fortunately, I could still buy a house or two and start the work, complete the licensing process, and by then start selling the updated homes. I didn't want to rent them out. I would clean them up, refurbish them and sell them. That was the plan.

I didn't sleep in, but spent the morning researching my employment options. I found the card Frank's shill had left me. James Kennedy, Land and Property Consultations. I called the number and left mine with the secretary that answered. It seemed unlikely I would ever hear back, but maybe I could pick up a couple houses without Frank Jeffries being involved.

After lunch I called Edith Templeton. She said she had some errands to run and would drop off copies of the bank statements she had. I was a little surprised she was willing to drive over, but she said she could find my place, no problem. I suspected that Eddy was around, and she didn't want him knowing what we were up to.

I spread out everything I had on the kitchen table, the notebook, the cards and the old bank statements Sam had given us. Some of the bank statements went back fifteen years. It was a history of how Davey had accumulated his wealth. A lot of the deposits were paychecks from his employer, a monthly salary plus bonuses. The first couple of years the totals were modest. By 2005 the amounts started to be more substantial and his payroll was supplemented by cash deposits, usually ten thousand dollars, sometimes twenty. The amounts snowballed and each year the totals increased until the account was closed in the fall of 2013 with just over three million dollars in it.

He'd managed to put that amount away, working at a job that paid just over a hundred thousand a year, in under ten years. Obviously, the math didn't work. A hundred grand was a lot of money to a sailor, but considering Davey's lifestyle, it wouldn't have been a huge amount to him. The confusing thing was that in the last two years, as far as I could tell, every dime he made working at the talent agency had gone into the bank. How did he eat?

There was a knock on the door. I pushed the cards into a pile, covered them with the bank statements, then picked up the notebook and slipped it into my back pocket. I presumed it was Edith Templeton and I wasn't ready for her to see everything I had taken from Davey's room.

Angela Jeffries stepped through my door looking as ethereal as the first time she had climbed out of the Templeton's pool that day so many years earlier. She smiled dreamily, and it didn't take a lot of imagination to see what she had in mind. I fought the impulse to give in to my demons, but she made it difficult. She looked incredible. Gone were the dark circles around her eyes, the gaunt look I had noticed that first night when we had talked about Davey's death. If it was sleep or the miracle of cosmetics, I wasn't sure. I didn't have time to wonder.

She rushed into my arms, smelling faintly of some exotic perfume and put her arms around me as she pushed me back against the kitchen wall. Without explanation she pulled my face down and kissed me, a deep penetrating kiss full of emotion and desire. My brain told me one thing but every other part of my body was screaming something else, and I gave into that urge for longer than I should have. Finally, I pushed her away, holding her at arm's length while she tried to continue the assault on my self-control.

"Angie, what the hell? What is this about?" I asked.

"Maggie told me what happened in Miami, how you almost got run over down there. It made me realize how I feel, how I really feel. It should have always been you, Eric. I want to be with you."

"Did you drive here? You don't taste like booze, but are you drunk, or high? Did you take something?"

"Is it so hard to believe that I would finally realize how much I care about you?" She was stuttering ever so slightly, and a second look at her eyes confirmed that her pupils were enlarged.

"Yes, as a matter of fact it is. Did you take something?" I asked again. I looked closely into her eyes and she smiled happily, gazing vacantly at some point behind my head. I took her hand and led her to the couch.

She looked up at me again. "I love you, Davey. Please don't go away, please?" With that she flopped over onto her side and closed her eyes.

"Angela, wake up!" I shook her shoulder several times, but she was out cold. I called Maggie. "Angie's here and I think she's messed-up. She wasn't making a lot of sense. She just passed out on my couch."

"Shit, she must have found Mom's keys and took her car. She took something, sure as hell. Is she breathing alright?"

"Best I can tell, but she's out cold and I can't wake her up. Should I call 911?"

"I'll do that and head over there. Get her on her feet, Slater. Make her move and don't let her fall asleep."

"Got it." I tossed the phone down and went back to the couch. I tried being gentle, but she wouldn't respond and a quick search for her pulse scared the hell out of me. I ran back to the sink and got a glass of water. I pulled her forward and shook her, roughly this time. No result. Desperate, I upended the glass of cold water, pouring the contents on her head, across her shoulders and down her back. She moaned softly and I grabbed both her hands and dragged her to her feet. She nearly collapsed, but then seemed to come to a little. I started walking her back and forth across the room, yelling her name every few seconds to try to keep her from going under.

Maggie burst through the door just as I heard the wail of sirens and helped me keep her on her feet. She snorted once, then seemed to wake up and turned to me, smiling. "I love you, Eric, more than anybody. I do." Then she dropped her head and was out. Maggie and I were carrying her at that point.

The EMT's came running in shouting instructions and asking questions. Maggie told them what she thought Angie had taken and they gave her a shot, then loaded her on a gurney. They had her in the ambulance within two minutes of the time they arrived, and Maggie climbed in beside her. She tossed me the keys to the rental. "Can you bring the car to the hospital, and call my Mom?"

"On my way. Don't worry, Maggie, she'll be okay."

She looked at me dismally before the doors of the ambulance closed. "I don't think she's ever going to be okay, Slater."

I grabbed my phone and called Rita Jeffries who was oblivious to the fact that Angie had taken her car. I explained and told her I would be picking her up. As I locked the door, Edith Templeton was stepping out of her car, a small bundle of papers in her hand.

"Sorry Edith, there's an emergency going on with Angie. She took something and they just left for the hospital."

"What can I do?" she asked anxiously.

"Any chance you'd pick up Rita and bring her back here to get her car?"

"She probably won't like that, but I'll do it. Which hospital? I'll follow her after we get back here."

"Memorial. I'll head straight up there."

***

"She's staying in treatment this time, Mom. To hell with Dad, she needs to be under constant supervision. He gets no say in this." Maggie was pacing the floor in front of her mother. I wasn't sure if Frank even knew his daughter was in the hospital. Maggie glanced at me. "Every time this happens Dad says that she doesn't need treatment, and that we can deal with it. Except he doesn't have to deal with it. You need to commit her, Mom, don't even tell Dad. He'll just sign her out first chance he gets."

"Okay, Maggie, whatever you think is best," Rita said dully.

Maggie stared at her like she might respond with violence, then spun and ran off in the direction of the bathroom. Edith Templeton got up from her seat and handed me the wad of papers she had continued to carry since her arrival, then hurried off after Maggie.

Rita sat in her chair looking at her hands for a while, then looked up at me. "I told you to let this go. Now you have Angie all worked up."

"There's more to this than her being worked up, Rita, and it sure as hell isn't my fault. Your daughter has serious problems. I'm sure the bipolar thing is hard enough, but there's more than that going on. She needs real, professional help. Davey's dying has her tied in knots, and she's starting to lose touch with reality."

"Maybe." She actually laughed at me. "Maybe that's a good thing."

I was too mad to talk. I got up and found a coffee machine, then went downstairs and out into the street. I couldn't stand hospitals. They brought back the memory of my mother's death.

Maggie found me after fifteen minutes and sat beside me on the bench in front of the hospital. She bumped my shoulder and gave me half a smile. "She's going to be alright, they got to her in time."

"That's good. I hope your mother listens to you and she gets some real help."

"Mom just doesn't have the strength to deal with those two. Usually, after a few days Angie cries and begs and my Dad brings her home. Then he yells at me because I didn't watch her close enough, and it starts all over again."

"Sorry. Sometimes I'm glad I'm an only child. An orphan at that."

"It's a hard knock life, right?"

I smiled, and looked into her eyes. "I really like you, you get that, don't you?"

"I like you too. So does my sister, from the sound of it."

"She's messed up, Maggie. That was just the pills talking."

"Maybe. Why'd she come to your house?"

"I really don't know."

"You have lipstick on your face, Angie's shade."

"I stopped her, like I said. She was confused. She called me Davey at one point."

"I just can't, you and I, not until I know she's alright."

"I get that. Just so you know, nothing would have happened even if she hadn't been doped up. I'm past that."

"Maybe. Maybe you are." She reached out and wiped the lipstick stain from the edge of my mouth. "For now, until we all know how we feel, you and I are just two gumshoes working the same case."

I chuckled and took her hand. "Partners. But remember, I'm a private investigator, not the Chubby Gumshoe."

***

I didn't get home until almost midnight. I gave Maggie a wave and stumbled to the door, half awake. I turned the lock and walked in, tossed my keys on the table, and reached for the light switch. I had a split second of warning and managed to get my shoulder up. A fist, or possibly a club glanced off my collarbone and caught me on the side of the head, almost knocking me to the floor. It was enough of a blow to confuse me, but I lashed out and made some contact. I grabbed for clothing or hair, any way to get ahold of my assailant to control the fight. I took another shot to the head that put me down, then the front door banged open and my assailant escaped into the night.

By the time I got to my feet and turned the outside light on, he was long gone. I stumbled to the bathroom and assessed the damage. Luckily, I have a hard head. I had a jagged cut above my eye that bled a little, but a cold compress took care of that. I checked out the house. My computer was undisturbed, as was the small cache of cash I had hidden in my bedroom. The appearance of Angela had been unexpected, and all the cards and bank statements I had laid out had been forgotten in my haste to get to the hospital.

A quick glance confirmed that all the cards were missing, but the bank statements were scattered across the table and floor. I remembered the notebook suddenly, and reached back quickly. It was still there, tucked securely behind my billfold. Hard to say what they were looking for, or if I had interrupted them before they could finish. I walked out and did a quick perimeter search, but happily my burglar had fled. I needed a gun.

Chapter Eleven

How's your head, Slater?"

I was trying to fix my front door that had shattered when the burglar ran through it. Maggie wasn't helping, she was just talking a lot.

"Sore, but better. If I was you, I wouldn't hang around me. Whoever killed Davey doesn't seem to like me."

"Not necessarily the same person. There are probably a lot of people that don't like you."

Since romance was off the table, we were back to her being a smart aleck. "Funny. Your Dad doesn't like me. Kennedy's guy called and said they want nothing more to do with me. I think he heard about our incident in Miami."

"I'll bet Angie told him. I asked Mom not to tell him she was back in the hospital but she did anyway. I give it a week. She'll be back home and I'll be babysitting again."

"How long until you get your car back?"

"Not sure, at least a few more days. But guess what? I may have another case for us. The word is getting out that we're private investigators."

"That's not surprising, since you keep telling everyone."

"I'm the PR person, you're the muscle."

"You're the dreamer, I'm the sane one."

She ignored me. "Five grand in it if things work out, plus expenses. Do you know who Maryanne Thatcher is?"

"No, I don't know that many millionaires."

"How'd you know she's a millionaire?"

"If she's willing to give us five thousand dollars, she has to be rich."

"We have an airplane, that's the important part."

"I have an airplane," I corrected her.

"I had a car," she deadpanned.

"Alright, you have a point. What's the job?"

"Maryanne's granddaughter is going to be in Atlanta next week. She called Maryanne and talked her into letting her stay at their summer place north of the city. I guess she's fallen in with some biker, a guy twice her age. But Maryanne thinks she's ready to dump the guy and come back home."

"Why wouldn't she just send her a plane ticket like a normal grandmother?"

"The girl's mother is Divine Thatcher."

"The one on the internet? Porn star turned business tycoon?"

"Same one. The girl left home two months ago and she's been a wild child ever since. Divine wants nothing to do with her, but she doesn't want any bad publicity either."

"Divine and Jasmine? With names like that, how could anything go wrong?" Maggie scowled at me. "So, two things. Why doesn't Grandma just call her daughter and have her deal with it? And if there's a biker gang going to shack up in Maryanne's house, why not just call the cops and have them tossed out."

"Publicity. Don't you read?"

"I don't read about celebrities. Just how many Kardashians are there? Divine Thatcher sure wasn't worried about publicity when she was showing her girlie parts in all those movies. I know that's sexist, I just don't care."

"Granted, but the point remains, they want to keep Jasmine's name out of the press. She just turned seventeen and she's shacking up with a thirty-four year old Henry Fonda wanna' be. It doesn't look good."

"Peter Fonda. Henry's kid, Peter, was the guy in Easy Rider. Henry rode horses, not Harleys."

"Slater, I'm too young to know the difference, and I don't really care. The point is, it's a job."

"It's a job for the cops. Thirty-four and seventeen, isn't that statutory rape?"

"Probably, but they don't want to press charges, they just want her out of that mess."

"Seems like if this girl wants to come home, she would just do it."

"She needs a little convincing. Maybe she's like Davey, maybe she's been brainwashed."

That earned her a dirty look. "Not fair using that. I'm not kidnapping anyone, even with her mother's permission. How does the Piper figure in?"

"There's an airstrip at the house. It's a big place, and that's why the bikers want to stay there. I thought we could fly in and land, maybe act like the plane's having trouble and we had to put down. That'll be our cover story. We hang out, I convince Jasmine to leave with us, and we fly back home."

"What if Jasmine has had a change of heart and tells these bikers what we're up to? I'd get beat up and you might get worse. How many bikers are we talking?"

"Where's your sense of adventure? Isn't that why we want to be private investigators, to have adventures and make a few bucks?"

"We again? I would be perfectly happy to figure out what happened to Davey and call it a day."

"Slater, the poor girl is only seventeen."

I knew she was playing me, but I couldn't look in those blue eyes and tell her no. "Why is the grandmother letting them stay there in the first place?"

"Part of the plan. If Jasmine's there, at least we know where to find her. And if things don't work out, we can always call the cops."

"Maybe, alright? Tell Maryanne to get on the phone and keep trying to convince her granddaughter to come home on her own. Your plan sounds pretty shaky to me."

Maggie was excited. She jumped around and hugged me and gave me a kiss on the cheek, so it was kind of worth it. The whole thing sounded like trouble to me.

***

I worked around the house all afternoon, dwelling on what we'd uncovered in Miami, and what it might mean for my future. Being a private investigator sounded romantic and fun, especially if Maggie Jeffries was my partner, but I knew the realities would be different. Most of the time investigating anything took months, maybe years, and the conclusions were seldom what you hoped for. More often, they were what you expected.

Every day the newspapers or the internet detailed stories of abduction and murder, of bodies found and identified to stop the wondering, but not the grief. I wasn't sure that was something I wanted to be a part of.

Rita Jeffries had been right. Investigating Davey's death was shedding light on things that might have been better left in the dark. She was right for the wrong reason, and I wasn't sure I wanted to know what she'd been talking about. More secrets undoubtedly, secrets that were only going to make more people unhappy.

The truth had always been the ultimate goal when I was in the Navy. People's careers hung in the balance sometimes, but things were usually black and white. If Petty Officer 1st class had indeed smashed a bottle over the head of that Marine in that bar, then he would spend thirty days in the brig and come out a Petty Officer 3rd class. I talked to witnesses and gave the evidence to the officer in charge. It was black and white and there were no choices for me to make. That was the beauty of it, simple. Luckily, I seldom knew the Petty Officer who lost rank and pay due to his night of stupidity, so I never had to make any moral judgment as to whether or not he deserved his punishment. The Navy did that for me.

But the truth about Davey was getting complicated. It wasn't one mistake made during a drunken night on the town. I couldn't hand my findings off to JAG and wash my hands of his Discipline Hearing. My findings this time, if I decided to share them, would define the remaining years of a mother's life. If Davey had done what it seemed he might have, it wasn't one night of drunken debauchery, it was a pattern, and possibly a lifestyle. I had promised Edith Templeton I would tell her what I found out, good or bad, and I already regretted that. I would lie to her if necessary, to make Davey seem more the victim than he appeared.

What I really regretted, was even starting the investigation. The truth, it was turning out, might be worse than anything I could have imagined. But, unlike a drunken seaman's wild night, this truth was nuanced. Life had been more difficult for David Templeton than I had ever imagined.

Somewhere along the line he had fallen in with, or fallen victim to this White Devil person. Everyone has neuroses and most of us cope with the minor ones; they don't affect our lives much, or at all. But some people need help and don't get it, and sometimes other people recognize whatever need that is and take advantage of it. I could see how that might have happened to Davey. He had needed help, and all I ever did for him was hit a kid that called him a name. The truth was that clocking Tommy Ackerman had been more for me than for Davey, and just because I could.

By the end of the day, I had talked myself full circle. The Davey Templeton I knew hadn't been capable of what Rosalyn Cabello said he'd done. Somehow, through threat, intimidation or brainwashing, the Diablo Blanco had made Davey do things that he would never have done under normal circumstances. If after years of abuse, the White Devil had killed Davey, I was going to find him and make him pay dearly. That was my truth.

***

The next morning, I pulled everything out I had regarding Davey's case again, minus the missing cards. There was one question that plagued me. If you were looking for something that Davey had hidden, why look at my house? Since the intrusion I'd taken to hiding things in case my curious assailant returned, and I had ordered a good handgun, a particular model that I was familiar with and very good at using. I had a permit to carry and if I stayed in the detective business, having a gun would come in handy sooner or later. But breaking into my house indicated the person knew that I was looking into Davey's death, probably knew I was his friend, and might even know that I had cleaned out Davey's room. That had to be a short list.

Maggie had called. As predicted, she was busy picking up her sister and moving her back to the house. I would be alone, which meant I could look over the bank records without the pleasant distraction of the Jeffries sisters. My brain definitely worked better that way. I made coffee and started going through them line by line, comparing what Davey had done prior to changing banks, with what he had done recently.

I had already looked at the statements that I got from Sam closely. Davey had amassed three million dollars in a hurry. But the statements Edith supplied me with told a different tale. The account didn't continue growing. There were months when he added pretty good sums, thirty, or forty thousand dollars. But there were months when that same amount, or more went out. Most of the deposits were cash, but a lot of the withdrawals were cashier's checks. Good as cash once he signed them, but a safe way to move money around.

Over the five years I had records for, he had added just over a million dollars and paid out a half million over and above that, all in cashier's checks, most of them written to himself. But, the signature on two of the checks had a different name, a familiar one. It meant a leap of faith on my part, but I had to know if my hunch was right. I grabbed one of Davey's cards and dialed the number.

"Hello, Miami Talent, this is Susy." I recognized the voice.

"Hi Susy, I didn't get your last name when we met, it's Foster, right?" There was a Foster on Davey's list of seven women.

"If this is a sales call, I'm not allowed to take those during business hours."

"No, not a sales call. My name is Eric Slater. I was in last Friday with Maggie Jeffries, the pretty woman with the red hair?"

"Oh sure, I remember. Has she changed her mind about dancing?"

"That's a big no. I actually wanted to talk to you."

"Yeah? I don't date guys with girlfriends."

"That's not it either. I need to talk to you about something else, something important. Is now a good time?"

"Andy's out of town and I'm running the place, such as it is. What's up?"

"We misled you the other day, and I did when we talked about Mr. Templeton. I knew Davey very well, spent half my childhood swimming in his pool most summers. Truth is, we're looking into his death. I don't think it was a suicide. I think he was murdered."

"Are you trying to con me? I know Davey had money, but that all went to his folks, I don't have any of it."

"Edith and Edward, they live at 4028 Point Road, and they have a horse barn in the back where he supposedly hung himself. Only he didn't. And I also know he gave you money, Susan. I really am an old friend of his and I'd like to figure out who killed him. He got involved in some really bad things. He maybe even did some bad things himself, and I think it got him killed."

"That money wasn't for me, I just delivered it."

"Obviously he trusted you. I need to know what happened to him, Susy, how things went so bad. I've uncovered some things that are very ugly. I'd like to think the man I knew couldn't have been involved in something that horrible, not Davey."

"Mister Slater, do you know where Titusville is?" she asked quietly.

"Sure, just off 95, near the Space Center."

"Could you meet me there today? There's someone I would like you to meet. I know it's a drive, it is for me too, but I'll close up shop right now and head up there."

"It's about the same for both of us. Will one o'clock work for you?"

"Take 406 east off 95. There's a Seven-Eleven about two miles down on your left. I'll be waiting in the parking lot. It's just a few blocks from there."

***

I was early, but so was she. She was standing by her car waiting and told me to park my pickup and ride with her. Susy Foster was all business, chewing her gum obsessively as she drove through the back streets to a quiet neighborhood half a dozen blocks from the main road. She glanced at me as we walked up to the single-story stucco. "Did I tell you I'm from Los Angeles originally?"

"No, and you still haven't said what we're doing here."

She smiled and pushed the doorbell. "I wasn't completely honest with you the other day either. I want you to see who David Templeton really was."

The door swung open and a pretty young girl pushed the screen door open and stepped back. She looked a dozen years younger than Susy but she had the same light brown hair and as soon as she spoke, I knew they were sisters. We sat down in the living room and she came back from the refrigerator with sweet tea. She poured us each a

191

glass then sat in a chair across from us, perched on the edge, rocking back and forth nervously.

"This is Sandy, Eric Slater. Sandy is my younger sister, and she's one of the girls that Davey Templeton brought back from hell." Susy paused to let that sink in, then nodded to her sister. "Tell him everything, Sandy, you said you could do this. It'll be okay."

The younger girl tried to smile. I've seen dogs, shy and nervous because they've been kicked one too many times show their teeth, and people think they're snarling when actually they're just afraid of being kicked again. That's how she smiled at me, like a dog that's afraid of being kicked. Her sister reached out and handed her a stick of Juicy Fruit. She popped it in her mouth and started chewing. Her next smile seemed more genuine.

"I quit smoking six months ago, and when I get nervous, I really want one."

"No problem." I tried to look reassuring and sympathetic. "Take your time, whatever you need."

She took a deep breath. "We lived in LA when I was a kid. Susy was already gone and my folks didn't get along so great. I was fifteen and out of control, drinking and running around with older guys. A lot of older guys. It got to where I wasn't ever going home. I always said I was at a girlfriend's house, when really I was shacked up with some idiot twice my age, snorting coke and getting so wasted I got passed around like a party favor when the money ran low."

I nodded. "It happens, you're not the first teenager to go down that road."

"One night, I was all dolled up for some reason, don't remember why, but my asshat boyfriend, Adrian, introduces me to this guy. Whitey his name was. Really big, heavy guy, and his hair was snow white, like he was eighty years old, only he wasn't. Anyway, they're both talking shit about how he's a big time Hollywood agent and he can make me a star." She stopped and took a swallow of her tea, then glanced at her sister.

"Go ahead, Sandy, I've heard this, and Slater's a big boy."

She cringed again, then continued. "So, before I know it, Adrian's gone and this Whitey guy, he says, come back to my place. I don't promote girls unless I get something out of it. Right then I knew I had to fuck him, if I wanted to be famous. By then I'd already slept with lots worse guys, so I thought what the hell, who doesn't want to be famous? We went back to his place and had a couple drinks. Next thing I know, I wake up gagged and hogtied in the back of an airplane."

"On the way to Dubai?" I guessed.

"I wish. Not sure, but some place over there, in the desert at least. There were six of us, locked in an old palace that was more like a prison. Two of the girls were from Taiwan, a couple from Brazil,

193

one girl was from Seattle. Chrissy, the Seattle girl, she was thirteen. Thirteen years old and she's a sex slave for some Sheik. He mostly kept her to himself, the rest of us were just there for general entertainment, for whoever wanted us." She wiped her eyes on the back of her sleeve and continued. "Other than the fact we were prisoners and basically sex toys, we got treated okay. We got fed and could listen to CD's and watch movies, and talk to each other as best we could.

Sometimes they drugged us. I'm not sure why, because we couldn't go anywhere anyway, but I had stretches where I couldn't remember anything for days sometimes. Sometimes the guys were decent, but we were never supposed to speak to them. Mostly rich old guys. If you talked about being a prisoner, or wouldn't do exactly what you were told, it didn't turn out good. One of the girls told a client she had been kidnapped. She trusted him because he seemed really nice, and they came and took her away. The guards said she was executed for being a spy."

"My God, where is this place? How can this happen in this day and age?" I asked.

"I never found out, not even what country I was in. Can you imagine? For a year and a half, I was a slave, raped on a regular basis until I was rescued, and to this day I couldn't tell you for sure where I was."

"How? How did you get out, and back here? Jesus, we're at war all over the world. Why aren't we there, killing the bastards that did this?"

"War? Some of the girls, the girls that were from Taiwan, they were servicing rich Americans!" I couldn't speak, I had no idea what I would have said.

"One night, out of the clear blue, one of the guards woke me up and took me out of there. I was sure he was going to rape me, then just kill me and leave me somewhere out in the desert to rot. But we drove into the desert in a jeep and he put me on a helicopter with a couple of other girls. I don't know where they were from before, but they were slaves too. They didn't speak any English and I'd never seen them before. The helicopter took us to another place, an airport somewhere and they gave us clothes and fed us. Then they put us on an airplane, like a corporate jet. There was a man on that plane, and he told me that I could never tell anyone about what had happened. He said that if I told, all the girls who were left behind would be tortured and murdered. He said if he could do it, someday it would be their turn to be rescued."

"That man, it was Davey Templeton?" I asked.

She nodded, tears streaming from her eyes. "He brought me back to Miami and even let me stay at his place for a couple days while I got my head on straight."

"His place, with Sam? How long ago was this?"

"One year, one month, and a week, but who's counting." She laughed and seemed to really relax. She fell back into her chair, sighing loudly. "I've never told that to anyone besides Susy. It feels good to get it out."

Her sister picked up the story. "Once she got back, Davey set her up with this place and gave her money to help her get going. I came out here to help her at first, then I went to work for Davey, trying to do whatever I could to help. Sometimes I delivered money for him. He'd been doing it for a while, burning the candle at both ends, and trying to get as many kids out as he could. That's the man Davey Templeton was, Slater. Great guy, like I said before."

I fought the emotions. "You have no idea how much I needed to hear that."

"Sandy's story isn't unique. There's an underground slave trade going on all the time, all over the world. Women, kids, girls and boys, sold like livestock to the highest bidder."

"But what about this Whitey guy? Could he be the same person that Davey knew?"

"Diablo Blanco? I don't know. Davey had bruises, all the time. That's why I asked you if he was with someone the day we first met. He told me he had a blood disease, poor clotting or something. Maybe the HIV, or maybe someone hitting him, I don't know. Why would you think he was with the same guy that took Sandy?"

"Davey was involved with someone like that years ago." I decided not to say more. "So, his roommate, Sam, he knows about all this? I talked to him, but he's a pretty good actor. I never had a clue."

"Did you meet his girlfriend, Dedra? Davey pulled her out of a brothel in Singapore two years ago. There were things Davey kept to himself. Sam didn't know everything that was going on, but he knew enough that he was willing to help fund what Davey was doing. Now with Davey gone, the whole network has kind of fallen apart and he's scared shitless. So of course, he doesn't know who to trust. These people have a lot of power and a long reach. That's why it's hopeless going to the cops. It's global. They've been talking about it at the UN for years, but people in this country refuse to acknowledge it could happen. Most people can't even imagine that it's real and they don't want to believe it."

"What about Gleason, he didn't strike me as a nice guy."

"He's more likely to be part of the problem. Over the years, a lot of these kids have come through the Agency's doors. That's why Davey asked me to start working there, to keep an eye on Andy and talk to some of the girls at the other branches. To try to figure out how the Talent Agency figures in and who knew what. There's a connection, but nothing I can prove yet."

"Holy Shit. I don't know what else to say. More than anything else, more than ever, I want to find the bastard that killed Davey. It sounds like he turned into kind of a hero. You too, Sandy, to come through everything you did and survive. It took a lot of courage."

"I didn't have a choice. I was just trying to stay alive." We stood and she walked with us to the door. "I still worry that someday they'll find me, so maybe I'm not that brave."

"What about my partner, can I tell your story to her?" Sandy looked stricken, but her sister nodded to her.

"If Slater trusts her, so can we, alright?"

Susy drove me back to my pickup and we talked on the way.

"You don't think they would come after her, after all this time, do you?" I asked.

"They got what they wanted from her. They'll just go a find a younger girl or boy to brutalize. I think that's why Davey was so careful, and he never told any of them where they had been. If they went to the US consulate or even the UN and started raising hell, trying to name names, who knows who'd end up dead? Don't think for a moment they would hesitate to kill people over this. Davey was taking a hell of a chance every time he rescued one of those kids, and I think he finally paid the price."

"Is what you're doing safe? You start digging around, they might come after you."

She hugged me quickly. "I can take care of myself. He was a good friend, and I really miss him. Helping girls like Sandy will be my way of paying him back."

"Thank you, again, knowing what Davey was doing really helps me. I was about ready to give up on humanity in general."

"Don't do that, Slater. Maggie will never marry you if you do that."

I laughed as I walked over to my truck and unlocked it. "That was just part of our cover story. We're not really engaged."

She grinned back at me as she put her car in gear. "Maybe just not yet."

I watched her drive away. Dedra. Sam's girlfriend's name was Dedra.

She was the third girl on Davey's list.

Chapter Twelve

Maggie wasn't thrilled to hear that I had met with Susy by myself, but she was happy that David Templeton wasn't quite the guy both of us were starting to think he was. Or maybe that was just me.

"I told you, Slater. I knew there had to be more to the story. People are basically good if you give them a chance."

"Right, Mary Poppins. Don't forget about all the slimy dirtbags that are abusing these kids to start with, and don't forget that Davey might have been involved with some of it, at least early on. Back in the day, he conned Rosie Cabello into thinking she could trust him."

"I don't think he did that willingly."

"I agree. I think this Whitey guy had some sort of a hold on him. This is starting to look worse than I ever thought, Maggie, really dangerous. I think I should keep digging, but maybe for now you should take a break."

"You ass! Davey was my friend too. Oh, I'm a poor little girl, and I should just run home and hide under my bed so the bad men don't get me. Fat chance of that happening! How can you..."

I threw up a hand. "Alright. I shouldn't have even suggested it. But neither one of us is bulletproof, and somebody already tried to run me over and knocked me in the head. We both need to be more careful, is all I'm saying. Don't forget what Davey told Angie the last time he was home, that you should move away from Point Road, that it isn't a safe place."

The redhead nodded. "Turned out he was right, it's where he died. He flies all over the world, all these dangerous locations, lives in Miami, then he ends up dead in his own backyard. What does that tell you?"

"That we should be looking around here?"

"Somebody we probably know, someone who knew about the barn. It always comes back to that. Even if they killed him somewhere else, they took him out there to make it look like a suicide. They knew where he lived and knew that barn was out there. Like I said before, not some complete stranger, and not some Sheik that caught him interfering with his whore-mongering. It was someone from here."

"Is that supposed to make me feel better?" I asked.

"Does this?" She slid aside the light sweatshirt she was wearing and I could see the outline of the shoulder holster and the small Glock through her top.

"Yeah, as a matter of fact it does. I'll have mine in a couple days, then we're going to the range and start practicing."

"I've been there already, but you can probably show me a thing or two." She grinned at me. The entendre had been unintentional. "I'm talking about shooting."

"I didn't think you were flirting, but it's good to know it crossed your mind."

"Not a hint, Slater. You'll know when that happens."

***

I spent the next couple of days filling out forms and mailing checks, clerical things that we all have to deal with. It was starting to look like I was going to be a licensed private investigator and contractor in the state of Florida. As far as I could tell, there was no reason I couldn't be both. The State might doubt my sanity, but they were still likely to cash my checks.

My plane needed some minor attention. A storm had blown through and tossed a couple of limbs down, smashing one of the exposed lights on the tail section. I spent a couple hours fixing the light, cleaning, and wondering how much bikers knew about airplanes.

It sounded like the trip north was going to happen, which didn't please me. Maybe it was part of the business, getting in the middle of complicated domestic situations, but there was a reason cops didn't like doing it. When you injected yourself into any kind of disagreement between family members you were asking for trouble. The irony of that thought had occurred to me, considering my relationship with Maggie and her sister.

But they were known elements, not some undoubtedly spoiled wild-child that had a thing for Harleys and men twice her age. I didn't have the details, but it seemed likely that if there was a bike rally, there might be more than a few bikers at the Thatcher's cabin. Jasmine had said a few bikers. That probably meant something different to a seventeen-year-old than it did to her grandmother. It was like having a few friends over for a party after school, but forgetting to tell your parents you were buying a keg. It was possible we'd find a small gathering, but much more likely we'd drop into a Sturgis-like setting of drunken mayhem and more alcohol and testosterone than we could possibly handle. Trying to take a young girl out of that mess wouldn't be easy, and it might be dangerous.

But she was a young girl, that was the thing. Granted, she wasn't a fifteen-year old that had been drugged and dragged halfway around the world while she was unconscious, but she was still too young to be straddling a Harley or the middle-aged dirtball that was driving it. As an investigator, was it my job to make those moral judgments? Or should I just do what the client asked me to do, take my twenty-five hundred bucks, and move on to the next case?

Bottom line, it wasn't the upcoming case that had me going in circles second guessing everything I was doing, it was the case I was already working on. Davey Templeton had almost certainly died at the hands of someone from the area, someone who knew about the horse barn.

I pondered all the reasons someone might have for killing Davey. It was possible he had taken the three million dollars he had in the bank from someone he shouldn't have, got caught, and paid the price. That was one theory.

Then there was Rosalyn and her over-protective boyfriend. Odds are Manny and his compadres would have been more than willing to extract their revenge on Davey if someone hadn't beat them to it. But if they had killed him, only a few hungry gators out in the 'Glades would have known about it. There would have been no pretense of suicide. Still, remotely possible, another theory.

Davey's dad had come and gone as a suspect. Three million dollars wasn't motive enough to kill your own son, even if he wasn't Captain of the football team or quite what you expected him to be. There may have been something going on between them that I didn't know about, some horrible truth as yet undiscovered. Still, probably the least likely of the options I had laid out in my head.

Then there was the Diablo. Davey had somehow gotten himself hooked up with the mysterious Whitey, or Diablo Blanco, if they were the same person. It seemed, perhaps for a while, he had been party to the horrors the man was perpetrating. I had to set that aside for now, and not think about the how and why of that, but concentrate on the good things he had been doing in the last couple years.

It seemed like more than a coincidence that Davey's onetime abuser matched the description of the man who had kidnapped Sandy Foster. Perhaps that was Davey's introduction into the world of child abduction. I had to think that it was that knowledge that had gotten him killed, that the Diablo learned what he was up to and killed him because of it. That seemed like the most likely theory.

Sandy had said that even in some God forsaken child prison in the Middle East, there were rich Americans. It's all about the money, that's what Davey had said. The degradations of a teenage whorehouse out in the desert somewhere were directly connected to the obscene amounts of money trading hands between assorted men with too much power. It was hard to imagine men sick enough, who felt self-entitled enough, that they would rape a child. Just because they could.

The idea sickened me. It sickened me more that I had one more theory. A new suspect to add to my list. There was one person I knew who ran in the circles of obscenely wealthy, self-entitled men. Someone who lived on Point Road, knew all about the horse barn, and was no fan of Davey Templeton. He was a man bereft of common decency according to Stacey Lane, and a man who seemed to be trying to block my investigation. It wasn't something I even wanted to consider, the least acceptable of all my theories. Yet a lot of the pieces fit. Could Davey's killer be my new partner's father, Frank Jeffries?

***

"You need to make us an appointment with this Maryanne Thatcher." The date of the bike rally was getting close, and my red-headed partner was eager.

"Slater, I have everything we need: GPS coordinates, Google map of the airstrip, and all the property nearby, even a picture of the girl." She handed me a photo of a young blond girl with pigtails.

"When was this picture taken? She looks ten years old in this. Of course she was cute and innocent back then. By now she's probably covered with Python tattoos, has a stud in her tongue, and spiked blue hair."

"I happen to think blue hair is sexy. I talked to Maryanne and everything is set, Partner."

"Well, Partner, I'm not risking my airplane, or my ass until I've talked to Grandma and she's convinced me we aren't going to have to kidnap little Miss Patty Hearst at gunpoint in order to get her away from her Biker-daddy. Call her, please!"

***

As Davey and I had observed from our bicycle trips up and down that stretch of road, most of the residents of Point Road were rich. In the vernacular of a thirteen-year-old, the Thatcher's were stinky rich. Obscenely so. In fact, they had gone beyond obscenely so by a few hundreds of million of dollars. With tongue firmly planted in my cheek, I referred to them as pornographically rich as the iron gates parted and we drove down the tree lined lane toward the big house. Not surprisingly, my partner didn't appreciate the pun.

"If Maryanne had a son in the business instead of a daughter, you wouldn't say a word about it."

"Right. I'm sure Ron Jeremy's mother is proud as hell."

"That guy really needs to lose some weight," she offered.

"That's your only problem with Ron Jeremy?"

"It's a case, Slater. The Thatchers made their money in oil. Divine's money is peanuts compared to Maryanne's holdings in the Dakotas."

"Oil trumps porn. Get it?" She rolled her eyes, but I was pretty sure I'd won that round.

Whatever the origin of the Thatcher's fortune, there was no denying it had to be considerable. Much like the Templeton's, the Thatcher's drive was at least a quarter mile long. Unlike the old plantation, there was no rock wall. The drive was lined with shrubs, all exactly the same height, all trimmed exactly the same way, all in groups of three, all of the groups spaced evenly. I looked out at the field on my side and saw that inside the shrub line was a white fence, and inside the fence were half a dozen well-groomed, well-fed horses.

It was an idyllic scene: the green grass, the white fence, the horses; like one of those paint by number sets you do while discovering you have absolutely no artistic abilities. The horses seemed excited by our presence and trotted along on the other side of the fence, keeping pace with the car. Every few seconds the painting changed, rearranging itself when the shrubs blocked our view. First there were six horses, then four, then two, then just one. One horse, standing all alone as we neared the big house. The tall animal ran out of pasture but stood in the nearest corner of the fencing, poking its head over the top railing and staring at us intently.

It looked sad to me. I wondered if that had been Jasmine's horse, and it followed each time a car came down the driveway, hoping it was the blue-haired wild child come home to saddle up and go for a ride. Beyond the white fence and the horses, there was a bright red barn with white trim. A shiny new John Deere tractor stood just inside and a farm hand was loading hay into the small wagon behind it.

We pulled up to the big house, following the circle of the cobblestone driveway to a front porch that was flanked by two enormous white pillars. I thought about how Angela would have looked right at home on that porch, drinking a mint julip and waving a fan at her face while she complained to Mammy about the heat and waited for gentleman callers.

"Slater! Did you doze off?" Maggie dragged me back to reality.

"Just a minute." I jumped out of the car quickly. "I'll be right back."

She stood there watching me as I trotted down to the fence. Who in their right mind would leave a place like this, ride on a Harley with a smelly biker, when you could relive a scene from National Velvet anytime you wanted? Funny, how easy it is to imagine someone else's dream, or what you think it should be. The reality is never as good.

The horse flipped its head as I walked up to the fence and reached out. "Hey, watch it! That's mare's mean as hell." I jerked my hand back just in time as the glue factory reject took a vicious swipe, trying to tear my finger off. A middle aged, brown farmhand walked up laughing. "I swear, old Dolly likes the taste of people. Never seen a horse that ornery."

I glared at the animal. "I felt sorry for her. I thought she was lonely. Stupid horse."

The man shrugged. "Probably is lonely. These horses are just for show mostly, for rich folks to look at. They have a trainer that comes over twice a week and they behave for her, and they love my son, but that one would bite me too if I let her."

The horse reached across the fence, trying for a piece of my shoulder and the brown man grabbed her nose and gave it a little twist. The mare jumped back, spun around and ran off across the pasture, then dropped and started rolling in the grass.

"See? She's laughing at us. I didn't hurt her, but she has to know who's boss. I'm no horse wrangler, but I know that much."

"What do you do, when you're not being a horse wrangler?"

"Carpentry, most of the time. Anything for a buck, like they say. I'm just helping out my kid today, filling in."

"Really? I'm looking for a carpenter, maybe pretty soon. Do you have a card?"

"Slater, what are you doing? We have an appointment. I'm sure Maryanne is a busy woman." Maggie had walked over and nodded to my new friend. "Is this man bothering you, Sir?"

He grinned and extended a hand. "I'm Luis, Luis Sanchez. And sure, I'll give you a card. I have a couple of guys I work with too, so we can handle pretty much any job."

"He'll need a lot of help," Maggie offered.

"Why are you always so mean to me?" I asked. I just got a shrug and a smile. We made all the introductions, exchanged cards, then Maggie and I walked back up to the big house and rang the bell. Wouldn't you know, they had a butler.

***

Maryanne Thatcher had been a widow for about eight years according to Maggie. If I was inclined to be a gold digger, I would have given up on carpentry, investigating, even Maggie, and pursued the sixty-year-old waiting for us in her office. She was stunning. I won't say she looked younger than her years, I'll just leave it at that. Stunning.

She sat behind a giant mahogany desk with papers strewn everywhere, half of which were beyond arm's reach. There was a huge map of North and South Dakota on the wall behind her covered with yellow and black stickpins. They created a bumblebee pattern that I presumed designated the locations of all her oil wells. She stood up as we were escorted into the office by the aforementioned butler. He announced us like we were royalty, halfway bowed, then pulled the door shut.

Maryanne shook our hands and laughed a little. "Edgar is ridiculously formal, he's old school from New York. We picked him up after the mess in 09, just before Reggie died. Reginald Muffin, if you can believe that for a name. I insisted on keeping my own, thankfully. How would you like to have a daughter in those damn porn movies named Divine Muffin? The company she worked for actually wanted to use it, but I had so many lawyers on their ass they had to back down."

I couldn't help myself. "Kind of catchy."

"Slater's a kidder," Maggie shared.

Maryanne motioned for us to sit, then walked behind her giant desk. "It's fine. I gave up being upset about it a long time ago. Divine's not a bad person, mostly. We talk, and she still flies down here once in a while. She was a wild one too, but she didn't leave home until after high school. She still calls her movies art." She caught me looking at the big map and spun her chair around. "That is my art. The black pins are wells that are shut down, temporarily. Sooner or later the Saudis will get the price back up where I can make money again."

"North Dakota is a long way from Florida," Maggie pointed out.

"My grandfather started buying land up there years ago. He loved the cold. I still own his old cabin. That's how Jasmine got hooked up with this Cletus fellow. She met him at Sturgis last summer."

"When she was sixteen?" I asked, ignoring Maggie's look.

"Divine had a boyfriend that was at the rally and she took Jasmine along. She did a piss poor job of keeping an eye on her, apparently. She met this guy and they stayed in touch, then she ran off a while ago with him to find herself. And do a lot of drugs, I'm guessing. Her mother has given up on her, but I'm not going to."

"Did you call the cops? She isn't eighteen."

"The house in Georgia is my summer place, but Divine lived there full time up until a couple years ago. She would fly out to do some movies and send Jasmine down here for a month at a time. But Jasmine's a legal resident of Georgia, and the law there is sixteen. My lawyers could make a case for crossing state lines, but what's the point? If I drag her back here kicking and screaming, she'll just run away again. She's incredibly smart, but horribly stubborn."

Everyone thinks their grandkids are incredibly smart, even the really stupid ones. Running off with a thirty-four-year-old biker didn't strike me as a sign of genius. "If we get her away from this guy and bring her back, won't she just run away again?"

"She ran away from her mother, but I think she'll stay here for me. We always talked about a good college for her, and she always said she wanted that. I never reined Divine in enough when she was that age, but it's time I do that for my granddaughter. I've talked to her by phone and it seems like she's almost ready to cave, but I'd like it to be her choice. I think if you and Maggie go up there, maybe put on a little show like we talked about, she'll see what she's missing and want to come home."

"What do you mean, a little show?" I asked.

"Maggie? Is he on board with this?" They both looked at me.

"Here's the deal, Slater." Maggie took a breath. "We go up there, come in like the plane is having trouble, then call for a mechanic. Only not really. So, the mechanic can't come until the next day, and we get ourselves invited to hang out, maybe stay there because there's six bedrooms."

"Wait." I stopped her. "What if there are forty bikers and no place to sleep? We camp out?"

"Jasmine called me to ask if they could use the place, Mister Slater. She doesn't seem to have much respect for her mother, but she and I communicate very well. I told her that if there were more than ten people at the house, I would have the cops there in half an hour. She is surprisingly responsible about things like that. She promised me, and I believe her."

"She's seventeen. You don't see the problem with that?"

"I had to get her somewhere safe, and I'm a little desperate. Like I said, she's teetering. I think she wants to come home. She just has to get away from this Cletus character and figure out that it's not the way normal people live."

Maggie took over again. "That's where we come in. We go in there and act all happy and lovey-dovey, like we're the all-American couple. We'll say we're engaged. Whatever her happily ever after is, she'll realize she can't have that with the old dirt bag on the motorcycle, or at least figure out that she needs someone closer to her own age. We'll pretend you're closer to my age, not an old pervert like her boyfriend."

"You are closer to my age. Lovey-dovey? That doesn't sound too hard. How lovey-dovey do I get to be?"

She ignored me. "We have to make her understand that she should finish school, go to college, then meet somebody nice if that's what she wants to do. She can't be planning to ride around on the back of a Harley for the rest of her life."

"She's too smart for that," Maryanne said. "But part of the problem is that she doesn't want to hurt this guy's feelings. She can be a handful, but she has a good heart."

"Yeah, we all know somebody like that, right, Maggie?"

The redhead ignored me, again. "It sounds like she just needs a nudge in the right direction. Once I get her alone, I can convince her she should ditch this guy, then we wait until everybody's asleep and fly out of there. Any better ideas, Slater?"

"Nothing comes to mind, but if anything happens to my airplane..."

"I'll buy you a new one." Maryanne smiled pointing at the map behind her. "There's still a lot of yellow pins up there. I could buy you a dozen airplanes."

Chapter Thirteen

It was just past three in the afternoon when we made our first pass, plenty high up and a quarter mile away. Maggie had my binoculars and was inspecting the field. "Looks good to me, Slater. Maryanne said the airstrip itself gets regular maintenance. Where are all the bikers?"

"The rally starts tomorrow, you'd think they'd be piling in. You don't really believe that girl is going to keep all her boyfriend's buddies from staying there, do you?"

"It does seem out of character for a seventeen-year-old. This guy she's with is supposed to be kind of a badass."

"I'll bet you can take him," I said.

She dropped the binoculars onto her chest. "No violence, and you should leave your gun in the plane. I'll keep mine on me, just in case. Don't bother telling me that's sexist. Any greasy biker puts his hands on me, I'm shooting him."

"Now you're being judgmental," I mocked. "Most bikers aren't the guys you see in the movies. Most of them are eight to five working people that are just trying to get away."

"Those aren't the kind of bikers that take a girl who just turned seventeen for a ride, in the literal sense. Maryanne had this guy checked out before she knew about us, and he's bad news. He's been busted for drugs and assault, twice. Big too. Six-one and three hundred pounds, according to his driver's license."

"How'd they get that information?"

"I don't know, the internet maybe? Maybe they're better detectives than us. We need to get on it and learn all the tricks."

"You really enjoy this don't you, this playing detective?"

"It beats spending my days trying to keep Angela from going over the edge. I'd do anything for her, but it gets to be a grind. This seems good, we're helping people. Davey's Mom would have spent the rest of her life thinking he may have been a drug smuggler and hung himself if not for the fact that we looked into it. That's important, isn't it?"

"I haven't explained all that to her yet. I think we need to dig a little more and verify everything."

"Really? You don't believe Susan's story?"

"Yeah, I think. There are some strings I'd like to tie up before I take her off my list."

She lifted the field glasses up again, peering at the distant airstrip. "You have a list of people you think might have killed Davey?"

"Of course. This Diablo, or Whitey guy, he's top of the list. It's kind of a big coincidence, him taking Susy's sister in California, then being the same guy that was involved with Davey. That's why I'm still wondering about Susy."

"That's what I thought. Pretty elaborate story though, if she was just trying to cover her tracks. Who else?"

"There are a lot of people on my list."

She dropped the binoculars again, letting them hang by their string and asked the question I didn't want to answer. "Where's my Dad on your list, Slater?"

I shrugged. "You're the one that wants to be a detective, where is he on yours?"

***

We made several passes at a considerable distance. Unless you have the eyes of a raptor, a plane on the horizon half a mile away is barely noticeable, but the field glasses I'd brought were hi-definition Vortex 12x50. From four thousand feet I could see Manatee swimming with their pups in the Saint Johns River or spot big alligators in the Everglades. They hadn't been cheap, so finding a practical use for them was nice.

"I only see three motorcycles down there and one of them has a sidecar."

"Really? Anybody out in the yard?"

"I don't think so. How do we make sure they see us come in?"

"I'll buzz the house, get in close and hit the throttle, then go to the far end of the field and do a low turn just over the trees, cut the power and coast in."

"That should get their attention. Will that duct tape hold up?"

"You're a laugh a minute. Wind is right to get around quick, but we'll have to takeoff downwind tonight or in the morning. Hopefully by then we'll have another body, which means more weight. Still, we're not carrying a lot of fuel, so it shouldn't be a problem."

"I'm not worried, you're the one that said flying comes natural to you."

"I might bounce us in a little just for show, so don't get nervous, okay?"

I dropped the flaps and came in as slow as I dared, just clearing the brick chimney that protruded above the roof of the two-story structure, then went to full throttle to be sure to make as much noise as possible. I flew to the other end of the big field, wobbling my wings, then banking sharply to get lined up with the small grassy runway. I glanced toward the house and saw several people running out onto the porch.

Whoever was in charge of mowing hadn't gotten around to it lately. The grass was so long it was hard to find the ground, and the first bounce was unintentional. I gave it a little rudder which cocked the plane over and corrected with the ailerons to make it look like I was doing a lot of maneuvering, then as we lost speed, braked hard and spun the plane off the runway, hoping it looked unintentional. If any of the people watching us happened to be a pilot, they might have suspected our trouble wasn't real.

Maggie tucked the binoculars under the seat, threw the door open and rolled down off the wing, then fell to her hands and knees. Three of the six people watching us started running, and by the time I climbed out they had Maggie sitting in the grass a short distance away. She was sobbing like a pregnant teen on Doctor Phil. Very convincing. I ran over, playing the concerned fiancé.

She was being dramatic. "Oh my God, I thought sure we were going to die! The damn plane just lost power, then it was roaring like it was going to blow up. I was never so scared in my life."

A middle-aged man with very little hair and two women were leaning over Maggie, making reassuring noises and trying to get her to drink some water. The balding man was likely the driver of the BMW with the side car, and the short plump woman at his side was undoubtedly his wife, since they were already bickering about the best way to make Maggie feel better. The second woman, big and tough looking, turned to me.

"We heard you come down. I thought sure you were going to pile that thing into the trees."

"I don't know what happened. We lost power, then the engine came back just long enough to get

221

us into this clearing. Just dumb luck there was an airstrip here."

"Bad luck, I'd say." It was a fourth voice, and I turned to get my first look at Cletus Johnson. He was all of three hundred, had just a little more hair than Sidecar, and wore bib overalls and a plaid shirt. If it wouldn't have been for the faraway look in his eye that indicated some form of intoxication, I would have mistaken him for an Iowa farmer down to look for that winter home he and the Missus had been talking about. He stared at the plane like it was a busted combine. "You need to get that thing out of here."

"Yeah, sure," I apologized quickly. "I didn't mean to land here, but it was that or in the trees, and this looked like the better option."

He frowned and spit a wad of snus on the ground between us, then cocked his head and looked back at me. "Are you trying to be a smart-ass?"

Jasmine Thatcher had walked up behind him. "Look at his wife, Dipshit. Do you really think he wanted to fly that wreck in here?" I was a little unhappy that Jasmine had referred to the Piper as a wreck, but I was glad she had shut down her belligerent boyfriend. He looked at me and frowned, then over at the plane and Maggie.

"Just didn't think you wanted any more people here, Jaz."

Jaz, as her behemoth biker mate called her did have blue hair, half a head of it, and it was spiked. The other side was shaved with a sizable tattoo imprinted across her skull. I couldn't read it and I didn't try, but my head hurt just looking at it. No Pythons or Dragons on her arms or shoulders anyway, and her eyes were clear and her smile welcoming. She was actually quite pretty, blue hair and all.

She held out her hand. "I'm Jasmine, this is Cletus. Brandon and his wife Gracie are looking after your wife. That's Tracy with them, and Doug." She looked around. "I guess Doug's too stoned to get off the porch. What the heck, we thought you were going to smack right into the woods over there. Is she hurt?"

"No, just scared the crap out of her, me too. Is this your place?"

"My grandmother owns it, we're just using it for the weekend. What's wrong with your airplane? Friday afternoon, it's going to be hard to find someone to work on it."

"Fuel, I think, maybe the filter or water in the tank. I'm not a very good mechanic. I'll call and see what I can do about finding someone."

"Sweetie?" Cletus smiled down at her and pointed at a small garage that was on the other side of the landing strip. There was no door on the old structure and I could see the taillights of an older car, probably a Toyota. "Maybe they could just use your Grandma's car and go in to town, fix the airplane tomorrow."

"You're welcome to do that if you want, but let's take your wife inside and let her relax a little. Maybe a cold beer would make her feel better."

I smiled over at Maggie. Sidecar and his wife had gotten her to her feet. "Not married yet, but she does like beer. And the carbs would probably calm her down." I went over and put an arm around Maggie and kissed her cheek. "Sorry about this, Hon, but no one got hurt and that's the main thing."

"I told you to hire someone to do the maintenance, but oh no, you had to try to do it yourself. The whole damn plane is held together by duct tape!" She smiled at Jasmine. "I'm Maggie, and this is Slater. We're getting married next Spring, if he doesn't kill me first. Men, right?"

"Idiots, the whole bunch of 'em," Jasmine agreed. I looked at Cletus, hoping to bond over our shared castigation, but just got an empty-eyed stare. He looked down and spit again.

We walked up to the house and met Doug. Doug looked like the biker in Maggie's head, the one the orangutan in the Clint Eastwood movie knocked off his motorcycle. Right turn, Clyde, and Doug would get knocked off his bike. Doug had taken a few too many shots to the head, or at the very least, too many wrong turns in his life. He smiled vaguely at us and nodded when Jasmine introduced us, then went back to humming and staring off into the distance. If it came to a confrontation, it didn't seem like Doug would be much of a threat. His wife looked like she would be more likely to hurt somebody than Doug, anchored to the rocker as he was.

Brandon and Gracie looked completely out of place in the company they were keeping. They were dressed like tourists and had a few years on Cletus. Neither of them seemed altered, drugs or otherwise. Then again, it was four o'clock in the afternoon. It wasn't anything like the scenario I had expected, but it was possible there were still more people coming. As it was, if we could convince Jasmine to leave, Cletus was the only major obstacle I could see. Granted, he was a very large obstacle.

"I have sweet tea, beer, diet soda, or water. Pick your poison," Jasmine said from the refrigerator. "Feeling any better?" She brought us both a can of sweetened iced tea. "Sugar will stop the shakes for now. We're grilling hotdogs and brats in an hour or so, and you're welcome to eat with us. Cletus, you should get the grill going."

"I'm fine now, sorry, I'm usually not such a baby." Maggie smiled and drank some tea.

I wondered silently what it would take to scare Maggie Jeffries, certainly not something as mundane as a plane crash. I sipped my tea and looked at Cletus again.

I'm not a judge of what seventeen-year-old girls find interesting in men, and I hadn't had any reason to wonder about it for twenty some years. Whatever it was, when I was that age, I didn't have it. Back then I was too busy mooning over the increasingly beautiful Angela Jeffries to be concerned about what mortal teenaged girls considered attractive. Pretty sure it wasn't obese bikers twice their age. But then, none of them had blue hair back then.

Cletus dropped into a chair and popped open a beer, glared in my direction for a moment, then went back to gazing fondly at Jasmine. I watched him watch her for a minute as she chatted with Maggie. His eyes followed her every movement and he smiled slightly at each new inflection of her voice. He actually broke into a small grin when she laughed at something Maggie said. Maybe that's what she liked about him; he worshipped her. He glanced back at me and saw that I was watching him. He leaned forward and stood quickly, then popped the clasps loose on his bibs.

"You probably want to call a mechanic about that plane. You might get somebody out tomorrow if you call right away. Saturday, it's going to cost you. Jaz, Sweetie, I'm going to get out of these bibs, they're too damn hot. Then I'll start the charcoal."

"Thanks, Babe." She called out as he lumbered back to a door on the far end of the great room that I presumed was a bedroom. The endearment made me cringe inwardly and I turned my attention back to what Maggie and the young girl were talking about.

"We're having the wedding outside and Slater's boss is going to marry us. I don't know if that's something lawyers can just do, or if he has to be an online minister or what. But he's making Slater partner in the law firm, as kind of a wedding present."

"That's so cool. How'd you two meet?"

Maggie threw her head back and laughed loudly. "Drunk one night at a frat party in college. I can't even remember it, but we woke up in bed together the next morning and we've been together ever since. Don't know what it is, but I love the big dope."

"She calls me things like that all the time." I smiled when Jasmine looked in my direction. I was feeling pretty good about myself, suddenly being engaged and a lawyer and all. "I don't think she really means it."

"Oh please, you know how much I love you." She made a kissy face, which I thought was completely over the top, but Jasmine laughed.

"Someday, maybe I'll have that. Cletus is great, but it's not a long-term thing. Kind of like the hair, just making a statement."

"I love your hair," Maggie gushed. "I would never have the guts to do that."

"I'm going out and try to call a mechanic," I said. "I don't need to listen to you two talk about your hair." The girl had given Maggie an opening and I wanted to leave them alone to let the girl-talk work its way back to their respective man troubles. Ideally, seeing how happy Maggie was in the white bread world we were presenting would send Jasmine running back to her grandmother, ready to go back to school and move on with her privileged life. Really, I couldn't imagine any girl not wanting to be like Maggie.

I walked out onto the porch with my cell phone in my hand. Tracy had joined Doug on the porch and they were both sprawled out in their rocking chairs passing a joint back and forth. Tracy held it up and raised an eyebrow. I waved a hand to pass and she shrugged and squeezed off the end of the doobie to extinguish it. Doug nodded at me and grinned. "Could you take us for a plane ride later? That would be far out."

"Yeah, maybe, if I can get a mechanic up here and get it running right."

"Far out!" He grinned and returned his gaze to the field and the green giraffes that were undoubtedly running around in his brain. I walked out toward the Piper and made a few imaginary phone calls, then I climbed in the plane, set the fuel mixture extra rich and turned it over a few times. It was still hot from the flight in, so it flooded quickly, coughed a time or two, then backfired sharply. All as expected. I climbed out and got on my phone again and paced back and forth like I was aggravated. Sidecar and his wife walked up, inspected the Piper, then came over to talk to me.

"No luck, huh? Are you going to take the car into town?"

"Not sure, pretty far out to call a taxi."

"We were thinking of going in tonight ourselves, but we can't find a place to stay this late without paying a small fortune. This isn't our kind of deal."

"Oh? I figured you were all old friends."

"Not really. Cletus worked for me a few years back. I'm an electrical contractor, and he invited us to ride down with him. He's not the same guy that worked for me. All the years of drugs and partying have changed him. He's gotten a little crazy."

"Batshit crazy, but I always said he was," Mrs. Sidecar agreed wide-eyed. I struggled, then remembered her name was Gracie. "He's always snorting something. I don't even want to know what."

"So, Gracie, have you talked to the girl? She looks pretty damn young to be running around with a guy like that. Is she okay?" I asked.

"I have no idea what she's doing with that moron. Good drugs? She seems really bright, and most of the time he acts like he's scared of her."

Sidecar snickered. "He's whipped, and that little girl is a ballbuster. He wanted to bring more riders, but she said no. They got into it on the way down here and it was ugly. She got right in his face and told him what for. We were close to just sneaking off and riding down to the rally on our own, but I don't know if I trust him alone with her. If the pea flips, he might do something to her. He's got a terrible temper and when he goes off it's not pretty. That's why I had to let him go from work. He got into it with two of my other guys and beat the hell out of them both. Put one of them in the hospital."

"Why are you even with him?"

"He apologized and paid the guy's bills. He's just one of those people that are really funny once you get to know him and great to talk to, but I think he's doing speed or something. When he's on that shit you just want to get away from him. You be careful if he gets mad. You're a good-sized guy and everything, but he's a whole lot tougher than he looks, and quick as a cat. I've heard of him all but killing guys before, and he's got a gun."

"Jasmine won't let him wear it. She makes him keep it in his backpack," Gracie said, then snickered.

"Ballbuster, like I said." Sidecar nodded. "If I was you, I'd take the car like he said. Once they get to drinking, they might start fighting, and you don't want to get in the middle of that."

I frowned for their benefit. "He's going to wind up hurting her at some point. How long have they been together? How old is she?"

"Jasmine says they met last summer, but they've only been together for a few weeks, shacking up. She says she's eighteen, but I wouldn't bet on it," Gracie muttered.

"Maggie and her are already yakking away like they're best buddies. Maybe she can talk some sense into her. This is her grandparents' place?"

"She told me it's her grandmothers, that her mom is out of the picture, but that she really loves her grandma. Said she just needed a vacation from it all."

Sidecar nodded toward the house where the overstuffed biker was squirting lighter fluid on the grill. "Cletus said her family has more money than God. I think he figures he can get his hands on some of it eventually. But I don't really think he's in it for the dough. I think the crazy bastard is in love with her. But she's a ballbuster, I'm telling you."

We walked back up to the house. Everything Brandon and his wife said jived with what I knew, which was reassuring. There was no way, psycho biker or not, that I wanted to take Jasmine out of there if she wasn't willing to go. I was hoping Maggie could work some magic.

As we walked up to the porch Cletus leaned in to light the grill. The evening sun still had some heat to it and the lighter fluid must have vaporized enough to create a sizeable fireball when Cletus put a match to it. He jumped back, swearing and shaking his hand. The air smelled of burnt hair and he slapped his hand against his leg quickly to quench a small fire that had started on the sleeve of the shirt he had just changed into.

From his observation post in the rocker Doug laughed wildly as if the whole incident was performance art put on just for his enjoyment. He couldn't or wouldn't stop laughing and even clapped his hands and said "far out" over and over like a scraggly haired John Denver wannabe. I was sure, if Cletus had the explosive temper Sidecar claimed he did, being laughed at when he was on fire would set him off.

I think it was close, but he and Doug must have had a history together, some bond formed over drug fueled episodes going back into their childhood. Cletus shot a dirty look at Doug, who, when he realized he had been noticed, laughed even harder. Rather than the explosion I had imagined, Cletus turned back to the grill and squirted more lighter fluid on the charcoal, running backwards as the flame chased him across the yard and attempted to engulf his arm, the can, and the dry grass at his feet.

At this point, we were all laughing uproariously. Doug had literally collapsed and fallen off his rocker, and even Cletus was giggling like a teenage girl. Unfortunately, the only real teenaged girl around was not amused.

Jasmine Thatcher came flying out of the house, screaming at the top of her lungs, calling Cletus, Doug, and all of us as a group, any and every name she could think of and a few she manufactured. Cletus looked like he had been poleaxed, and even Doug managed to swallow his mirth, containing it to an occasional snort while he listened to the tiny blue-haired girl deliver her lecture.

"You burn down my grandmother's house you dumb son of a bitch, and I will personally hire five guys to beat you to a bloody pulp before I send your sorry, no-good ass back to that shit hole where I found you." It was a lot longer than that, and there was a lot more swearing, most of which I can't remember, then she spun around and slammed her way back into the house.

Sidecar poked me with an elbow. "See? Ballbuster."

* * *

Maggie and Jasmine came out after another fifteen minutes with a plastic tablecloth and silverware and started covering a picnic table that sat in the yard. They were fighting the breeze, so I got up and went to help them weigh down the flimsy plastic with enough plates to keep it from blowing away.

Maggie surprised me by grabbing my hand suddenly and wrapping me into a hug, followed by a long steamy kiss. "Thanks, Honey," she said aloud, then leaned next to my ear. "We're the happy couple, Jasmine's watching."

"Anytime," I said aloud and leaned against her again, kissing her a little longer than necessary, considering it was just for show.

When she came up for air, she gave me an honest blush, and a bemused smile. "Enough. Save something for the honeymoon."

"You two are so damn cute together." Jasmine chuckled, throwing down more silverware on the table. I saw her looking at Cletus from the corner of her eye. I may not know seventeen-year-old girls, but I knew that look. Cletus wasn't going to last.

The hotdogs and brats were great and it seemed like we had all bonded over our shared experience of being schooled by an angry child. Her anger didn't last and soon we were all seated around the picnic table, gorging ourselves on the food, drinking beer, and talking like we were old friends. Even Cletus managed to break a smile and lift himself from his intermittent melancholy to talk and tell a couple of funny stories. I could see why Sidecar said what he had said, and I had to remind myself that the guy was basically a rapist in any state where it wasn't considered acceptable to marry your cousin. He could be engaging, and a small part of me felt sorry for him.

The pot came out after supper. We carried everything inside, then all sat around the big kitchen table to talk some more, and of course Doug pulled out a bag of his best. Maggie and I both passed. I never was a pot guy and I was relieved that Maggie didn't join in, if for no other reason than we both needed to keep our wits about us. I was sitting next to Doug who passed me the joint and mumbled something about being a bummer when I didn't take a toke. Surprisingly, Sidecar and his wife both inhaled eagerly.

He looked over at me and grinned. "What's a little marijuana? It'll make me sleep good." My guess was that Doug and his significant other wouldn't have any trouble sleeping. After a couple rounds, Jasmine and Cletus passed, then Sidecar and his wife. Doug kept smoking until he burned his fingers. Jasmine stood up and started picking up the plates and Maggie helped her.

"Maggie and Slater are staying the night," Jasmine said to no one in particular. "I'm going to hang around here tomorrow and skip the rally." That was directed at Cletus.

"We can talk about it," Cletus said levelly.

Jasmine was having no part of it. "What's to talk about? They may need a ride to town, and I'm sick of looking at motorcycles. Also, I'm sick of you thinking you can tell me what to do."

"Alright, Jaz, whatever you want." He said it calmly enough, then sat there like a petulant child, shooting ugly looks at me, Maggie, and Jasmine in turn. I could see it building. "I thought you and I were going to make a week of it." He finally erupted loudly.

"I don't want to go, so I'm not," Jasmine said matter-of-factly.

"Jaz, Honey?" Anger hadn't worked, now there was pleading in his tone. For a moment again, I felt bad for him. "What's going on?" He asked her softly.

"I don't think I can keep doing this. I told you that before. I think I have to go home."

She dropped the dishes she had in her hands and ran suddenly to the bedroom. He jumped up and followed, but she had locked the door. The rest of us sat there, trying to pretend we weren't listening as he pleaded with her to open the door, alternating between begging and demanding until she finally relented and let him in. I looked around the table. Sidecar put an arm around his wife and shrugged, Maggie basically made the same gesture, and Doug scratched his ragged beard thoughtfully and said, "Bummer."

I volunteered to help Maggie with the dishes since everybody else was stoned and only had enough energy to disappear up the stairs to their respective bedrooms.

"Where are we supposed to sleep, and what's the plan?" I asked her quietly as I took a plate to dry.

"She said she's been wanting to end it for a couple weeks, but that he's totally obsessed with her. She's afraid, not so much of him, but for him. A little of both. She really thinks he might flip out and kill himself if she leaves."

"So all this was for nothing? She was going to go home anyway?"

"Maybe, maybe not. Look at it this way, we're getting five-grand between us and you got to make out with me. Besides, wanting to leave and leaving are two different things. I wanted to leave Richie for two years and the only reason I finally did was because he told me he'd knocked up his secretary. A hundred bucks says he's in there being sweet and reminiscing, reminding her of all the fun they've had. If that doesn't work, he'll move on to begging, then probably anger and intimidation."

"That won't go well. Did you hear her before? Sidecar was right, that little girl's a ballbuster."

"Who the hell is Sidecar? And a what!"

"Okay, that's not politically correct, I know. Let's just say she's headstrong, like her grandmother said. Sidecar is Brandon. How could you not get that?"

"I don't get half of what you say, Slater." She flicked some soap at me. There was no noise coming from the other end of the house and I wasn't sure if that was a good sign or not.

"Did you tell her who we really are, and that Maryanne sent us?"

"No. That would just make her mad. Once she decides for sure to go home, maybe we can tell her. If we tell her before she makes up her mind about Cletus, she might run again and stay with him. Girls don't always think logically when they're seventeen."

"Does that ever change?" I got a soap bath that time, which didn't stop me. "At least the kissing was fun. Where do we sleep, Honey?"

***

It was a long night. There was a small bedroom tucked behind the kitchen that I wasn't even aware of, and there was just enough room for a dresser and a double bed. I suggested we sleep in our clothes just in case we had to make a run for it in the middle of the night. Really, I couldn't see both of us in that bed, undressed to any degree, without me embarrassing myself. Double beds are made for kids, not two full-grown adults that are painfully aware of every time their bodies come in contact. Again, maybe that was just me.

The yelling started about four in the morning and went on for an hour. I don't know how Maggie slept through it, but she did. She buried her face deeper under the covers and pressed up against me for warmth, which was excruciating and nice at the same time. I listened to the couple fighting on the far end of the house for another ten minutes, then there was an ominous silence. I got up and went out into the great room on the pretext of using the bathroom. No one was in the big living room when I went in, but when I came back out, I could see Cletus sitting on the couch. It looked like he might have been crying. At least his eyes were red. There was a line of white powder on the coffee table, so that's not all he was doing.

"You alright?" I knew he didn't like me, but we had bonded over a flaming barbeque grill.

He looked up at me coldly. "Go back to bed, Asshole."

At six-thirty I heard noise, footsteps on the open stairs that went to the second floor. I eased out of the bed and went out into the kitchen. The spot where Cletus had been on the couch was empty, and the master bedroom door was standing open. Sidecar and his wife, each with a small piece of luggage in their hands, were standing by the front door talking to Jasmine. I walked over and shook hands with the pair and remembered to call Sidecar by his proper name.

"If you're ever in Fargo, look me up. Kramer Electric. We're heading into town to the rally. You guys going to be okay, Jasmine?"

"No way he and I were going to last much longer anyway, you know that. He's outside sulking, but I'm done. I'm going to tell Doug and Tracy they can camp out here in the field if they want, Cletus too. I'll take Grandma's car and give these guys a lift to town, then head back down to Jacksonville and see if she'll take me back."

Sidecar and his wife drove away waving and Jasmine and I went back inside. Maggie was up and had coffee brewing. She hugged Jasmine quickly, which started a small waterfall of tears from the blue-haired teenager.

"I feel bad for him, but I can't stay with him just because of that. I don't love him. I don't know if my grandmother will take me back or not, but I have to get away from him. He's getting psycho, more than normal. I'm afraid of him."

"Your grandmother will take you back, Jasmine. She sent us after you." Being partners, a discussion before-hand would have been nice, but Maggie's instincts were usually right.

"Oh great! She sent you, and your plane isn't really broken?" I could hear the change in her tone, the headstrong girl returning.

"She loves you Jasmine. Real love. You said you were ready to go home anyway."

I could see her working it out in her head, then she gave in. "But, Maggie, I thought you really liked me."

"Of course I like you, Jasmine, that isn't fake."

"Are you two even a couple? Are you really getting married?"

"We are, but I'm not really a lawyer." I tried to help. "She's marrying a bum."

"Just because I'm a dummy, doesn't mean you should be." Maggie laughed and wrapped her arms around the girl as she winked at me over her head. "Pack a bag, we'll help you get out of here."

***

Cletus walked in fifteen minutes later, sweating and out of breath. Jasmine had roused Doug and Tracey and explained that she was leaving her middle-aged lover and that they would not be sleeping inside, but that they were welcome to camp on the property. Tracey was angry and Doug thought it was a bummer. Jasmine had a small bag packed sitting on the floor. Ideally, she would have gotten in her grandmother's Toyota, left Atlanta and Cletus far behind, and Maggie and I would get in the Piper and fly home to collect our five-grand. Cletus didn't see it that way.

After more pleading that was embarrassing for everyone, Cletus got stubborn and mean. I knew he had snorted something, probably not slept at all, and was fragile emotionally. I hoped he wouldn't get violent, but that didn't work out either.

"How you going to run back home, Bitch?" He demanded. "I went out to the garage, and your grandma's car is not going anywhere anytime soon." He pointed in our direction. "These two are leaving. I don't give a shit if they have to walk to Atlanta from here, they're gone. Doug and Tracey can go to the rally, and you and I are going to sit here until we get this figured out."

"What the hell did you do to my grandmother's car? Let it go, Cletus, I'm done. Did you think I want to ride around on the back of that stupid motorcycle my whole life? I'm going to finish school, go to college, and you're not going to stop me. Get out of this house, or I'm calling the cops."

"No! Come on, Baby." He stepped forward and reached out for her. Maybe he wasn't himself. But lack of sleep, his misguided passion, and the white powder all had combined to make him very dangerous in that moment. I could see it in his eyes, the maniacal certainty that he would have Jasmine one way or another. I stepped in front of her quickly.

"No way, Cletus, go sleep it off."

Most people that have been in a fight will tell you that whoever lands the first punch is the odds on favorite to win. Sidecar had done me the favor of telling me how tough Cletus was, so I didn't hesitate or wait for the bell to ring. Before I finished speaking, I hit Cletus as hard as I could, right on the side of the forehead. Normally that would be enough. I'm a pretty big guy and I can hit pretty hard. It dazed him, but the combination of adrenaline, drugs and just plain toughness kept him on his feet. Before I could try again, he was swinging. He didn't fight like a boxer. He just rotated his hips and flailed his arms and fists as fast as he could, using his size and weight to overpower me. He hit me so fast twice that I nearly went down. My ears rang and the colors of the room faded.

When boxers are outmatched by size or speed, they grapple. Get in close and hold on. That's what I did. I had him by the neck and pulled him in close as we hit the floor, not strangling him, but not letting him get far enough away to take a full swing at me. I could feel his breath as he gasped and did his best to push me away, and we rolled across the floor, both of us trying to get the advantage anyway we could.

From the corner of my eye, I saw Maggie run up with a bottle, presumably to use on Cletus. Tracey, in a show of loyalty, grabbed Maggie and doubled a fist. Beneath Cletus as I was, I couldn't see the result of that altercation, just a glimpse of Tracey going airborne and a loud crash. By the time Cletus had broken my hold, Maggie laid a beer bottle across his balding head, sending shards of glass everywhere. I pushed away from him and stood up. Surprisingly, he scrambled up and lunged at me again. The beer bottle must have had some effect, because he had slowed considerably and I tagged him a good one. He went down again, but reached out a meaty hand, yanking me to the floor with him. The guy was stubborn, I'll give him that.

Suddenly there was a roar that stopped the fight. A gunshot is pretty loud inside a house and there were bits of plaster falling from the ceiling. Maggie stood by the open door with her small Glock pointed at Cletus. Jasmine stood behind her, eyes wide. I lunged through the opening and Maggie and Jasmine turned and chased me across the field to the Piper. They clambered in as I primed, then fired the plane up. One revolution, and we were rolling. There wasn't time for a warmup, so I crossed my fingers as I spun the Piper onto the airstrip. I couldn't believe Cletus would want to continue the fight, but he was half crazy and I just wanted to get out of there.

We didn't get in the air as fast as I would have liked because of the long grass on the strip and the fact that we had a tailwind. By the time I got us off the ground I had to make a shallow turn to avoid the trees and put us into the wind to gain altitude. We started climbing and flew straight in the direction of the house. Doug and Tracey already stood on the porch, and Doug raised a hand and waved solemnly like we were all still best friends. I should have peeled off then, headed north and stayed away from the house, but I was using the wind to climb.

Far below us, Cletus came running out onto the porch, fell to his knees, and raised his hands. Over the roar of the engine I couldn't hear the gunshot, but against the darker background of the shadows below us, I saw the plume as he squeezed the trigger on the gun he had retrieved from his backpack. I realized it didn't help, but I yelled out to the girls. "That crazy son of a bitch is shooting at us."

I banked hard and he missed us but must have kept shooting. Just when I was sure we were out of range, I heard a sharp bang and knew that we'd been hit. Both the girls were screaming but the plane kept flying straight and no gauges were dropping. I thought he might have just tagged our wing. I kept climbing and watching the gauges, happy to get out of there alive.

"Slater!" Maggie said suddenly. I could hear the fear in her voice. I looked over at her, and she lifted her leg a little. There was a jagged hole in her calf the size of a dime pushing blood out as fast as her heart could pump.

Chapter Fourteen

Jasmine Thatcher was not your average seventeen-year-old girl. That had been obvious from the onset, but I had been too busy worrying about her self-entitled excursions with a middle-aged biker to realize that she had some amazingly good qualities. She was smart and fearless. While I got on the radio, reporting our dilemma and lining up help, Jasmine got Maggie's seat laid down with her leg as high as she could get it, made a half-assed tourniquet out of her sweatshirt sleeve, and kept pressure on her leg; all while covered with blood and continually talking to Maggie and trying to keep her from going into shock. Maggie was white, but conscious and the bleeding had slowed. She still had her sense of humor.

"Jeez, Slater, I can't even blame you for this. It was all my fault. I'm the one that wanted to be a detective."

"Blame, Cletus, he's the nut job that tried to kill us all."

"Blame me, I'm the idiot that ran off with him," Jasmine volunteered. "How long before we get there, Slater."

"We're going to Dobbins Air Base. It's the closest, and there's a hospital right there. Fifteen minutes."

"I don't know if it matters, but I have kind of rare blood if they decide to put some in me."

246

Maggie volunteered. "I feel pretty lightheaded, so maybe that would be a good thing." She paused and closed her eyes. "It's AB negative, and I guess it's kind of uncommon."

"One percent for Caucasians," Jasmine said, like it was something everyone should know. "The good news is you can be transfused with any of the negative blood types, or they might just do plasma."

"How the hell do you know that?" I asked.

"What? I stayed awake in biology class that day."

I knew we might have another problem. A warning light was on, indicating low hydraulic pressure. The gear had dropped, meaning all the gear lock lights should have been on, but the left main indicator wasn't. I kicked the rudder over both directions to no avail.

Jasmine noticed. "What are you doing?"

"He's trying to be sure all the landing gear locks." Maggie glanced at me. "Probably got clipped by a bullet and the fluid leaked out. Maybe do a flyby and have the tower look for damage."

"That takes time."

"So will scraping us off the runway if it collapses and you aren't ready. You can go on two wheels, as long as you know what's going on. Want me to show you?"

I tried levity. "Lots of things I want you to show me, but none of them have anything to do with flying."

She chuckled and closed her eyes again. "Just get me to a doctor. This hurts like a bitch, and I need some drugs."

***

I took Maggie's advice and called the tower. After a slow flyby, they confirmed that there was an issue with the gear. We still had the wheel but some of the linage looked bad. It was very possible the gear would hold up and absolutely nothing would happen. The good news in our case was that the wind had freshened, coming from the south at a pretty steady twenty miles per hour. With full flaps I could keep the weight off the right side throughout most of the landing.

"So, are we going to crash?" Jasmine asked, laughing nervously. "A month and a half living with a crack head, riding on the back of a Hog and getting shot at, I don't want to finally end up as a grease spot on a runway."

"Stop," Maggie moaned. "Don't make me laugh. I'm the one who has a hole in her leg, and I'm not worried. Slater's the best pilot I know."

I wasn't sure if she believed that, but it was nice of her to say. We had a choice of runways because it was an Air Force base, so I was able to keep the Piper dead into the wind. Once we were on the ground and slowing down, I eased us off the asphalt onto the grass and basically kept it flying on the ground at a low speed. As we got close to the control tower the fire trucks started running alongside. I killed the engine, shut off the fuel, and braked hard, trying to keep weight on the front gear. We were close to stopped and I was beginning to think I had worried needlessly when the gear collapsed and the Piper slammed down, digging the right wing into the ground and demolishing the prop.

"Good landing," Maggie said. "At least most of us can walk away from it."

***

The next couple of days were intense. When I wasn't in the hospital with Maggie, I was filling out police reports, getting my airplane transported for repairs, and fighting with Angela. It seemed like she was mad on behalf of her father, who was too lazy or disinterested to show up himself. She and her mother made it to the hospital the next day.

Maggie was tired and a little out of it from the drugs. Jasmine Thatcher insisted on staying for a couple of days until she knew Maggie was out of danger and her old boyfriend was in jail. I was a little surprised that Cletus hadn't burned the house down, but he had been picked up at the Bike Rally the next day without incident. He claimed he didn't know us or anyone else involved. He was too stupid or messed up to get rid of his gun, so his chances of getting off were slim to none. Jasmine called her grandmother and rented us a suite in a nearby hotel so we could both spend as much time as we wanted with Maggie and remain available to law enforcement. That, as much as anything, seemed to bother Angela.

"Doesn't Maryanne think it's unseemly, you and a seventeen-year-old sharing a room?"

"Jasmine's been riding around the country with a middle-aged crackhead for a month," I pointed out. "That was unseemly. Maryanne's not worried about it, so why are you?"

"She's jealous." Maggie chuckled through the fog of her medication. "She wants to keep it in the family. Guess what, Angie, Slater and I slept together."

"Fully clothed, you left that part out," I mentioned.

"I know. I left it out on purpose." She laughed again.

"I think you should stop playing Private Eye, both of you." Angela said. "Maybe Davey did kill himself. Maybe it's too dangerous to be snooping around."

"This had nothing to do with Davey's case," I said.

"You haven't told her?" Maggie asked.

"No, remember I told you I want to verify a couple things?" I couldn't fault her slip of the tongue, she was pretty out of it.

"Alright, this is bullshit," Angie snapped. "I gave you ten-grand to go to Miami and you haven't said one word about what you found out. Isn't that breaking the private eye code or some kind of a law? I'm the client. I should get to know what you're finding out."

Something in her eyes in that moment: the flash of anger, or just the right color of blue in the light of the hospital room; it triggered a memory. The sudden realization shook me to the core. I wanted to ask her right then, but I couldn't, not with Maggie in the room. I think Angela realized that something important was spinning around in my head, but I covered as best I could.

"Anytime you want your money back, Angela, just let me know. I'll tell you what I know when I'm sure it's true."

"No, I'm sorry. You do what you think is right." She reached out and put her hand on mine. Maggie snickered.

"See, Slater? Jealous."

***

By Tuesday, Maggie was ready to be transported home in a medical van. Rita and Angela had gone home on Monday, so it was left to

Jasmine and me to follow her back to Jacksonville. We went in the big house and helped Angela get her settled. Jasmine had volunteered to play nurse, but Angela hired an LPN since Maryanne Thatcher was paying for it anyway. We sat with Maggie for a while, then I was finally ready to take Jasmine back to her grandmother. She sat on the edge of Maggie's bed holding her hand.

"So, is it okay if I come see you? I love both of you, you know that. You probably saved my stupid life."

"You're anything but stupid, Jasmine," Maggie said. "Don't let anybody tell you different, and keep rocking the blue hair, okay? Come see me every day if you want, as much as you want. I'll be out of the detective business for a couple weeks."

I asked Jasmine for a minute with Maggie and she went out to the rental car to wait. I sat beside her and leaned down to kiss her forehead.

"What was that for?" She asked.

"You were amazing up there. You probably did save her life."

"Hey, we're partners. You were willing to get your ass kicked, just like back in high school."

"I had him right where I wanted him." I reached out and pushed a chestnut lock out of her eyes.

Her voice was a little husky when she spoke again. "I better sleep, these drugs are kicking my ass. Thanks, Slater. We need to talk about Angela. I

252

won't tell her anything, but she needs to know."
She dozed off and I walked out to the car to drive
Jasmine Thatcher back to her real life, compliments
of Maggie Jeffries.

***

I was glad to find my house in one piece and
undisturbed when I got home. I went straight to my
dresser and pulled out the small box I was using to
keep all my information on Davey Templeton's
murder. No doubt anymore, it was murder, and the
potential suspect list kept getting more
complicated.

I made the phone call, got in my truck and
drove the two miles to Point Road. I stared at the
stone wall as I drove up to the house, considering
all the ways Davey Templeton could have died. No
investigation and no autopsy. Maybe he had
stopped in the rain, or been stopped. Maybe
someone pulled him from his car, they fought, and
he banged his head on one of these rocks. An
accident of sorts. Then the fake suicide. But that
would take two people, or one very strong one.
Just another theory.

Claire La-font, Edith's long-time housekeeper
and best friend answered the door. She gave me a
small hug and walked me into the kitchen where
Edith sat with a cup of coffee. Claire handed me a

cup and filled it from the pot on the stove, then stood nearby, waiting expectantly.

"So, do you have news? Did you find something out about Davey?" Both Edith and Claire leaned toward me, hoping for any scrap of information.

"More questions than answers, I'm afraid. I'm sorry, Claire, but do you think I could have some time alone with Edith?"

"Claire knows all about Davey and what he might have done," Edith said quickly.

"Alright, the good news. Davey was definitely not selling drugs. The rest of it I have to keep in my head for now. I still have to verify some things. I'm sorry, Edith, but I really need to talk to you, and it has to be alone."

Claire spoke up. "It's fine, Eric, don't worry, it's time I was getting home anyway."

"I'm sorry, Claire, I'll tell you all about it tomorrow," Edith said. She glared at me as the other woman left. "Really, Eric, there isn't anything Claire doesn't know about Davey."

"Maybe, maybe not." I pulled Davey's medical alert bracelet from my pocket and dropped it on the table in front of her, hoping a little theater would get a reaction. I wasn't absolutely sure. "Does she know Davey's real father lives half a mile from here, straight across Point Road?"

She took a drink of coffee and bit her lip, but she didn't seem terribly surprised. "Yes. As a matter of fact, Claire does know that Davey's biological father is Frank Jeffries. I trust her with everything."

"You didn't trust me, and I'm supposed to be your investigator."

"How did you find out? Did Rita say something? I think she always suspected, but she's never come right out and said it."

"Blood type. When Maggie got hurt up north, we thought she might need blood. AB negative is pretty rare. Not impossible for two neighbors to both have it, but usually the simplest explanation is the right one. I knew for sure the other day, looking in Angela's eyes. Maggie's eyes are a little different, but Angela's eyes are exactly like Davey's. I'm surprised I never saw it. Does Angie know, and Maggie?"

"I'm not sure. Davey had talked about telling Angela, but I think she would have said something when she called. They were so close, he must have told her."

"When did he find out?"

"A few years ago. I think it was the year he turned thirty-two." She bent her head and a tear slipped out. "We had a little party and of course Eddy was working and said he couldn't make it. He said it was stupid to have a birthday party for someone that old. Eddy was always so hard on Davey, and so callous. Davey tried not to let it show, but it hurt him. He told me not to worry, that he knew his Dad had always hated him because he was gay. I was upset. I couldn't admit to him that it might be true, so instead I told him that Frank was his biological father and that his Dad couldn't get over it. That he didn't hate him, he hated me. That much was true."

"Frank knew, obviously."

"No, not really. We only slept together one time and that was it. Davey was premature. There were problems early, so I was on bedrest for months. When Frank asked, I swore up and down Davey wasn't his, that he was Eddy's. The timing was off enough that Frank never questioned it. Eddy knew better of course. He's been shooting blanks his whole life because of some congenital birth defect. Davey ended up with two men that wouldn't accept him, his biological father and Eddy. But like I told you before, Eddy came around. He and Davey ended up being pretty close the last couple of years. Eddy goes out to the horse barn every time he's home now, sits out there and sobs for what he didn't do. Davey forgave Eddy, but Eddy never forgave himself, or me. I should ask him to leave, but there's the barn, and everything." She was crying softly again, so I sat waiting.

"No chance anyone else might know this?" I asked.

"No. Davey might have told Angela, but as far as I know, nobody else could know. Are you going to ask her, ask Angela if she knows?"

"I'm not sure. I can't tell you everything I know, Edith, not yet. But I can tell you that you should be very proud of your son."

"Thank you, Eric, but I didn't need to hear that from you. I was always proud of him."

***

I had a lot to think about on the drive home. I kept going back to Davey's last letter and his father issues.

Every mother is proud of their children; every father too, or should be. I thought back to the day my mother sat me down to ask if I was gay. She assured me she would love me no matter what, even if I was gay. At the time it didn't matter to me the way she said it. But in hindsight, wasn't that like saying she would love me in spite of the fact that I was gay? Had Davey's mother said that to him? Or his Dad? What unintentional message would that send?

Every time I thought about Davey being involved with Rosalyn's kidnapping, I went down the same rabbit hole, questioning what could have caused him to go along with the man I now called Whitey. Had his control over Davey been purely psychological, driven by some need in the younger man, or was there more to it? Did Whitey threaten his family, or blackmail him to keep that control?

Very possibly it had been a combination of both. But why the change?

If I put together what little I knew and pieced it into a timeline, it seemed like Davey had been drawn into the dark world of child abduction by the man Rosalyn called Diablo Blanco at some point after leaving Point Road and going to Miami. If not an active part, certainly he was complicit, or as I hoped, forced into it somehow. Rosalyn had been put in that cage almost five years ago.

Sandy Foster found herself on that airplane bound for the middle east roughly two and a half years ago, but taken from Los Angeles, half a continent away. Somewhere during that time, coincidently or not, it appeared Davey had turned things around. If he was the villain Rosalyn claimed, what had changed to suddenly make him the hero of Sandy's story? Guilt? Some epiphany? Or was it the absence of an outside influence?

If, as I believed, Diablo Blanco and Whitey were the same man, perhaps that was the key. Maybe the man left Miami and set up shop in Los Angeles and went about his dirty business across the country allowing Davey free will. It made a certain amount of sense, if even half my guesses were right. Perhaps freed from whatever control he was subjected to, Davey had turned his life around after Diablo Blanco left town and tried to redeem himself. It didn't exonerate him completely in my mind, but then I hadn't lived his life.

The timing worked with Rosalyn's story and Sandy's, it worked with Davey's bank statements and his move into Sam's apartment. The common thread throughout Davey's story and possibly Whitey's, was the Talent Agency. Granted, there were bound to be a lot of talent agencies in Los Angeles, but the stories Sandy Foster told included girls from a lot of the cities where the company Davey worked for had agencies. It was one thing they all shared and something to go on.

I wanted to move forward. Much as I liked spending time with Maggie, Angela was right. Investigating Davey's death was becoming dangerous. Seeing Maggie lying across the seat of my airplane, in pain and covered with blood had scared me like few things ever had before. It was like the day my mother called. That gut wrenching fear for someone you love. Cancer, and it's terminal.

We're all terminal, and when we're young we don't think of it as being real. But time passes and people disappear from our lives, my mother and Davey were gone, and others I hadn't known quite as well. I couldn't imagine having to miss Maggie that way. She was lying in bed with a hole in her leg because I had gone along with the whole crazy rescue idea, mostly because it meant getting to spend a lot of time with her. It was all exciting and romantic, and I was glad that we had pulled a wild young woman back to reality. But the possible consequences had really hit home when I looked down and saw that blood pumping from her leg. She could have died, and part of that would have been my fault. I would have been the complicit one.

I felt like I had to find Davey's killer if I could, I owed him that. But keeping his sister safe? I owed him that too.

***

I went through all the cards, the notes, and the bank statements again and everything seemed to fit the scenario I had worked out in my head. One of the reasons I didn't want Maggie involved was the fact that her father was on my list of possible suspects. It would be a horrible twist of fate if Frank Jeffries had inadvertently killed his own son.

Frank had always rubbed me the wrong way, even as a kid. Maybe Maggie was right and Angela did get her bipolar tendencies from her father. He was never warm to Davey or me when we hung around their house, and I attributed it to the fact that he thought of us as just teenage freeloaders using his pool and eating his chips. But too frequently he would blow up for no apparent reason, order us off the place, and not allow Angela to come over to Davey's house for a couple of weeks. Quite probably that was why I didn't care for him.

When I got older, I heard some of the rumors. He had a reputation as a ladies' man. Even in our public high school there were stories whispered about him, how he had had affairs with married women and that he spent time in Lauderdale so he could chase after college girls. I had blown the stories off as gossip, normal people being jealous of anyone who lived on the Point. Now I wasn't as sure. The gossip might have had a grain of truth to it.

He was gone a lot. Even when Angela and Maggie were young, he spent more time in Fort Lauderdale than at home. Now it was most of his time, and any pretense he had of a normal marriage had disappeared. Business kept him away. That's what he said, and what Angela seemed to believe. I doubted Rita or Maggie were that naïve. If I considered him a suspect, maybe I would have to visit Fort Lauderdale and do a little surveillance. With Maggie laid up, I would have time to see what her father was up to without her knowledge.

But my priority had to be on what I knew. I knew Davey had worked for Miami Talent, I knew Susy Foster hadn't told me everything, and I knew there was plenty Sam hadn't mentioned as well. Susan Foster's boss Gleason might be involved. He seemed sleezy enough to send girls too young for the strip clubs down a more dangerous path. It was all about the money. I had to find out more and track down the mysterious Whitey if that was possible. It meant another trip to Miami, and that meant talking to Maggie first.

I texted her, then locked up and drove over to the house. There was a car in the driveway that I didn't recognize when I pulled up, a new Audi. Angela surprised me by opening the door. "Eric. Here to see my sister, no doubt?"

"I have to go to Miami; more questions about Davey. At least if someone gets shot this time, it'll be me."

"I'm sorry about the other day. Maggie has always been the brave one. It isn't your fault she's reckless."

"I don't know about reckless, maybe a little too enthusiastic."

"She really likes you."

"I really like her. Is that okay?"

She leaned forward suddenly and kissed my cheek, then actually blushed. "I think I missed out, but she's my sister, and sisters do stuff for each other. She's out on the porch with her new best friend. She fired the nurse because she wouldn't let her get out of bed."

The exchange surprised me. It was nice and normal. Not like Angela at all.

Maggie's new best friend had half a head of blue hair and a familiar face. She smiled up at me when I walked out of the house. "Like my new car?"

"It beats the back of a Harley. Shouldn't you be in school?"

"Calm down, Dad. I've had a traumatic experience. I'm rehabilitating."

"Maggie had a traumatic experience. You went on a month-long joyride that could have gotten you killed."

"He's been like this ever since we stayed in the hotel room together," Jasmine said. Maggie was laughing at us. "He thinks he's my big brother now. For what it's worth, I have a tutor and I'm going to GED my way into college. Gram says if I don't get good grades, the car goes away."

"A's. Good grades are A's." She bent the finger I had pointed at her.

"Do you want to be alone with your girlfriend?" she asked.

"I'm not his girlfriend," Maggie said loudly.

Jasmine leaned over and whispered. "I hope you're working on that?"

"I'm working on the case," I said. "The one we were on before we had to stop so we could rescue your punk-ass."

"You realize it's totally inappropriate to talk to me like that. Legally I'm a juvenile in this state."

"Juvenile delinquent. Maggie, help me?"

"She's my new nurse, Slater. You should have seen us getting me down the steps. I'm going to move into my Dad's room until I can do the stairs without help."

"I thought he might call and yell at me for breaking his daughter, but not so far."

"If you took Angie bowling and she chipped a nail he'd have the cops after you. I get shot, and it's crickets."

"That's not true. Have you talked to him? Is he in Lauderdale?"

"He did call and express concern, almost like a real father. I don't know where he is, Lauderdale usually. Is this Slater the Investigator asking?"

"He might know somebody who knows something. It might be worth driving by the house down there."

"Diplomatic. But I can see why he's on your list. Do what you need to do to eliminate him as a suspect, Slater, I'm fine with that. Did you talk to Angie on the way in? She'd be more likely to know where he is."

"She's good today. I don't think I should risk riling her up."

"She doesn't like my hair," Jasmine interjected.

"Go figure. I'm going to run back down to Miami and talk to Sam and Susy again. I didn't want you thinking I was sneaking down there without telling you."

"Do you want my car? It's back from the shop and it's in the garage."

"That's a big no. We got you shot and almost totaled your ride once, that's enough damage for a while."

"Give me a week, a week and a half tops, then I'll be good to go."

"Yeah, whatever," I mumbled, looking at my shoes.

"Slater, I can see the screws turning in your head. My getting shot was not your fault, and I need this. You don't have to protect me or worry about me. Look what we did. This beautiful little girl is back with her family because of us."

Jasmine posed for me, a huge grin plastered across her face. If it was hard for me to deny Maggie anything, it was doubly hard to deny them both.

"Alright, we'll see. But you need to be healed up completely before we take on anything new. I'll fly down there and rent a car. I might stay a day or two, or maybe not. It depends on what I find." Jasmine looked like she was about to speak. "No, I don't need any help. Maggie, don't encourage her. I have to go home, I'll call you."

There was an awkward moment. I knew what Jasmine expected, but I wasn't sure about Maggie. I finally leaned down and kissed Maggie's forehead, then turned and quickly headed for the door to the sound of Jasmine's laughter. No wonder Cletus did drugs.

***

It was about two that afternoon when someone knocked on my door. I pulled it open just as he was about to rap again. James Kennedy stood there, looking nervous and bobbling his head like there'd been an earthquake. I stood aside and he took the opening, rushing past me to the kitchen table. He was even more fidgety than his previous visit, and fumbled to open his soft sided briefcase, then dropped several folders on the floor. Finally, he composed himself, looked over his reading glasses at me, and apologized for not having an appointment.

"I believe my assistant gave you the wrong impression on the phone the other day, Mister Slater. Our firm is still very interested in doing business with you."

"Hard to get any impression but the right one. He said your company was definitely not going to do business with me. Not a friendly tone either."

"Oh gosh, my goodness! I will have to speak to him. After speaking with another individual, one with holdings much more substantial than Mr. Jeffries, we are prepared to offer you the same deal. Even a better deal."

"And who might this client be?"

"I'm not at liberty to say." His voice rose an octave, more a question than a statement.

"You can tell Maryanne Thatcher that I appreciate it very much, but she's done enough. She has been very generous already, paying for

Maggie's hospital bills and my airplane's repair. Any more, and I would consider it charity."

"A simple business deal, like we outlined before. She moves substantial amounts of substandard housing and you split the profits with her holding company."

"She has the perfect guy already working for her. Why wouldn't she give Luis Sanchez the same deal?"

"He had some trouble a few years back. He is documented, but he isn't eligible for a contractor's license. We tried to help him straighten it out, but the immigration laws are dysfunctional, miles of red tape. I can't volunteer anything more than that. I can tell you that your contractor's license will soon be valid. The process has been expedited. Mrs. Thatcher wants me to assure you that this a win-win. You will both profit from this."

"What's the timeline? I have a small crew of carpenters in mind, but it will take a while to get up and running."

"We need to see progress of course. We will sign on each house case by case and expect delivery within ninety days. I have a sample contract along and we could go take a look at some of the homes today if you have time."

"I'll make the time. Mrs. Thatcher must be a good client."

"As I said, Mister Jeffries is a very important client. But Maryanne Thatcher, she owns the company."

Chapter Fifteen

I didn't get out of town on Thursday. I spent all day with Kennedy and Luis, looking at houses, signing contracts, and shopping for tools. It was hard to say how busy I could stay as a detective. If we figured out who murdered Davey, I'd be willing to walk away. But I had no desire to walk away from Maggie Jeffries and she could be very persuasive.

I wasn't sure going back to Miami was going to produce any results. It was an excuse to some degree, for myself, and something to tell Maggie. Miami and Fort Lauderdale are called sister cities, and I was beginning to think that the solution to this case, in a wry juxtaposition of my own life, might be a visit to the little sister. Perhaps metaphor was the better word, but I found the comparison humorous and sometimes you need that. The point being that Fort Lauderdale was the location of Jeffries and Jeffries, the firm founded by Frank Jeffries' grandfather.

The name of the firm had originally been coined by Hugh and Ernest Jeffries back in the days when Fort Lauderdale had been much smaller and quieter, long before the hordes of college kids discovered the beaches and turned the town into party central in the mid-Eighties. By then Hugh had passed away, unmarried and childless, leaving the brothers' burgeoning real estate empire in the sole hands of Ernest and his son Clarence.

Clarence got a law degree and married well. He used his law school connections to expand the business and cozy up to state and local politicians, bribing officials when necessary to buy large quantities of undeveloped land to the west of the city. He expanded the family fortune by building tract homes on property ill-suited for that purpose, shortly before stricter building codes would be enacted. His wife's family lived in Jacksonville, a burgeoning area south of town known as The Point. He shipped her and his sons up to north Florida, built the ten-story building that still housed Jeffries and Jeffries, and continued draining the swamps.

I knew all of that from stories Gary had told us when he took us on short hops in his float plane. Gary was the youngest of the Jeffries boys. There was quite a spread in their ages. Three boys, each born eight years apart. The oldest brother, named Clarence after his father, defied his parents, joined the Marines, and volunteered for Vietnam. He flew a Medivac helicopter until a Chinese rocket found its mark. It was too much for his mother and she committed suicide shortly after, leaving Gary and Frank in the sole care of their father. Gary always wore his brother's purple heart around his neck on a gold chain and often cried when he showed it to us. I remembered thinking it was odd, because I was thirteen, that a grown man would cry like that.

He was that kind of a guy, hot and cold, like another Jeffries I knew. Sometimes we would show up to ask for a plane ride and he would blow up and chase us away as fast as our bikes would carry us. Two days later we'd be swimming in Angela's pool and he would come to find us, all smiles, reminding us he was only there for another day or two and that he would be happy to take us flying. Davey was afraid of him and his flying, but he always went along to keep me company. I was a little afraid of Gary myself, but getting to fly his airplane occasionally was worth being a little terrified. He wasn't much of a pilot and I wasn't surprised when I heard he had dumped his floatplane into the Everglades.

That left the family business to Frank, and by all accounts, it wasn't going great. Maggie had hinted that he might be struggling financially, which might have been motivation to get his fingers into things he shouldn't have. It was a big jump from shady real estate mogul to child slave marketeer, and I really didn't think he would be directly involved. But he might know someone who was. He might have a rich client who was that seedy, who knew what Davey was doing and demanded a favor. Frank wouldn't necessarily have even known the particulars, or that Davey was in mortal danger. Unlike most of my suspects, what separated Frank was the fact that he knew about the horse barn. That seemed key. From the details Edith Templeton had shared, it was also where Frank's only son had been conceived.

The Jeffries building was all office space. A quick computer search confirmed what I had overheard in conversation at the Jeffries dinner table over the years. Gary had a beach-adjacent home in Lauderdale that they used to entertain rich clients and politicians, and at one point it slipped out that there was a boat docked in a private slip. Remarkably, neither Rita, nor either of the girls had ever been there. With Gary dead, I wasn't sure if Frank still had the property or not, but he had to live somewhere.

It took a while, but I found the county records and its location. I had searched for it in Frank's and the business's name, then every shell corporation I could dream up that he might have used. Finally, I had a thought and searched for it under Angela Jeffries. The house and boat were both in her name. Perhaps that was to avoid eventual estate taxes, although I doubted it. Considering the usage, I figured it should be listed as an asset of the corporation, but I was no tax guy. It was possible, considering her dead husband's fortune, that she had bought both the property and the boat as a loan to her father.

If that was the case, it seemed to me he should be a whole lot nicer to her. But then it was my opinion he should be nicer to both his daughters. He was sixty-three years old, but it had crossed my mind more than once that it would feel good to punch the guy. I had never liked the way he treated his wife or either of his daughters. I knew I was letting my disdain for him taint my objectivity, but my gut kept telling me he was involved somehow. I canceled my flight to Miami and the car rental. I decided I would take my old pickup and just drive to Lauderdale.

* * *

Since I had to go right by Titusville, it seemed reasonable to stop and pick Sandy Foster's brain for any more details she could remember. Our meeting had been stressful for her, and I knew it was possible she had thought of things after the fact that might be helpful. A part of me wanted to just sit and talk about Davey. Knowing what he had done for her and others took the edge off Rosalyn's story. Now that I knew that Maggie and Angela were his sisters, his being a good guy had become doubly important.

I had pictures of Frank I'd found on his website, and I figured it wouldn't hurt to show them to her. I called Susy first, just in case Sandy would be uncomfortable with me calling directly. I had nothing to compare it to, but being held captive for that long had to change your perspective on life, and on men in general.

"I'll call her and tell her you want to stop by." Susy said. "She liked you, so I'm sure she'll be okay with it."

"Want to have lunch tomorrow? I'm curious about your boss, Gleason. Maybe you could bring me one of your flyers with Gleason's picture on it. I'm checking on some things in Lauderdale after I leave Sandy's, then I'll stay over in Miami."

"You can Google him. I'm actually going up to stay with Sandy tonight, and probably stay the weekend with her. She's having a tough time. PTSD, more or less. She thinks she saw the guy that kidnapped her at the local Walmart."

"Wow. Any chance she did? Maybe he's back in Florida."

"Seems unlikely. She admitted she couldn't be sure. She said he looked completely different."

"Maybe I shouldn't stop there today."

"No, go ahead. She needs to work through this and learn to trust people again."

"Anyway, I'm going to be in Miami, maybe talk to Sam and check on a couple of other things."

"I told him we talked, so he knows you're one of the good guys."

"On the way back north, I'll call you and we can grab a bite. There is something I wanted to talk to you about, and I can tell you the story about how Maggie got shot by a psycho biker. She's fine, but it was a little too exciting."

"Wow, sounds like it. When are you heading home? I'll stay at Sandy's all weekend, then drive in to work on Monday morning. We can't talk over the phone?"

"Maybe not the best idea. I'm starting to wonder if my cell phone is hacked. I'll probably drive home Sunday. We could meet early afternoon."

"I'll text you an address, a decent restaurant that isn't too busy on Sundays. Just let me know what time."

"Maybe just you and I, if Sandy will be alright alone. I don't want to worry her any more than she already is."

"Yeah, sounds good, I'll see you then. I'll let her know you're coming by today."

***

Sandy was nervous. She pulled the curtain aside and peeked out at me hesitantly, looking in both directions beyond me as far as she could see before opening the door. I stepped in and she slammed it shut quickly, dropped two chain locks into place and spun the deadbolt before turning back to me. Every shade in the house was drawn. I was a little startled when she walked over to the end table of the couch and put down a small revolver that she had been carrying.

"Is that a good idea?" I motioned at the gun as she opened the refrigerator to grab me an iced tea.

"I saw him, day before yesterday. He looks different, but I know it was him. First thing I did when I moved here was bought a gun and learned how to use it. I had a boyfriend for a while and I felt a little safer then, but I ran him off with my craziness."

"Sorry. I can't imagine what you went through. Still, be careful you don't shoot yourself."

"Do you own a gun?" When I nodded, she said, "Be careful you don't shoot yourself."

I chuckled. "Good one. My bad. I'd say shoot me, but I'm afraid you might just do it."

We joked about the state of feminism and the world in general and after a while she calmed down. "He looked completely different. He shaved his head and he lost a lot of weight. I didn't see his face, but he was talking to a clerk and I recognized his voice. I just turned and ran out of there fast as I could."

"Hard to be sure without seeing his face, right?"

"That's what Susy keeps saying. Trust me, I know. I just know."

"Can I show you a picture? Maybe not Whitey, but maybe someone who knows him, or someone you might have seen."

She took the picture of Frank and stared at it for a long time, then handed it back. "Something about him is familiar. Has he been on television?"

"It's possible he's done some commercials. He is a real estate guy. I just moved back here about six weeks ago, so he might have had something on television that I don't know about."

"Looks like a car salesman. I probably saw him on some ad or something. He's definitely not the guy that doped me and threw me on that airplane."

"Well, that's good, one person off my list." We talked for half an hour about her captivity and if she had seen the faces of any of the Americans who came to the brothel that was her prison. I left feeling angry again, but with little new information.

I got in my pickup and backed out, thinking to drive back to the Seven-Eleven for gas and a coffee. There was a dark colored sedan parked up the street. I had driven by a municipal playground across the street from the car, so I thought that maybe it was just a lazy father letting his kid swing by himself. I drove slowly in his direction and looked the playground over. There wasn't a single kid in the park. I pulled up across from him and stopped. He glanced at me and I glared back at him, waiting for some sort of a reaction. Just a brief wave, a nod, even a middle finger. Nothing. He wore a plain dark suit and had a book spread out across his steering wheel. The easiest way to find something out is to ask, so I got out of my truck and walked across the street toward the car.

He barely acknowledged my existence, but I saw him reaching into his coat pocket. Had he rolled his window down I would have been pulling my new gun. He didn't, just flipped his wallet open and plastered it against the glass of his side window. The shield was big enough to read from where I stood. FBI. He spared me a glance and I nodded to him, then got in my truck and headed for Fort Lauderdale.

Apparently, I wasn't the only one interested in Sandy Foster. It seemed odd that my stopping at Sandy's hadn't pulled the agent away from his book. But then maybe he knew who I was, and that I was coming. Maybe my phone was hacked. And maybe we weren't the only ones investigating Davey Templeton's death.

***

First thing I did in Fort Lauderdale was locate Frank Jeffries slip. The estate that Gary Jeffries had owned and now belonged to Angela, was off the water, tucked a quarter mile west of the Atlantic in a plush neighborhood of cobblestone driveways, fenced yards and electric gates. The good news was that it wasn't inside a gated community with a logbook. Getting close without being noticed might be difficult and I had decided to wait for the cover of darkness to do my snooping. The last thing I wanted was for Frank Jeffries to see me.

The boat slip at the marina was empty, which I considered good news. I knew the boat was a day cruiser, a thirty-two-footer, only capable of limited sea travel and not likely to be gone overnight. Odds were that it would be back in by dark, carrying Frank and some rich client, or possibly a small-time politician that had borrowed it to try to impress his girlfriend. I looked around for a place to wait without being noticed. There was an open-air restaurant on the roof of the marina that looked like a perfect observation point. It seemed reasonable to me that people would sit up there and watch the boats and wait for relatives to come in off the water.

I hadn't expected it to be overly fancy, but the maître d' looked at me and sniffed when I walked up the stairs with my binoculars in my hand. "I just don't want to miss my friends when they come in," I explained.

"This is a private club, sir. Your friend's name?"

"Jeffries, Angela Jeffries' boat, but it might be under her Dad's name." It was a calculated risk, but I couldn't imagine he really cared. He flipped a book open and must have found their names in the roster. I was a little surprised when he asked for my name. "David Templeton," I said. I could only hope Frank might see that entry at some point. I couldn't punch the old guy, but maybe I could get his attention.

I took a tiny table on the far side of the roof, trying to be as unobtrusive as possible so the maître d' wouldn't have any reason to chase me out of there. I nursed a drink, then another, then ordered a small dinner. By the time I had finished eating the sun was creeping down to the horizon behind me, and I was wondering if I'd been wrong about them bringing the boat back in. Every once in a while, I'd been scanning the little harbor with my field glasses. None of the other diners seemed to find it odd. One woman even commented that she wished she had thought of it, but Mr. Maître d' kept shooting me black looks. I had just finished my bowl of ice cream, my girth notwithstanding, when I saw activity in the Jeffries' slip.

If I hadn't had the binoculars, it would have been too dark to recognize the people who climbed off the boat. As it eased up to the pier, a man with a shaved head and a slight, dark-skinned man jumped off the boat and tied it quickly to the dock. Then Frank Jeffries jumped down and helped three women down as well. I studied them all carefully. I knew Frank, but not the woman who wrapped her arm around his as they started walking toward the parking lot. No shocker there. I had no idea about the second man or his apparent date. Even though it was getting dark, he wore shaded glasses and tipped a hat onto his bald head as they followed

Frank. The third couple I knew, and I watched them through the glasses for as long as I could, just to be sure. Samath Chopra and the girl Davey had rescued from a brothel in Singapore walked along casually and chatted happily with the other members of the group.

They walked to the parking lot and got into two separate vehicles. I hurried to the counter and tossed a hundred at the maître d', then ran down and jumped in my truck.

**

When I was nine or ten years old, I started watching Magnum PI. The show had nearly wrapped up before I was old enough to stay up that late, so I had to start at the beginning, and watch reruns. Besides the fact that it was funny, Magnum always got the girl and there were a lot of scenes where the helicopter played an important part. I decided at a young age that being a PI might be a good job to have. By the time I was old enough to lust after Angela Jeffries, the idea had worn thin, but I still remembered most of the episodes.

Magnum always seemed to stumble his way through any kind of crime and come out a winner. Often as not he got beat up along the way, was occasionally shot, and once even appeared to die; then they renewed his contract. But there was one chink in his mustachioed armor that he never seemed to be able to circumvent, and they used it a lot. Dogs.

I had parked my truck down the street a good distance from the Jeffries' property and walked casually down the street like I belonged there. I was going in blind and had no idea of the layout of the place, if there were motion sensors, outside lighting, or any other kind of security. It was possible there would be a fence to scramble over. I knew nothing. It was a poor plan, but I had driven all the way from Jacksonville so I decided I was going to at least try to get a peek at the house.

I didn't dare just walk down the long driveway in plain sight of the front window. The property was surrounded by thick palms and shrubbery six feet high, and after a quick look around for a friendly tree, I dropped to my hands and knees and shuffled along on the sidewalk, trying to find a hole big enough to squeeze through. I had to be quick because the street was well lit. In the corner of the lot, where the shrubbery met the neighbor's wooden fence, there was a small opening between the bases of the shrubs. I got down on the ground and bellycrawled through the tiny opening, then pulled my feet through and peered around, trying to decide how close to get.

That's when I thought about Magnum. When I smelled the distinct odor of dog feces. It was bad enough that I was covered with dirt, but the indignity of having my elbows in Fido's remains made it infinitely worse. What troubled me the most was that because it was dark, I couldn't tell if it was it a big or small dog. Any dog might be bad if they decided to let him out to do his business while I was lying there. But Magnum had ended up head to head with Dobermans and Mastiffs a few times, and I really hoped that wasn't what I would be up against.

Google Earth had showed me the main house with the garage attached and a smaller building behind that stood close to a small channel or backwater. I would have thought it was a boathouse, but there was a light on and I glimpsed movement. Maybe a maid's quarters? It was pitch black, no moon, and only the porch light illuminated a small part of the yard. As I watched, the garage light winked on and the door started to lift.

I scurried into the corner of the yard and backed into the palms as far as I could, then held perfectly still. Frank Jeffries walked out of the garage to the end of the driveway and grabbed mail from the mailbox, then went to the front door and stood there waiting. The woman I had seen him with earlier walked out of the service door of the garage and joined him. She was slender and looked to be in her mid-twenties with dark hair, possibly Latino. He bent down and kissed her and opened the front door.

A boy, maybe four or five rushed out and started chatting with them. I could see a girl inside, probably the babysitter since she was blond, smiling and greeting the pair. I also spotted the dog, a German Shepherd cross of some variety that looked like he was eager for his evening walk. As soon as the door closed, I belly crawled as fast as I could back through the opening, made it to the sidewalk and jogged the block and a half to my pickup. I climbed in and turned around so I wouldn't have to drive past the house.

Being a private investigator didn't seem like such a good idea right about then. I had branches in my hair, my shirt was ripped, my pants were filthy, and I reeked of dog shit. On top of it, I had uncovered the fact that Maggie's dad was an even bigger scumbag than I thought. He had a second family and they were living in Angela's house. I would have almost preferred that I found proof that he was a murderer than to have to tell Maggie and Angela what was going on. I couldn't help wondering what Magnum would do.

Chapter Sixteen

I slept in the next morning, then stayed in bed thinking about what I'd found out the night before. The internet was full of stories of people who were leading double lives, of men married to several women at once. I couldn't imagine anyone having that much energy. My guess was that Frank told his Fort Lauderdale family the same story he told Rita and the girls. Business. It was business alright, funny business.

The reality was that Frank's and Rita's marriage had ended years before, and the girls were both adults, able to fend for themselves. The right thing for Frank to do was get a divorce, give up his free house and yacht, and be straight with both families. I didn't think that was my call to make and I wasn't sure what the private detective handbook said about it. True, I was working for Angela, but on Davey's murder, not on uncovering the fact that her worthless, borderline abusive father had another family. I decided at the least, I would put it on the back burner and concentrate on the main reason I had come to south Florida. Which was to find Davey's killer.

Sam being with Frank Jeffries didn't add up. From what I could see from my vantage point at the restaurant, all three of the men had seemed to know each other. They appeared comfortable and friendly, chatting like old friends. The bald man and his female companion had climbed in the Escalade with Frank and his amour, and Sam and Dedra had driven off separately. A pleasure cruise on a sunny day, at whose expense?

After another long shower I was reasonably sure I didn't smell like a kennel anymore, and decided to walk down to the hotel restaurant for breakfast. I was just about to leave when Maggie called. I didn't want my tone to give anything away, so I joked.

"Yes dear, bread and milk on my way home?"

"Just checking in. Jaz says hi, and to get working on it, whatever that means."

"Who knows with her." I knew.

"I get the impression you two are conspiring against me, but I'm at her mercy for the next week, so I'll roll with it. Did my Dad kill Davey?"

"Jeez. Nice segue. I don't know much more than I did. The one weird thing is that Sam and Dedra seem to know your Dad and..." I stopped talking, but not soon enough.

"My Dad and who? You almost said, and somebody."

"Sorry, but he was with a woman. Does that surprise you?"

"He's been with the same girl for a while, unless he recently traded her in for a younger model. He doesn't usually let them stick around very long. I was wondering if you'd see her, and if you'd tell me."

"Does Angela know?" I stopped myself from volunteering too much.

"Yeah, and she bought him out of the house. I know about that too. Angela knows he's messing around. Mom too, though she likes to pretend she doesn't. What would be the point? She doesn't want anything to do with him, but neither one of them will agree to a divorce. I feel more sorry for his girlfriends than either one of them."

"No offense, but your family is messed up. What do you think about Sam being friends with your dad?" I asked. "Coincidence?"

"Might be, stranger things have happened. Sam's family has money, so my dad would be trying to get some of it. They wouldn't necessarily know that they both knew Davey."

"You don't really believe that, do you?"

"Unlikely as hell. But do you really think my dad would traffic kids? Father of the year he's not, but I don't think he's capable of selling kids into slavery, or murder."

"I don't think so either, but it might be someone he knows. I'm going to talk to Rosalyn again, then I'm going to see Sam, and ask him about their connection. I saw Susy's sister yesterday and the FBI has her house staked out. She claims she saw the guy that kidnapped her at Wal-Mart."

"That poor girl. Funny that the FBI would do that, tight as the budgets are anymore. Just sounds like her imagination working overtime unless they looked at security footage or something. There must be some special circumstance for the FBI to show up, don't you think?"

"I know. And I have my doubts that Susan Foster is telling us everything. You really are a natural at this detective stuff."

"Stick with me, Partner, we'll bust this case wide open."

"Yeah, you just worry about not busting your stitches wide open. I'll stop over when I get back and give you an update."

"Don't get in any trouble down there. I don't want to have to send Jasmine down to bail you out of jail."

"None of us wants that. I'll talk to you soon."

***

The timing was right, so I drove into Miami proper and wound my way through the side streets until I found Rosalyn Cabello's house. I knew Billy's didn't open until noon, and there was no need for a dishwasher before then. If I was lucky, Manny and his posse were somewhere else. If not, I had my new gun loaded and tucked into a shoulder holster. I didn't know if Manny was the one who had tried to run me over, but I had no intention of taking a beating.

I walked up to the broken screen door and rapped on it. Rosalyn opened the interior door and looked at me dourly. "Senor, no quiero hablar contigo. No Senor."

"Don't give me that no Ingles crap, Rosie, you spoke perfect English the other day."

"Go away! If Manny sees you here you will not like what he does to you."

"I just need ten minutes, the faster you give that to me, the faster I'm out of here. Please."

"Alright, but hurry. He went to the store with his compadres. What is it?"

I slid onto a chair and she sat down across from me. There was no offer of a drink this time. "I need to talk to you about some of the details from when you were taken by the Diablo. I know it's painful, and I know you blame Davey for a lot of what happened, but can we talk about that time?"

"Like I said, Templeton was there when the smugglers brought me to this country. They raped me first, then it was the Diablo's turn."

"The smugglers raped you?"

"I was young and very pretty, Senor, alone with three men for several days. Of course they forced me. I could not help it. I could not tell, or I would have been sent home and it would have all been for nothing. If I say the truth, I think David paid extra for me so they would not keep me for their own pleasure. Perhaps I owe him for that. But the Diablo, what he did was worse, much worse."

She took a shaky breath. "He forced me, every way a man can force a woman. And he didn't do it for his pleasure, he did it for my pain." She spat the last words out, staring at me with her eyes empty, looking back to that moment.

"And David, you said he tried to stop him?"

"He was like a child against the Diablo. The Diablo, he was older, but tall. Tall as you or more, and he weighed, who knows? One hundred and twenty kilos, maybe more, maybe three hundred pounds. Templeton tried, but he slapped him and kicked him until he could not stand. He tried maybe, maybe he tried. But when Diablo said watch, he watched."

"I'm sorry, Rosalyn, really. What about the other man? Was he there every time?"

"No, only once."

"And David, he watched while they forced you?"

She stared through me again, and seemed to be questioning her memory. "Only the one time, maybe. I think it was when the Diablo was there. The other man, I can't be sure. They had given me the drugs so I wouldn't cry out. Maybe, the time when the other man was there, David was not. I have tried so long to forget, now it is hard to remember. I am not sure. Once David was there, once the other man. Always the Diablo."

"Did you see the other man at all?"

"A glimpse, perhaps. Perhaps it was in my mind, because of the drugs."

"Could this be the man?" I slid a picture of Frank Jeffries across the table.

"No, he was not a white man. He was dark skinned. Skin darker than mine, perhaps a black man." She buried her head in her hands. "I am sorry, I cannot be sure."

"Is there a chance that it was the other man all along? Because of the drugs. Is it possible that it wasn't Davey with you in that room? Could it always have been the other man?"

She smiled at me sadly. "I know what you want me to say, Mister Slater, so that you can have the good memory of your friend back. I cannot say it, it would not be true. David Templeton was the man who took me to the Diablo. He turned away when I screamed, but he watched when the Diablo said watch. I don't know why he would do such a thing. I will pray for his eternal soul. But it was him, at least the one time. I swear it to you."

"Alright, I really appreciate you talking to me. Nothing I can say to you will ever make this right. I think the person who did that to you also killed Davey. If I can find him, I will do everything I can to make him pay, for you and for Davey."

"I hope he does not kill you too, Mister Slater. You must go now. Manny will be back soon."

I walked out to my truck and unlocked it, then dropped my keys and bent down to pick them up.

From the corner of my eye, I saw a black Escalade turn the corner and drive slowly down the street. I waited until he was even with me, then stood quickly and looked at the driver. It was the man from Frank's boat. When he saw me stand, he spun his head away before I could get a good look and stepped on the accelerator. He was wearing his dark glasses and hat. I wouldn't have been able to identify him, but the front of his shirt hung open and I had just a moment to see a flash of color. A plain bright gold necklace with a bright pendant hanging from it. I knew it well. I had delivered a few during my time as a Master Chief. The pendant hanging from the driver's neck was a purple heart, just like the one Gary Jeffries had refused to ever remove from his neck. But Gary Jeffries had died in the Everglades years ago. Hadn't he?

＊

The details of the crash had been sketchy, and the body had never been found. When we were kids, we used to joke about people who disappeared into the 'Glades, never to be seen again. We called them alligator bait, in the cruel, macabre way kids talk when it's not their body parts being ripped into gator sized bites. More than a few bodies had disappeared into the Everglades, and after a few days, when no bones or jewelry were discovered, the unfortunate individual was presumed dead and the life insurance paid. The alligators were good at disposing of evidence, or in this case, the lack of it.

I hadn't seen all of his face, not in the car, but I was sure it was the same man that had climbed out of Frank Jeffries boat. The gait was right, the height and the build, all the little things that fell into place when the purple ribbon triggered my memory. His hair, the last time I'd seen him had been light, although not snow white like Roslyn had described it. The years might have made it so, or he might have dyed it. It seemed impossible, yet not, that the Diablo Blanco, the person Sandy Foster called Whitey, the person who had done unspeakable acts to so many people; that that person could be Gary Jeffries come back to life.

I sat in my truck, dumbfounded. The consequences of that fact, Davey's murder, the twisted relationship between them, it all crashed down onto my chest until I felt buried by it and sat there fighting to catch my breath. Davey had learned of his true parentage when he was thirty-two years old. He may have told Gary at that point, he may not have. Shortly after that, Gary had faked his own death and disappeared, probably resurfacing in California to eventually kidnap Sandy Foster. The question I had was, did Davey know that Gary wasn't really dead? If so, why keep the secret? Then I knew. Angela.

Davey hadn't told anyone. He had carried that around with him because of Angela. He had to have thought that the twisted tale of kidnapping and child abuse that he and her uncle, his uncle as well, had perpetrated would have unhinged her permanently should she find out. She was never close to Gary and had a tumultuous relationship with her father, but Davey was the one man she loved and needed most in the world. Knowing what he had done, even in spite of his redemption, would have broken their bond. And it was a bond she desperately needed.

She had clung to Davey, as a sixteen-year-old girl screaming when the tide tore at her, and as the woman she now was; a woman constantly fighting the demons in her head. Was that what he finally told her that last trip home when they cried on each other's shoulder? And did she suspect, as I did, that her uncle might be the person responsible for Davey's death? Perhaps even her own father?

I mapped it all out in my head. Davey had finally sickened of the hold Gary had over him, perhaps threatened to turn him in. Maybe that was the reason Gary had faked his death and left for California. Then Davey had turned his life around and started trying to help some of the people he had wronged. But something had changed and Gary came back. He had changed his appearance somewhat and hid out in his brother's guest house. Was it about money? Was it too hard to get away with kidnap and rape in California, forcing him to return to spiriting helpless immigrant children into the hands of the monsters that were his clients?

I was too involved with my thoughts to notice that Manny and his small posse had surrounded my vehicle. Maybe the look on my face spoke to him, because they didn't try to drag me out of the truck and beat me to death. Instead, he held up his hand and approached my window. I dropped the glass and he just stared at me. Undoubtedly, I was as white as the ghost I thought I had just seen.

"Manny, listen very closely. I am almost positive that I just saw the man we are both after. I thought he was dead many years ago, but I'm sure that I saw the man that Rosie calls the Diablo Blanco. His head is shaved and he looks different, but I know it was him. And he just drove down this street. Never, ever, leave Rosie alone again, alright? Promise me! If he drove by here, it's because he wants her dead. Carry a gun, and never leave her alone. When we catch him, I will call her and tell her it's safe."

"Si, Mr. Slater. If that Diablo comes for her, I will send you his skin."

"I kind of hope you do."

I almost turned around right then and just drove home. I could have gone straight to the Jeffries, had some sweet tea and spent some time being harassed by Maggie and her new best friend.

That would have been a lot easier and I wouldn't have ended up in jail.

***

I got back on the highway and drove across Biscayne Bay. Miami Beach is a very different place than the backstreets where Manny and Rosalyn lived. Their broken storm door and the screen with holes in it were a far cry from the fifteenth floor with the electric blinds and the window overlooking the beach where Samath Chopra and his girlfriend lived. But Rosie and Dedra were linked somehow, seemingly tied together by a haunted past of abduction and unspeakable horror at the hands of a man who had once taught me to fly. And the list.

From what I had been able to learn, the list of girls spirited away into a life of slavery and degradation was considerably longer than the seven names in the back of Davey's notebook. Sandy Foster had seen the man she thought was her abductor recently, the man I now believed was Gary Jeffries. Now, he had shown himself in front of Rosalyn Cabello's. Was Sam's girlfriend next? I pushed the gas pedal down and started passing cars. It had to be about the list. But what separated those seven girls from the countless others that had been abducted? Perhaps Dedra could tell me that.

The doorman gave me a dour look and tried to reach Sam's apartment without success. "I know he's busy and doesn't want to be bothered. The I.T. guy from his father's firm is up there."

"I need to talk to him and it's urgent," I pleaded. "Can't you override something, or just let me go up? You know I was just here the other day, for Christ's sakes."

My annoyance didn't sway him, and we stood there looking at each other. I was seconds away from pulling my gun when the exterior door opened and Sam's girlfriend walked in with a large paper grocery bag in her arms. She recognized me immediately.

"It's alright, Jerry, I know this man."

"Are you sure? The I.T. guy from his father's company is up there."

I interrupted. "Doesn't really matter. It's you I need to talk to, Dedra."

"Oh? Let's go on up. I went and picked up some sandwich stuff for lunch, so you can have a bite with us. Sam is so fussy I got three different kinds of everything. We can talk while Sam and the computer guy are working. Something about the feed from his father's company computer I guess."

As we rode the elevator up I explained briefly what I was hoping she could tell me: why she was on a list of seven women that Davey had hidden in his childhood bedroom. She shrugged. "I can't imagine anything I went through that the other girls didn't. Maybe Sam has some ideas, and I can think better with a full stomach."

She laughed a little and pushed against the door, then pulled her keys out and shifted the groceries onto her left arm. All that bread and salami probably saved her life.

As the door swung open I stepped up behind her, following closely as she walked into the dim room. The blinds had been closed and she bumped the light switch. Sam Chopra stared at us from his huge leather sofa with eyes that would never see again. He was stripped to the waist, eviscerated, and covered in blood and skin fragments. Dedra saw him and drew a breath, a scream rising to her throat. Instinctively, I reached for my gun.

There was a short wall that divided the kitchen from the rest of the room and a shadowy figure burst forward suddenly, slamming into Dedra. She turned her shoulder as he raised his arm and tried to plunge the knife he held into her neck. Luck was on her side and he inadvertently drove the blade into a tall salami that extended above the groceries. She stumbled and threw herself back against the wall as he raised the knife to continue the attack. I don't know if he ever realized that I was there, laser-focused on his intended victim as he was.

My first bullet knocked him back against the kitchen wall, but it didn't stop him. Possibly he was stunned and didn't realize that he had been shot, or possibly he was just that determined. Dedra was close, and I had to hesitate just a fraction of a second to be sure I didn't hit her. When he lunged again, I put two shots into his chest. The force drove him back into the kitchen where he fell to the floor. I stepped on his hand quickly and kicked the knife away. The nine-millimeter had done its job. He was stone dead.

Sam was equally dead, and Dedra stood staring at him, screaming over and over. I pushed her into the hall and sat her down on the floor, then went back inside. I needed just a moment to look at the would-be assassin.

He was middle eastern, that was all I was sure of. He had no phone, no passport, no wallet; just a plastic name tag that identified him as a technician from the Chopra business firm that had been ripped almost in two by one of my bullets. By the looks of Sam, he hadn't said what the assassin wanted to hear. He had not died quickly, cut apart piece by piece for information he probably didn't have.

I put my gun on the floor and stepped back into the small lobby, crouching in front of Dedra. She had a small cut on her forearm but was unscathed otherwise. Physically at least. The neighbor pulled his door open a crack and looked out fearfully. "Did you call the cops?" I asked. He nodded and pushed the door shut. I heard the chain lock drop into place.

Five minutes later, five cops, two from the elevator, three from the stairs, burst in wearing riot gear and shouting orders. They pulled Dedra from my arms, slammed me to the floor and handcuffed me. It didn't help that Dedra pleaded with them, or that I explained what had happened. Another ten minutes, six more cops, and I was in the back of a police van on my way to a holding cell.

I expected to be questioned and released, knowing that Dedra would explain the circumstances. If nothing else, I was sure the Stand Your Ground rule would apply. The man did have a knife and it was pretty clear he was trying to kill us. But hours passed and I still sat in the cell without any idea if I was being charged or not.

By evening I was livid and started calling for the jailer. A large, square jawed Sergeant walked back to my cell and scowled at me. "You keep yelling and you aren't getting any supper."

"I want my phone call. I want to call my lawyer, right fucking now."

"You cuss at me again and a phone call will be the least of your problems. Phone calls are a courtesy we don't give murderers until they're charged. Besides, I don't know that you need a lawyer. You haven't been interrogated or charged."

"I still get a phone call. I was an MA in the Navy. Everybody gets a call within twelve hours."

The Sergeant leaned against the bars and nodded like he was interested. "Military man, huh? Where'd you serve?"

I was hoping he was going to relax and let me make my call. "Here and there, San Diego my last few years. Come on Sarge, everybody gets a phone call."

"Not tonight," he said stubbornly. "This isn't San Diego and it damn sure isn't the Navy. I got word you're not to get a phone call until morning, after they decide if they're going to charge you with murder or not. Are you going to yell and cuss some more, or are you hungry?"

* * *

My cot wasn't very comfortable, which was alright because I couldn't sleep anyway. The man in Sam's apartment had been a paid assassin, I was sure of it. And from what he'd done to Sam it was clear he was after information, information Sam either couldn't or wouldn't give up. The assassin hadn't had a lot of time, just the time it took to go to the grocery store and back. Maybe Sam had given the man what he wanted. Maybe that was why he went after Dedra right away. Kill her, silence her, and be on his way. Then what? Was he supposed to get rid of Rosalyn and Sandy too? Did Gary not have the stomach for cold blooded murder?

Gary Jeffries was a sick bastard, and very possibly responsible for several people's deaths indirectly. But as far as I knew, despite the way he had brutalized Rosalyn, he hadn't killed anyone. Davey might be the exception, but that remained to be seen. The fact that he seemed to be stalking Sandy Foster and Rosalyn didn't necessarily mean that he was trying to kill them. Granted, it was likely, and I planned to alert Susy the minute I was released that her sister was not delusional. As for Rosalyn, I didn't want to imagine what would happen to the individual that Manny and his compadres caught trying to hurt her. Actually, I could imagine it. That's what I was doing when I finally drifted off.

"If I was you, I'd be calling my lawyer." It was a different Sergeant who took me out to use the phone after breakfast. "Somebody really wants to keep your ass in jail."

"I can do better than that," I said. "I have a friend with an army of lawyers."

Chapter Seventeen

Maryanne Thatcher's legal team had me out three hours later. The bespectacled man that stood beside me while I retrieved my belongings expressed his regret that it had taken so long. "I can't imagine why they even detained you. The law written the way it is, you had every right to shoot. How did a homeless man get up on the fifteenth floor?"

"A homeless man?"

"Yes, that's what I was told. I understand the doorman left his post and has been released because of it. Still, how did he get in the apartment?"

"They're saying he was a homeless guy?" I was dumbfounded. "Where is Dedra?"

"Dedra? Was she the prostitute that was at the apartment?"

"She wasn't a prostitute. She was Sam's girlfriend. What did they do with her?"

"I was told she gave her statement and was released. She exonerated you, so that should be the end of it. I don't expect you will face any further charges."

"Listen, I appreciate what you've done, but there's something really wrong here. That guy was a hired killer, I would bet anything on that. Would a homeless guy have cut Sam into little pieces? What about his parents, they have to have been told."

"I can't tell you that, and I have no way of knowing. I just know that the woman was released. She testified that you shot in self-defense, and no one will be charged."

"Son of a bitch! Sorry, but this stinks of a conspiracy of some sort." I was given my belt, wallet, and cell phone, and we walked out of the county building together. "Any idea where my truck is?"

***

The lawyer took me to the impound lot and I had to pay to get my truck released. Once out of the lot, I checked my cell phone. There were three messages from Maggie and two from Susy Foster. It was Sunday and I was supposed to meet Susy in Titusville on my way home. If she had heard about Sam, the afternoon lunch would be off and she had to be a basket case. I called her first.

"My God, Slater! Dedra called and told me what happened. She said she told them you had nothing to do with killing Sam and that you shot the man who did it, but they took you in anyway. She said Sam was dead and it looked like he'd been tortured. She's hiding out at a girlfriend's place because she's afraid they might be after her, but she wouldn't tell me where. She called on a burner phone because she thought someone might trace hers. She said she tossed it, just to be on the safe side."

"Smart girl, but I really would like to talk to her. They made damn sure to keep me locked up until today, almost like they wanted to do cleanup before I got out. The doorman's been replaced, so I can't talk to him, and they're claiming Dedra was just some random hooker that Sam had hired. That was no homeless man that killed him, he was a pro. And he cut poor Sam up pretty badly before he killed him, like he was trying to get information out of him."

"Oh, God." She didn't say anything for a moment, and I could hear her struggling to talk.

"The cops are covering things up, but any kind of autopsy would verify what I'm saying." I insisted.

"I talked to Sam's parents. His body has already been cremated. In his culture, they do it as soon as possible. They couldn't get out of India right away. Monsoon season, I guess."

"This is getting out of control. They're covering things up, Susy. Your sister isn't delusional. I think she really did see Whitey, or the man that used to be Whitey."

"What would make you say that?"

"I know someone else, someone who might have seen him too." My caller ID buzzed and I saw that Maggie was trying to reach me. "I have to go, but you be damn sure that your sister has protection. Someone is targeting women, just a

305

few that Davey had on a list, and I may know who it is."

"Who, Slater? What list? Eric?"

"I have to go. Maggie is calling. I'll call you back in a bit."

"What list? Is it about the White Devil? Is that who you're talking about?"

"Sorry, I need to talk to Maggie, she's called several times." She was still talking when I ended the call and answered Maggie's.

***

"What the hell, Slater, why haven't you been answering your phone?"

"You told me not to get in trouble, but that didn't work out." I told her the whole story, leaving out the fact that I thought her uncle was alive and might well be the Diablo Blanco. "I'm not a conspiracy nut, somebody is covering things up."

"Yeah, there's something going on. Edith Templeton called me. That's why I called you again. Claire picks her up for church Sundays and Eddy was out of town. Somebody broke into the house while she was gone this morning and tore the place apart. She said none of her jewelry was touched and nothing was taken as far as she could tell. She called me and I told her to call the cops and that I would call you."

"What did Eddy say?"

306

"I don't know if those two are talking. She said he's out of town and she wasn't even going to bother him. She also said the cops are worthless and she wasn't going to call them either. There wasn't any real damage, just stuff thrown everywhere. They were looking for something."

"My guess is they're looking for Davey's notebook. I think I know what this is about."

"Yeah?"

"I'm not saying any more over the phone. The cops had it overnight so for all I know it's bugged. How's the leg?"

"I'm a quick healer. The swelling is gone and I can manage the stairs."

"That's good. Can you manage to shoot a burglar if you need to? Keep Davey's gun handy. Whoever is behind this, they know we're all connected." I wasn't sure if it was even possible, but I really was starting to worry that my phone might be hacked. If it was, perhaps I could use that.

"If they know he and Angela were close, they might even go after her. She doesn't know anything, but whoever is behind this might think she does," I said. "Call Edith and tell her I'll stop over there when I get back. It'll probably be after six. I have one more stop to make. I'll go talk to her, then I'll come over and fill you in."

"I feel so bad about Sam, and poor Dedra. I'll have to call Susan Foster and get her number."

"Dedra's in hiding. How did you get Susan's number?"

"She called me the other day. She had my number from the time we went to the agency. She called to see how I was, if my leg was healing."

"Yeah? What day was that?"

"I don't know, Thursday, maybe? Yeah, it was Thursday, the day after I fired the nurse. Are you going to call her?"

"I suppose I'd better or she'll just keep calling me. I'll fill you in when I get back."

That was one too many coincidences. Now I was sure about Susan Foster.

***

I turned off the Coast Highway and drove into Titusville. I came at Sandy Foster's house from a side street and turned up the hill without driving directly past the house. Susy's car sat out front, but there was no sign of the agent from the FBI that had been keeping an eye on the place. I drove around several blocks, looking for anything that seemed out of place. It was a quiet Sunday in Titusville. I drove back to Sandy's house and knocked. I really didn't want to go back to jail, but I wasn't about to tell Susan Foster everything I knew.

Susy pulled the door open, looking surprised. "Slater, I called you back, twice."

"Right, like I want the FBI listening in when I incriminate myself. And thank you by the way, for making sure I sat in jail overnight."

"What are you talking about?"

"Diablo Blanco, Susan. You asked me about him that first day, the first time I met Sandy. Slip of the tongue, kind of like when I told you about the list. But then you already knew it existed, didn't you?" She looked like she might deny everything, so I continued. "How would a woman working at a talent agency have ever heard of the Diablo Blanco? It is a name you might hear down at Billy's at South Beach, if you knew to ask. I figured it was possible that Davey might have heard the name and said it to you, but there was more. You checked on Maggie after the shooting, a couple days before I ever mentioned it. Not like it was on the news down here. But then, being FBI, you probably have our names flagged on a computer somewhere."

"Maggie seems nice, I was worried about her."

Sandy delivered drinks, then glanced nervously between Susy and me. "Should I go watch television in my room?"

"No, stick around. You may be able to help." Susy looked back at me and nodded. "Okay, I was planning to level with you pretty soon anyway. I don't work for the FBI, but I do work with them. My agency is a part of Homeland Security. Child slavery isn't new, and it goes on more than you can imagine. I have seen children as young as ten in unspeakable situations, abused by people without a conscience. The talent agency got our attention because it was more organized and better funded than a lot of what goes on. There were girls being moved out of the US and taken to the middle east. Girls from Singapore and Colombia brought here to work in high end brothels, and girls from the middle east being sent to South America."

"That's what Davey's notebook showed. We thought it was drugs."

"He told me a lot of what was going on, but he would never tell me anything about Diablo Blanco. Do you know who he is?"

"No, no idea," I lied. "I thought it was an old boyfriend, but that doesn't add up. All of the people who knew Davey best swear he'd been single for quite a while."

Susy continued. "When Sandy disappeared, of course I went after Adrian. He told me this Whitey guy had connections at some talent agency, and that he really thought he planned to make her famous. Of course, he didn't know what Whitey's real name was and I never was able to find him. Now I think he skipped town when he heard I was looking for him and came back to Miami. Anyway, when Davey got Sandy out, she called me right away and I came here. Davey kept feeding me information and trying to get girls out, but he refused to ever say who got him involved to begin with."

"About six weeks ago a girl named Yi Chin was murdered in Panama City. She was in the same hell hole as Sandy, and Davey said she had seen some of the American clientele while she was there. Maybe they didn't plan to let her or the other girls out of there alive, I don't know. In hindsight, we should have done a better job of protecting her. Anyway, Davey thought it may have been why she was killed, because she could identify some of the rich clients. He thought there were others. He said that this Diablo lined up certain girls for a special customer. He said he would try to make a list of the girls who had been with this one particular guy, a man that would kill to keep his involvement secret. Davey said he didn't know who that man was. I'm not so sure that was true, but I'm betting the Diablo did. I never got that list from Davey because he was murdered when he went home that weekend. He did say Sandy would be one of the girls on that list."

Sandy spoke up. "There were guys I was sure were Americans, but they had me so doped up I could never have identified them. Most of the time I had my eyes shut anyway."

"So he went home, made the list, and hid it under his dresser, where I found it. Is my phone hacked?"

"Not by us, or the FBI. Despite what you hear there are legal channels we have to go through. But there are ways to do it remotely, high tech stuff without actually putting a chip in your phone. You don't have to be in the FBI to have that equipment."

"Davey didn't do that great a job of hiding his notebook. I presume you searched the place in Miami and you had access to his computer stuff."

"Yeah, but he always said he liked to write things down. I wanted to look at his parents' place, but I couldn't get a warrant because it was ruled a suicide."

"He had a meeting that night. Did someone suspect what he knew?"

"I don't think so, not that he had made that list anyway. You saw Sam, they would have made him talk, or gone after his parents. But they might have found out he was the one pulling girls out. It was a complicated operation and a lot of people were involved. One leak would have been enough."

"So, when I started snooping around, they got nervous and started listening in on my phone, or bugging my house. I talked to Maggie about the notebook there one day and someone broke in shortly after that. Of course they couldn't find it, and this morning they tore Edith Templeton's house apart. Or was that you?"

"Edith Templeton? No, I swear, no one that works with me would do something like that. Not sure why anyone would. If you're right about your phone, wouldn't they know you have the list and come after you?"

"You would think so, presuming someone else isn't involved."

"What about this list? We need to know who's on it if we're going to protect them. Yi Chin is dead, we have Dedra, Sandy, Rosalyn. Who else?"

"You know about Rosalyn?" I asked.

"She was the first person Davey mentioned. How many others?"

"Three more. But if you want their names, I need something. Two things, really."

Her face hardened. "I can't see that you're in any position to deal. I could drum up some charges, toss you in jail, and tear your house apart."

"You wouldn't find it. I can be a very stubborn man, Susy, and the cot in county wasn't that hard. I even had some decent spaghetti for supper last night."

Susy smiled. "It would be better if you and I get along. I want to find Davey's killer as bad as you do, and the odds are that finding his killer will be a step closer to shutting down this group that are kidnapping kids. What is it you want?"

"You already gave me one of them. See how easy this is? Make finding Davey's killer a priority. So far, I haven't seen much effort by law enforcement to do that. The locals swept it under the rug and called it suicide. It should be an active murder investigation."

"Done. I don't think anyone believes it was suicide at this point."

"And Rosalyn Cabello, she needs her citizenship."

"I can't make that happen, not in this political climate."

"If you bring these people down, it will be in large part because Rosalyn was willing to tell her story. You need to make it happen, or no names."

"She'll have to go through the process, but I can make sure it's quick."

"And that's a promise?"

"Yeah, Slater. You have my word."

"Is she being protected?"

"Her boyfriend and his buddies are taking care of that for us. The detail I sent over there couldn't get anywhere near the house without showing their badges, and Rosalyn refused our protection. She said Manny would protect her or die trying. Let's hope it doesn't come to that."

"I'm not sure I know where to go next. I'm going home and get my real business going. I'm going to start remodeling houses while Maggie heals up. It seems to me these people aren't done. They're nervous or they wouldn't be breaking into houses and looking for that notebook. Maybe they'll come to me." I grabbed the pen and notepad that were on the table and jotted down the three remaining names. "That's all, just seven names, four that you already know. There were no phone numbers or addresses or ages. Just the names."

"And we're no closer to this Diablo Blanco. No idea?"

"Nope, just a guy from Davey's past." I knew I might sit in jail before it was all over, but I wanted to be the first one to talk to Gary Jeffries.

***

I knocked a couple times before Edith Templeton opened the door. She looked tired, but she smiled at me and shrugged when I asked her how she was. "Something like this happens I get mad, and it gets my blood pumping. What the hell is going on, Eric? I know you didn't want to tell me what David was up to before, but I think it's time you did."

"There are still things I don't know, Edith, but it was bad." She shrugged and nodded, so I continued. "Davey got mixed up in something, and I think he was controlled somehow. I'm not even sure if he knew how bad it was. He was lining up people at the talent agency for jobs, and a lot of them were kids. I think he thought it was for legitimate work at first, talent opportunities, but that isn't what it turned into. A lot of these kids were refugees, some of them homeless, some runaways. I'm sorry, but I said I would tell you, good or bad. It amounted to child prostitution."

"Kids. How old?"

"I don't know for sure, but I know of one girl that was fourteen. I think the talent agency he worked for was trafficking these kids, Edith. Kids as young as thirteen, maybe younger. I don't know how much he knew, or for sure when he realized what was going on, but I know of one time when he was personally involved. It was slave trading. Moving children to different countries and selling them into brothels. These people took young girls, maybe boys too, and sent them overseas to be sex slaves. They may have brought some of them into this country for the same reason."

"Dear God. And Davey knew all this?"

"I'm not sure he knew the details, or when he became involved. He may have been forced into it in some way or manipulated by someone. Maybe blackmailed."

"Is that what you really think, or is that just what you're telling me to spare my feelings?"

"There is good news. Starting a few years ago he turned it around. I don't think he could stop the people from doing it, but he started helping some of the victims, getting them out of those situations and helping them get their lives back on track. That's what all the money in his account was for. His roommate was helping fund things, and they even used his corporate jet. I think that's what got

Davey killed. Someone discovered what he was doing and it became a liability for them. They didn't want these kids back in the US telling their stories. Davey's roommate, Samath Chopra, was murdered yesterday."

"Oh my God. That poor man. You think they came here looking for something of Davey's? There wasn't much, and you kept some of it, right?"

"Yeah, they came to my place looking too. They got some of Davey's stuff, but I had the one thing they wanted in my back pocket the night they broke in. It was the night Angela went to the hospital. When I went home, they were in my house and I surprised them."

"Glad we were in church today. I wasn't going to go, but Claire guilted me into it."

"Yeah, lucky." I agreed hesitantly, but she could see what I was thinking. She answered my question before I asked it.

"I called her that day, right before I picked up Rita. I was afraid Rita would say something about all those years ago when I was with Frank, and I needed moral support. I called Claire and told her you were on the way to the hospital."

"I know you're close, and I can't imagine she would want either of us hurt. Maybe it was just a coincidence, or someone knew some other way."

"I'll talk to her in the morning, but I would literally trust her with my life, Eric. Why would she want someone to trash my house looking for

317

something? She cleans the place. She could look everywhere, anytime she wants."

"That's true. Maybe just be a little more careful what you say to her going forward. These people are serious, Edith. Maybe I should stay the night."

"Eddy is coming home. Maggie talked me into calling him. I don't know what's going to happen between us, but he said he could sleep here, just in case. He'll be here in an hour or so."

"Alright. I can help you clean up until he gets here, then I have to check in with Maggie."

***

It was after nine before I made the short drive across Point Road to the Jeffries' house. Most of the lights were off, but the main living room was lit up and Maggie opened the door before I rang the bell.

"Mom and Angela are already in bed. Angela drinks herself to sleep pretty early, but at least she isn't popping pills."

I sat down on the couch and watched her sweep a loose strand of hair from her eyes as she winced a little. She started pacing around the room in front of me, limping slightly. "What are you thinking, Slater?"

"I'm thinking you need to take a break. You should rest that leg. You can't be on it all the time and think it's going to heal."

"Movement is the best thing for it now. It can heal while I sleep. I've been trying to locate Dedra, just to give her my sympathies, but still nothing. Nobody knows where she is. I tried Susan Foster again and she doesn't have a clue."

"That's probably not quite true. I'd guess she has an idea."

"Yeah? Why's that? What do you know, Slater?"

"I know that Susy's job at the talent agency is temporary and totally not real. She works for some federal agency and she and Davey were working together trying to stop all this."

"Yes! I told you there was more to it. Davey got roped into something, but he was a good person at the end."

"Don't gloat, it's unattractive. Yes, Davey turned it around and that's what got him killed. It probably got Sam killed too. Honestly, I'm worried about you being here by yourselves. And so help me, don't even tell me that's sexist. I'm scared. This has gotten really dangerous and whoever this is will kill anyone to get that list. They may be bugging my cell phone, all our phones. They seem to know things they couldn't, unless they have us hacked somehow.

"The girls on Davey's list were all raped and beaten by someone, one man I think, that thought they would never see freedom. Then Davey started bringing them back to the States. Now this guy wants them all dead because of what they might have seen. Because they might be able to identify him. What kind of a person rapes a child and is willing to kill her, just on the off chance that she saw his face?"

"The kind of a person that we have to lock up, Slater. We can get them and get whoever killed Davey. We have to keep trying," Maggie stated.

"You didn't see Sam gutted like a fish, and you didn't hear Dedra screaming. I'm sorry, Maggie, but there is no we, at least not for a while. What if they come after you? I couldn't live with that." My voice broke.

"Alright, calm down, Slater." She sat down beside me, put her arms around my neck and pulled my head down onto her shoulder. "I'm the one being sexist now. I should have realized you couldn't see Sam like that without it tearing you apart."

"If I hadn't started digging into this, maybe they wouldn't have known about the list. Maybe Sam would still be alive."

"And everything would have gone back to the way it was. How many kids' lives might be saved if we can stop even some of this? Davey knew that and so did Sam. They made their choice, and that isn't your fault. And it's not your fault there are people like Diablo Blanco in the world. But we, and I do mean we, have to try and stop them."

I couldn't hold it in. The image of Dedra screaming while Sam laid there covered in blood was too much. Maggie held me for a minute while I let it out.

Finally, I sat back. "You need to improve your security. If someone from the Point is involved, they would know how close Davey and Angela were and they might come here."

"We have some, but we could sure make it better. I'll get someone over here tomorrow, put in motion lights and cameras, whatever it takes. I can throw Angela's checkbook at them."

"Sooner the better. And keep that gun handy."

"Do you want to stay tonight?" she asked. "Not in my room! I can make up Dad's bed and you can sleep in there."

I smiled, feeling better. "Seems like a waste of blankets."

She laughed as she stood up. "Just don't let me catch you sneaking into Angela's room."

"Never crossed my mind." And for once, it hadn't.

Chapter Eighteen

I wasn't surprised the next morning to discover that my house had been ransacked while I was gone. I had planned to look for bugs, but that seemed pointless now. The notebook was right where I'd left it, tucked into the plastic bag that was adhered to my water heater, right behind the owner's manual. Sometimes it's the things that are in plain sight that you don't see.

I thought about that as I started to clean up the mess. Had I missed the signs? At some point in time, Gary Jeffries had developed an unnatural hold over Davey, some sort of twisted, domineering parental relationship. I was sure it hadn't been anything sexual. From my memories of the stories Gary told, it was clear that he only liked women. It seemed more about Davey and his desperate need for a father.

At his best, Eddy Templeton was a cold man. When I first started hanging around with Davey, he had been openly hostile to me. Looking back, I'm sure he thought Davey and I were more than friends. It took the addition of Angie Jeffries and my transparent crush on her for Eddy to accept the fact that I was straight. He never accepted the fact that Davey wasn't, and he went out of his way to show it.

Unaccepting was an understatement. Cold and occasionally cruel would be closer to describing the way he acted. I remember thinking at the time that I was better off. Better to have a father that was gone, or to not have a father at all, than to have one like Eddy Templeton. In hindsight, I wasn't sure if he acted that way because he knew Davey wasn't his biological son or because he was gay, but neither was excusable. Whatever the reason, I knew his indifference and hostility hurt Davey on a daily basis. He needed a father, and he needed a father who could accept him for what he was. At eleven, I had watched him cry more than once because of it, and as we grew older, I watched it make him angry.

Somewhere along the line, between plane rides and flying lessons, Gary Jeffries must have recognized that anger and used it to take Davey down a dark path. Some people have the innate ability to spot those individuals that can be manipulated into doing things that they might never do otherwise. Hitler and Charlie Manson both come to mind. Gary Jeffries was neither, but he must have intuitively started Davey's training back during those airplane rides and strengthened it in the years after high school.

Gary was my most likely suspect and I was pretty sure he was staying at the house in Fort Lauderdale that Frank Jeffries called home. I would have to confront him at some point soon, without the help of Susan Foster and her friends from the FBI, and without the help of my partner. I didn't know what to think about Frank Jeffries. Was it possible that Frank still didn't know that Davey was his son?

The intruders had dumped out every box and drawer in my house, and it took the best part of the day to put it back together. As far as I could tell, nothing was missing. Even the cash I had stashed was left in the pile of papers in my bedroom. Maybe they were just leaving a message. You keep digging, so will we.

Just after noon Edith Templeton called. "Claire finally admitted that she talked to Eddy the night you went to the hospital. Eddy wants to find out who did this, same as us. He'd prefer the more direct approach when it comes to justice; just shoot the bastards. He admitted he had thought about trying to find out what you knew, but he swears on a stack of bibles he didn't go to your house that night."

"Someone was here when I was out of town and went through everything. By now I would hope that they're tired of digging through my underwear drawer."

"I don't think it was him, but I wouldn't swear to it. He's so eaten up by guilt because he wasn't a better father to Davey, anything seems possible. He's not rational right now."

"Are you and Claire speaking?"

"She loved Davey almost as much as I did. She just wants to know what happened."

"We all do. But tell them to let me handle it. It's hard enough to figure out what's going on without more people in the mix."

Luis came by at four o'clock and we drove to the small duplex we were going to start renovating. I planned to let Luis run his crew and just show up to help when I could. It would be a good way to stay busy for a few days, and I didn't want to go back to Miami until I knew the Jeffries house had been secured. The security people were working on lights and all kinds of alarms, but the work wasn't complete. Angela had agreed that I could stay in her Dad's bedroom until the work was done, just in case. Rita wasn't thrilled, but nothing I had done lately thrilled Rita. Jasmine thought the arrangement was hilarious.

"Slater, I said work on it, I didn't say move in." I found myself on the porch alone with her shortly before turning in.

"I'm just sleeping here for a few nights, you're the one that moved in."

"Couple more nights, then Maggie will be able to fend for herself."

"She already can, you just don't want to go home."

"She's the big sister I never had," Jasmine admitted. "It's like one big slumber party."

"That would make Angela the other sister you never had."

She snorted loudly. "That woman hates me. She keeps staring at my head."

"I see you're letting your hair grow out. It's your head, but you did look kind of lopsided."

"Just a thing. I can change my hair, I'm not sure Angela can change her personality."

"Don't be mean. She's jealous of you because you don't have to try with Maggie. Angie's always loved her, but she never was good at showing it. They can't talk for more than five minutes without fighting."

"Maggie thinks you still have a thing for Angela."

"Are you spying for her now?"

"She thinks Angela has a thing for you too."

"She'd be wrong on both counts. You can tell her I said that."

"I tell her everything. That's what sisters do."

"Some sisters." It reminded me that I still wasn't sure if Angie knew about Davey being their brother. It wasn't really my business, but I cared about them both and I thought they both deserved to know. I suspected Davey had told Angie at some point in the last few years but that she hadn't shared it with Maggie. Maggie hadn't told me that they both knew about their dad's girlfriend until it had slipped out that I'd seen her, but it had probably seemed unimportant to her. But finding out that Davey had been her brother would have been a major event in her life. I was sure she would have mentioned it.

It made me wonder, did the private investigator's code say that partners should tell each other everything? If that was the case, I would probably get tossed out of the union, because there was a lot I hadn't told Maggie. And I was very sure she wasn't going to be happy about it, if she found out.

I was certain that the person in Frank's boathouse was his brother Gary, and I was nearly as certain that he was the Diablo Blanco. But before I told my partner, or Susy Foster, or the FBI what I knew, I wanted to look him in the eyes and make him tell me everything. I needed to know how I had failed Davey Templeton and how he had become the man doing the bidding of the Diablo Blanco. And I needed to know if Gary had killed Davey. If I could make him tell me that? I wasn't sure what I would do then.

***

I had come up with a plan of sorts, but I put things on hold for a few days. Luis was doing a great job and the crew would have done fine without me, but doing physical labor took my mind off things. Sometimes that worked. It was like the name of the guy in that movie you couldn't remember. When you stopped thinking about it, it came to you suddenly. Rational or not I felt a degree of responsibility for Gary's control over Davey. And always in the back of my mind there was the scene of Samath Chopra, lying dead and bloody on his leather couch.

Neither of the Jeffries brothers struck me as the kind of people that would hire a killer. No matter how narcissistic they might be, it was impossible to believe they could have had supper with Sam one night and then have him butchered the next. It had to be someone else. Probably it was the same man who was determined to find the list and eliminate the girls on it.

I wasn't sure how Gary had managed to fake his own death or why he had done so. He had fled to California for a couple of years, then apparently moved into the boathouse at Frank Jeffries' compound. He had changed his appearance, but it wasn't like he was unrecognizable. I had realized it was him, but that had a lot to do with the fact that I spotted his brother's purple heart. I couldn't help wondering what the war hero, Clarence Jeffries, would think of his brothers.

I spent the week playing carpenter during the day and sleeping at the Jeffries at night, still worried about intruders. Jasmine decided to go home to Maryanne and the angry mare that was waiting for her. She said she was scared of horses and I told her I didn't think she was scared of anything. She promised to try riding if I would keep working on it. Maggie said she still didn't get it.

Rita loosened up and seemed able to tolerate my presence. She even invited me to supper on my last night there. Rosa had to leave early, so after giving Maggie instructions, she went home. I helped carry the food out and we sat down with Rita. Angie appeared after a couple of minutes, stumbling slightly and slurring her words.

Maggie started in on her right away. "Nice Angela. Six-thirty. Another couple of drinks and you can go pass out in your room."

"It helps me sleep," she mumbled. "Would you rather I take something?"

"Maybe if you did what the doctor told you and quit drinking so much you would sleep like a normal person."

"I'm not a normal person. Normal is boring. Do you like boring, Eric?" She reached out and laid a hand on my forearm and laughed again.

"I guess there's a sweet spot somewhere between boring and crazy, that's what I shoot for," I tried.

"We all know the sweet spot you're shooting for." She threw an exaggerated wink at Maggie and tipped her glass up.

In all my years of being around that household I'd never seen Rita try to discipline her daughter, or even offer an opinion about her behavior. That's why it was so shocking when she did. She reached out suddenly and snatched the glass from Angela's grasp and set it on the table. When Angela reached for it, Rita grabbed it again and tossed it in the general direction of the fireplace, ignoring the noise as it shattered.

"Enough of your damn nonsense, and your vulgarity. If you can't show up for dinner sober, then at least sit here and pretend to have some respect for this family and for yourself. As I remember, Eric spent half his life chasing after you, and you never gave him the time of day. If he and Maggie have something now, it's none of your damn business."

Angela didn't back down. "Jesus, I was just teasing them. You don't get to lecture me about men, you're the last person I'd listen to about that. That's why Daddy is always gone, and it's why he is the way he is. He's never home because he needs to feel something real, and he sure as hell can't find that here."

"He won't find it with her either," Rita returned. "There's always the next tramp willing to fuck him, but he always moves on, doesn't he? I know all about the whore he has down in Lauderdale."

"You know what, Mom? I've met her. Maria is a warm, loving, happy person. And she makes him happy. Can you say that? Even if it doesn't last, maybe he deserves to be happy for a little while."

"I don't care what makes him happy. There's been too much crap over the years, too many other women. He's too arrogant and twisted for me to ever care what makes him happy. Besides, our relationship is none of your business."

"Really? It really is Mom. It started being my business a long time ago."

"What the hell does that mean?"

Angela had tears running down her cheeks and she paused, staring at her mother for a long moment, then spoke. "Who pays for everything? It's my money that keeps this house going. It's my money that pays for the Lauderdale house. If I hadn't married Charlie we'd be living on the street."

"Fine. I'll divorce your father, sell the house, and go live in a condo. I wasn't hungry anyway." Rita slammed her chair back and went to her bedroom on the east end of the big house. The room echoed when she shut the door.

Angela sat there for a few moments then got up and walked to the steps. As she climbed to her room, she looked down at us and smiled. "I need a drink."

I didn't say anything as Maggie picked at her food. She pointed at my plate. "Eat. Rosa worked hard on this; somebody has to eat it."

"Should I go home, or stay the night?"

"You can stay, it'll be fine. By tomorrow they'll be back to normal. Angie will be sober and Mom will shut down again. I'd like to lock them both in a rubber room somewhere and let them fight it out."

"Are you going to walk the road in the morning? I'll come with you if you want. I can be late for work."

"Walk? My leg is good to go. I'll leave you in the dust."

***

I woke up early in Frank's bed, surprised to find Angela sitting on the edge of it with two cups of coffee. I slid up against the headboard and rubbed my eyes.

She smiled her lovely smile. "Some bodyguard you are, Slater. I was banging around the kitchen for half an hour and you were still sawing logs when I came in."

"It's early," I grumbled, taking the cup she handed me. I glanced at the bedroom door. It was open.

Angela snickered. "Times have changed, right? Not too long ago you would have preferred that door was locked. But we wouldn't want Maggie to get the wrong impression."

I nodded and waited for her to say something more.

"I wanted to apologize for that scene last night. I shouldn't have said those things to my mother. Daddy and her just never had what you're supposed to have in a marriage. Not that I'm an expert, but there never was any passion. He's like me, up and down all the time. I think she decided that if she just ignored it and never reacted, they could make it work."

"She shouldn't have to be what he wants."

"That's what Charlie always said about me. Nobody understood us, but I really did love him, and I miss him a lot. I'm sorry I act so crazy sometimes, but I really miss Charlie, and Davey too." She teared up when she said his name.

I nodded again. "I know how close you and Davey were."

She smiled sadly and looked into her coffee cup. "Nobody really knows how close we were, not truly."

She was so beautiful, and so broken. It hurt me to look at her. I put my hand on hers and spoke softly. "Yeah, Angie, I think I do. I know he was your brother."

She lifted that beautiful face and stared into my eyes. "How?"

"Despite what you may have heard, I'm not bad at this detective thing. Blood type. I knew Davey's from an old medical alert bracelet, and when Maggie got clipped by that bullet fragment in the plane, she talked about hers."

"You told her?"

"No, I think you need to do that. If you don't, I will, but it would be better coming from you." I tried to make my question sound casual. "Your Dad, he has a girlfriend?"

"Yeah, really young, but that's what he likes. She's Latino, Colombian I think, and she has a four-year old boy."

"Maria, pretty name."

"Yeah, Maria Lopez. I never really met her. I lied to Mom just to make her mad, but I did talk to her on the phone a couple times. Daddy wants to bring her up here so I can meet her, but that would be too weird, even for this family. I think he might really care about this one."

"Kind of late in life to find the right person, but better late than never."

"I could say that about you, Eric." There was a sound from the kitchen and I leaned forward. Maggie was pouring herself coffee and glanced in our direction. Angela laughed at her expression. "Don't worry, Maggie, I'm not in here molesting your boyfriend."

"Not my boyfriend," she called out.

Angela giggled and looked back at me. "You better get working on that, Slater."

I nodded. "Yeah, that's what everybody keeps telling me."

***

I was ready to go when Maggie came down dressed in her running gear. She gave me a small smile but didn't say anything right away. She started at a slow trot and gradually worked up to half speed.

"I'm still a little weak, Slater, sorry if you don't like the pace."

"Suits me. Another week and I won't be able to keep up with you."

"Not if you get out here every morning at seven like we talked about. But you're going to have to drive over from now on. After what I saw this morning, I'm throwing you out of the house."

"Good timing. I was leaving anyway."

"I know, I was kidding. Don't get a big head, but for just a second when I saw you two this morning, I might have been a little jealous. Just a teensy bit."

"That shouldn't make me happy, but it does. Just a teensy bit."

She ran quietly for a bit, looking thoughtful. "I think my parents are going to get a divorce," she said.

"Probably for the best, right?"

"Probably. Dad's coming home Sunday night so they can talk. I think he's ready to just get it over with."

"Is he bringing his girlfriend?"

"No, I don't think so. Why the hell would he do that?"

"Just asking. Angela said he wanted you and her to meet this girl. I thought he might bring her along."

"Not that I know of, that would be too weird."

"Yeah, that's what Angela said too. Weird."

* * *

Maria Lopez was one of the remaining names on the list. I was well aware that it was a common name in the Latin culture and a quick Google search told me that there were over four thousand just in the Miami-Fort Lauderdale area. It seemed unlikely that Frank would be involved with one of his victims. But then, I still didn't know that he was involved in any of it for sure. I had to go back to Lauderdale, and I had to do it soon. If Frank was coming north on Sunday, I would be going south. If I had to, I would beat a confession out of Gary Jeffries.

Chapter Nineteen

I ran with Maggie Sunday morning and we chatted about her father's impending arrival. It had Angie tied in knots, so I knew Maggie would stick around to help her through it. He was flying commercial and his plane was due in at ten o'clock that evening. With traffic, boarding, loading, and unloading, I guessed that he would leave his house no later than six-thirty. If I left my house at two in the afternoon, I could be driving down his street by seven or seven-thirty. With luck, his girlfriend and her son would have taken him to the airport and Gary would be in the guest house alone.

There were a lot of things that could go wrong with my plan. But I was sure that if Gary hadn't killed Davey, he had to know who did. Considering just the things I knew he had done, without throwing in murder, I didn't plan to go easy on him for old time's sake. With Frank and his girlfriend out of the way, I would have time to sweat a confession out of Gary.

There was still a piece missing in the puzzle, someone pulling strings that none of us could see. Gary, and possibly Frank might have been involved in kidnapping young girls and selling them, but someone with a lot of money was buying them. Whoever that was, might be the person that had killed Davey, with or without the help of Diablo Blanco. If he was willing to kill underaged girls just for looking at him, he would certainly try to kill me if our paths crossed. And people like that didn't do their own killing, they hired professionals. Men that were good with a gun. That didn't matter to me. I had been to the range and I was ready.

***

When I got to Lauderdale, I stopped at the Seven Eleven and bought a package of hot dogs: the really disgusting cheesy kind. Dogs love them. I didn't want to have to tell Maggie that I had shot her dad's dog on top of all the other explaining I would be doing. Hopefully, if I ended up nose to nose with the pooch, he would eat the hotdogs and not me.

It's surprising how oblivious most people are to the things that go on around them. In the absence of security lighting and motion sensors, people in a house with the lights on are blind to what's going on outside once the sun goes down. If there's no moon, you can tromp all over their yard and they'll remain unaware while they keep their eyes glued to the latest guilty pleasure on their screens. I expected the big house might have motion sensors, but I was hoping the guesthouse didn't have any outside lighting.

There were several lights on in the main house, which didn't strike me as being a good sign. If Frank had taken a taxi to the airport, that meant that his girlfriend was at home alone with the child. That might not matter to me if Gary was down in the guest house. I shimmied under the bushes again and crawled all the way down the hill, hugging the dark corner of the privacy fence until I was even with the window of the small guest cottage. It was overcast, pitch black except for the shimmering reflections from the water in the channel a few yards away.

The guest house's window had a cheap white lace curtain drawn across the opening. It was sheer enough to see through from outside. I didn't want to get too close to the window, so I used my binoculars. The light gathering capability works regardless of your location and by moving around I was able to get an idea of what was going on inside.

Nothing I saw made sense to me, so I decided to risk a look from a different angle. It took several minutes to relocate to the other side of the cabin. I had to go up the hill toward the main house and crawl along the edge of the deck. None of the lights were on in that part of the house and if there was security lighting, it wasn't sensitive enough to pick up my motion. I made a mental note to be sure Maggie's house had a better system.

From my new location I could see more of the room. The curtains on that side were open. I had to stay well back or risk being spotted, but I had a better view of the room. It was definitely Gary

Jeffries. Without his hat and sunglasses there was no doubt that it was him, just older and with less hair. Andy Gleason sat across the table from him and there was a gun lying between them. From the other perspective I had thought they were just sitting at the table having a conversation, but from my new angle I could see that Gary never put his hands on the table. His arms never moved and appeared to be stretched around the back of the chair. I watched them for several minutes until I was sure. Gary was restrained; it was the only explanation. Yet it looked like they were carrying on a normal conversation. Andy even smiled and laughed a couple of times. That didn't make a lot of sense.

You don't have to be a detective to know that if you tie someone up, you probably don't plan to shoot them. No need for restraints if someone is dead. Much as Gary Jeffries' second passing would please me, I needed to find out what he knew about Davey's death. I watched for a few more minutes and the scene never changed. Andy sat there chatting with Gary like they were old friends. It was as if they were waiting for something.

When it occurred to me what that was, I scurried up the hill as fast as I could. Andy was waiting for an execution.

The north side of the house backed up to another privacy fence, just a few feet from the building. I ducked under a couple of unlit windows and made my way to the frontside of the house. The overhead light was on in the main part of the house and from a small window in the laundry area I could see a small portion of the living room.

The first thing I saw was a pair of Nikes, shoes too big to belong to a child, protruding from beyond the doorsill. Two other sets of legs dangled from a chair directly in front of the shoes: children's feet. I presumed it was the little boy I had seen before and a babysitter, probably the same little blond girl. One of the feet was bouncing nervously, so at least they were still alive. Undoubtedly, they had been spared as hostages should the shooter need them. They were waiting too. Everyone was waiting for Maria Lopez to return from taking Frank to the airport.

The German Shepherd mix was stretched out on the kitchen tile with a small puddle of blood pooled beside his head. Damn. No more mister nice guy. The bastard had killed the dog.

I pulled back and sent a text, then hunkered down to wait. I really hoped Maria would stop for groceries, go dancing, or use her free time to cheat on Frank. Anything but come straight home from the airport. I needed twenty minutes.

What I got was fifteen. When I heard the garage door start to open, I moved along the sidewall and waited until the vehicle was almost inside. Maria was driving the big SUV I'd seen at the docks, an Escalade or a Suburban. I ducked around the corner and followed it in. Fortunately, it was a big garage. Even more fortunate was the fact that she had stopped for groceries. She opened the rear side door and reached in for the bag as I walked silently up behind her. When she stood up, I reached around and clamped one hand over her mouth and put my other one on her throat. She reacted as I expected, and as she should, by struggling and trying to bite me. Silence was my goal and I increased the pressure on her throat until she stopped fighting and was close to passing out. Then I whispered in her ear.

"There's a man inside that has your child and the babysitter. He was sent here to kill you, and he will kill them too. I'm here to help. If you scream, they are dead for sure. Do you understand me?"

She nodded and I let her go. She turned to me wide eyed and whispered, "Is it the man who killed Sam?"

"No, he's dead. I shot him, and I'm going to shoot this asshole too. But I need him out in the open. I need you to open the door and say something, whatever you want, just be casual. Push the door all the way open and then jump back out of the way. If it doesn't go right, you get my gun and start shooting, because he'll never let any of you out of here alive. Can you do that?"

"Si, I will do my best."

"Give me just a second," I said quietly. There was a small bucket near the door and I used it to unplug the opener, plunging the garage into darkness. I wasn't about to give the shooter a silhouette. He would be expecting a helpless young woman with a bag of groceries, and he would probably not start shooting until after she had walked through the doorway. But a pro would have a back-up plan, and I had to be ready for that.

Plans. His, mine, they never work out quite like they're supposed to. Maria did a good job. She threw the door open and called out something about having popcorn, then lunged to the side. I expected a hail of bullets, but that's not what happened. The gunman stepped out into the room and started to lift his gun as I took the one step up into the entry. With his free arm he held the babysitter in front of his body for a shield. I could see the surprise and his momentary indecision; shoot me or use the kid for a hostage to get the woman. I had just a split second to look into that young girl's eyes and make my choice. Really, there was only one choice.

I had told Maggie that I was good at two things: flying and shooting. I'm a pretty damn good pilot. You spend enough hours in the air and the plane becomes a part of you. But as instinctual as flying is for me, as naturally gifted as I am at that, I am much, much better with a handgun. With a Glock in my hand, I don't miss.

The girl was struggling a little and the assassin wasn't able to get her up high enough to shield himself completely. As he started to swing his gun in my direction I put a shot six inches over the top of the girl's head, somewhere between the gunman's nose and left cheek. There was no need to wonder if he was dead. I knew. It threw him back into the living room and I stepped aside as Maria Lopez rushed past me to gather up the two children. I flipped the light switch off and walked over to her.

"This isn't over. There's another one down in the guest house. Lock the door and call the police. And throw a blanket over that poor dog."

***

I couldn't be sure that Gleason had heard the shot. If he had he would think it was his accomplice, completing his work. My backup hadn't arrived, and I was beginning to wish I hadn't sent that text. I walked down the hill with my gun in my hand, throwing caution to the wind.

When I got close to the cabin, Gleason stepped into the dim light from the window. "Everything taken care of?" He asked it casually, as if a woman and two children's lives meant nothing to him.

I stepped into the light with my Glock pointed at his face. "Not quite. Just give me any kind of reason to finish it up." He had the gun I had seen on the table in his hand and I could see he was thinking about trying to use it. "You have two seconds," I said. He tossed the gun before I had finished the sentence. "Now your phone."

I followed him into the room and pointed to the hardwood. "I'm going to talk to your friend here for a minute. Get down on your face and spread eagle in the middle of the floor where I can see you." He obliged slowly while Gary Jeffries looked on calmly. I positioned myself where I could see them both, then warned him again. "You move one time and I'm going to shoot you right in that fat ass of yours. No second chances. Got it?" He moaned something that I took for a yes.

I pointed my gun at Gary Jeffries. "Is it murder if somebody is already dead?"

"Eric. Long time. You might as well shoot me because I'm as good as dead already."

"You better hope the cops get here soon. If Rosalyn's boyfriend shows up first, I wouldn't want to be you. Rosalyn Cabello, remember her? Did Frank get in on that too?"

Gary stared at me for a minute, then shrugged. "He likes the young ones even more than I do. Couple different guys had a turn with her. That whole deal got out of hand, but I couldn't help myself. She was just too hot for her own good."

"Don't blame her, you sick piece of shit. She was a child! Did you kill Davey Templeton? The two of you?"

"Of course not. He was a pussy, but I liked that kid. He didn't care for it when I got rough with the girl. That was when he started to man up, when he finally figured things out. He liked all those bonus payments he got for finding me pretty young girls, but once he realized those kids weren't going off to be runway models somewhere, he flipped out. Then he just kept sticking his nose in where it didn't belong. When I came back to town I tried to knock some sense into him, but he wouldn't listen. He would have been alright if he'd just minded his own business."

"What you were doing, Gary, that's everybody's business. Civilized people don't do that kind of shit." I wanted to tell him that Davey was his nephew, but in that moment, I decided he didn't deserve to know.

He kept talking. "The guy we're dealing with, he's very serious about his privacy. Some of those girls had seen him, and he wasn't happy when they started showing up back in this country. Once he figured out it was Davey bringing those girls back, the kid was as good as dead. He didn't like that Frank took Maria in either. She was supposed to disappear. That's why Frank went to Jacksonville. It was Maria or his daughters, he was told to make a choice."

"He left his girlfriend here to be butchered?"

"He's in over his head, same as me. I didn't want to go along, and that's why Andy tied me up like this. I was going to try to stop them from killing Maria. But somebody had to die to teach Frank a lesson, and Maria had seen too much. She was dead either way, so Frank made the only choice he could. Honestly, Eric, it wasn't me that killed Davey. This guy we're dealing with, anybody is expendable if they make too much noise. There is so much money involved, here and overseas. Turned out Sam was working with Davey, which was news to me. When they killed him, Frank and I knew we'd be next if we didn't do as we're told. We go along or we're dead."

"A name, Gary. Who is this scumbag that's willing to have a four-year old murdered, along with his babysitter and mother."

"I always liked you, Eric, so I'm not going to tell you that." I stepped back and leveled the gun at his face. He actually chuckled. "We both know you won't shoot me. Really, Eric, this guy would kill you, me, and my nieces if we get in his way, then go have a cold beer and laugh about it. I know you think Frank and I are bad people, and no doubt you're right. But we're boy scouts compared to the man I'm talking about. Believe me, there is nothing he won't do, and there's no perversion that's too far. And he has all the money and rich friends he needs to get away with it."

"How did you do it, Gary? How did you get Davey to ever agree to any of this?"

"Little of that in all of us, Eric. It feels good to have that power over someone else. Davey never had that. He got kicked around in school and his old man wouldn't even look at him. I just did what his father should have done, I treated him like a man, then I pushed him to prove it. But when it came right down to it, he couldn't. Pussy, like I said. He didn't like the rough stuff. Then all of a sudden, mostly because of the Cabello girl, he grew a set of balls. He was going to go to the cops and turn me in, but I talked him out of it. He let me disappear and make a run for it instead. The feds were closing in on me anyway."

"Surprised you didn't just kill him," I said.

"Like I said, Eric, I liked that kid. I've never killed anyone."

"Maybe you didn't squeeze the trigger, but how many people are dead or ruined for life, because of what you were doing? You're going to pay for that, Gary."

I heard a sudden noise. The door was open and my backup stood just inside. "Yeah, my Rosie, she has nightmares and screams in the middle of the night because she remembers you, Diablo."

Manny and four of his compadres poured into the room and surrounded us. "You owe her a great debt, Senor Diablo, and I am here to collect. Sorry, Mister Slater. It would be better if you don't have to see this." I should have realized what they had in mind, but there were too many of them. There was a blinding flash, then darkness.

***

"Slater! Slater, wake up! Wakey, wakey."

I struggled to open my eyes as someone slapped me on the cheek. I was sure that if I moved, the pain in my head was going to kill me. It took a full ten seconds to get my eyes to focus. Susan Foster stood over me smiling.

"I knew that head of yours was too hard to do any serious damage, but you were out for quite a while. You are lucky I like you, Sailor, or I'd have you in jail for a very long time. You did manage to save another woman's life, so you get a pass, again. Good thing we had somebody tailing Manny or he would have done something you'd regret. If we'd have been a couple of minutes later he'd have used his knife, then you'd all be in prison."

"Where's Gary?" I muttered.

"Who's Gary?" she asked as she pulled me to a sitting position and handed me a bag of frozen vegetables she must have taken from the refrigerator.

"Gary Jeffries, the Diablo Blanco? Manny came here to skin him." Manny and his crew were sitting on the floor on the other side of the room. Their hands were cuffed behind their backs and two uniformed officers were kneeling down talking to them. Andy and Gary were nowhere to be seen. Susy popped a piece of gum in her mouth, then glanced at Manny who was glaring at us coldly.

"We'll cut them loose and I'll stick to our deal. Don't worry, I have people watching Rosalyn. But who is this Gary Jeffries you're talking about?"

My head hurt and nothing she said was making sense. "Gary, Maggie's uncle, the Diablo Blanco. He was going to kill Sandy, and Rosalyn."

"See, the story I heard was that this Diablo guy was trying to warn them about the assassin that was coming after them. It might even be true. And it might be that he knows all the names of all the people I want to know. But Gary Jeffries? He's been dead for years. Alligator bait is what I heard."

"Alright, I get it, he's your star witness. What about Frank? What about the girls?" I tried to stand up, panicked, but Susy put a hand on my shoulder. I tried to explain. "If they couldn't get Maria, they'll go after Angie and Maggie."

"Relax, Eric. Having Gary gives us leverage, and it was never about Maggie and Angela. My old boss, Andy, he'll be going into witness protection too. The guy with the real money, the one I really want, he and his bunch are running back to their sandcastle for now, and the locals that were involved are too busy trying to cover their own asses to come after Frank."

"And Davey? Any idea who killed him?"

"If Gary knows, he's holding out on us until we cut a deal."

"Alright, what about Frank?"

"I'm going to let him sweat it out for a while and see who he runs to. Maybe he'll finger Davey's killer, if his brother doesn't."

"Maria, what about her and the kid?"

"She'll disappear until everything shakes out with Frank. Far as he knows, they're all dead. The man you shot was a hired gun, and nobody will get too excited that he didn't call in. Frank was willing to give her up and let them kill her. Couple of fine brothers, those two."

"They told Frank it was Maria or his daughters. He'll think she's dead because he chose Angie and Maggie," I explained.

"You make a deal with the Devil, you have to expect to get burned." Susy leaned toward me suddenly, real anger on her face. "I know your head hurts, Slater, but you listen very closely to what I'm about to say. Dozens, possibly hundreds of kids from all over this country and plenty of immigrants, some of them young as ten years old, have been kidnapped, raped, and brutalized. Two of the people I loved and respected most in the world were extinguished, just so people like Frank and Gary Jeffries could get their nut off." She snapped her gum once, then put her face inches from mine.

"I'm cutting you loose, only because Maria Lopez and those kids are still breathing. That's the only reason. But if you give Frank Jeffries any indication of what happened here tonight, if you fuck up this investigation any more than you already have, I will have you in jail every day I can for obstruction and be waiting for you when you walk out of prison to make your life a living hell. Do you understand me?"

I didn't argue. "Yeah, perfectly. Can I go now or am I under arrest? It'll be a long drive home."

She wasn't quite done. "Not a word to anybody about any of this, and that includes Maggie." I nodded and tossed the ice bag in the sink as I walked to the door. A uniformed deputy handed me my gun and held the door open.

"Hey, Slater." I turned around and Susy Foster gave me the slightest smile. "Nice shooting."

Chapter Twenty

It was a long drive back to Jacksonville. I had to stop at a convenience store and buy another bag of frozen peas to hold on my head as I drove. I swear, thinking made it hurt more, but I couldn't help that.

All things considered, it could have gone worse. Not much, but I had managed to keep Maria Lopez and the kids alive, so that was a win. Gary Jeffries was in custody, and that was another good thing. He would cut some kind of deal, probably be a protected witness and get another new life. We should have called him El Gato. My guess was that his brother was burning up his phone trying to find out what had happened. It was a tossup between the two which brother I hated more at that point.

I had thought that Gary had been the one to pull Frank into everything, but now I wasn't so sure. It might have gone the other way. They both seemed to have a pathological need to dominate and I wasn't about to try to analyze where that came from. One night at the dinner table with Frank spoke volumes about his personality. He was the one that had supported his brother in hiding, and the one that had fooled his family all those years. I could begrudgingly give him credit for wanting to save his daughters, but that didn't begin to make up for the horrors Rosalyn Cabello and countless other girls had gone through. Susy Foster was right, he didn't deserve a word of warning from me. I would protect his daughters as best I could, but Frank Jeffries could go to hell.

***

I got home at four in the morning and took another handful of Ibuprofen. I didn't bother reading the label; kidney damage seemed worth it if my headache would go away. I got in bed and tried to fall asleep, but the throbbing got worse, so I got up and wandered around the house for a while with an ice pack. Standing seemed the least painful and moving around helped. By six o'clock the pain had subsided some and I contemplated the fact that it was Monday morning. Maybe a walk would help.

Luis and the crew started at eight, but he wouldn't be counting on me to show up until later, if at all. Maggie would be expecting me to run with her at seven. I decided to walk over to her place and attempt it. Walking in the cool air felt pretty good, so maybe a run wouldn't be too bad.

I was wondering what Frank had said the night before, and if he was still talking about a divorce. As far as he knew, Maria Lopez was lying dead in Angela's house. Maybe he planned to play it off as a burglary, act shocked when he heard the news, and continue on as if he weren't the monster I knew him to be. Davey's death was still unexplained, and at some point, Frank Jeffries and I were going to talk about that. Maybe Susy Foster would give me another pass. If not, the food in jail wasn't that bad.

It wasn't a long walk to Point Road and I jogged a couple times to warm up and make sure my skull would take the bouncing. I made it to the end of Maggie's driveway half an hour early, so I decided to walk back to the Templeton's and say good morning to Edith. There was something I wanted to talk to her about anyway. It was getting light, but the kitchen lights were still glowing in the window when I walked up.

Edith Templeton swung the screen door open and stood there in her housecoat smiling at me. "Well, Eric, going for a run with Maggie this morning? I told you she's the one you need to be chasing."

"Morning, Edith. I'm too early, so I've got a few minutes. Any coffee?"

"Sure, come on in."

I sat down and started awkwardly. "I want to talk to you about Davey's money." I explained what Davey had been doing with the money, how he had been helping some of the girls, and how Rosalyn Cabello was living in poverty. "Maybe it isn't my place to say, Edith, but I know it would have made Davey happy to give some of that money to Rosalyn and the girls like her."

"It sounds like a great way to honor his memory, Eric. You and I can sit down together and figure out how to do it. I'm sure Eddy will be fine with it. It was Davey's money, not ours. Eddy and I are trying to work things out. We both made a lot of mistakes over the years, and we're going to try to get beyond that." Edith had left the front door open to let in the cool morning air. I heard a sudden shout, then another. Edith stood quickly. "Eddy went back to the barn, and he took his gun."

I opened the screen door and turned back to her. "Wait here, I'll see what's going on."

Funny, how sometimes you just know things.

The big door of the barn was standing open and Eddy Templeton was staring up at something with a shotgun dangling from his hand. He heard me coming and turned slowly, then motioned into the barn.

"I walked out in the hayfield to see if I could jump some quail. I was on my way back and I just now found him."

Frank Jeffries hung from the same high railing where they had found his son two months before. It seemed likely he had done it himself. He must have known one belt wasn't enough because he had tied three of them together and stepped off one of the old chairs. He hadn't bothered to kick it away.

I walked over to him with Eddy a step behind. I lifted him high enough for Eddy to stand on a chair and loosen the makeshift noose, then lowered him to the ground. I didn't need to wonder if he was dead; he was stiff and his skin was an ugly bluish grey. He must have walked over in the middle of the night. Eddy was shaking and started to cry as I rolled him over.

"Son of a bitch didn't even give me the satisfaction of beating his ass for what he did to Davey."

"What do you mean, what he did to Davey?"

"Davey knew I wasn't his biological father, and he told Frank. The bastard told Davey no son of his would be a damn queer. If I'd known he was going to do this, I'd have come to watch." He spit in Frank's general direction and then turned and started walking away.

"Eddy, Davey told me you were always the man he considered his father. He said he loved you a lot." It was a lie he needed to hear.

"Really? I didn't deserve that, but then, that was Davey. Thank you for telling me that, Eric."

"I'll call the cops. Can you bring a blanket back so I can cover him?"

When we were getting him down, I had noticed a piece of paper protruding from his pocket with Angela's name on it. Even in death he had managed to discount his youngest daughter. I was damned if I was going to let him get away with that. I pulled the note out and read it.

357

"Sorry, Angie, for everything I did and the things I can't undo. This will end it. They won't come after any more of the people I love. Daddy."

To hell with Frank Jeffries. He didn't get to hurt Maggie like that and still play the hero. I crumpled the note up and pushed it into the pocket of my shorts. Edith came out with a blanket, handed it to me and walked away without a word. I walked to the end of the driveway and waited for the ambulance to come and haul Frank Jeffries out of our lives forever. I heard the wail of the siren and could see the lights flashing as Maggie came trotting down her driveway. She looked down the road, then lunged into my arms, sobbing.

***

I went with Maggie and Rita to tell Angela. I've never seen anyone grieve like that. By the time you're nearly forty most people have experienced death, be it grandparents, parents, or for the unlucky few, loved ones younger than themselves. The slow onslaught of cancer, difficult as that is, gives loved ones a chance to adapt to the reality of a life without, Grandpa, Uncle Jim, or as was my case, Mom.

It's harder, having a person ripped from your lives in the space of a sentence. "Thank you for your son's service, Mrs. Johnson, we are sorry to inform you..." I had to stand beside a Chaplain on a few occasions when they delivered that message. They always knew, when they opened their door and saw a Naval Chaplain and Master Chief Petty Officer standing there in his dress blues. They knew before we said anything that their child would never be coming home again.

Angela had that look when she saw the three of us together and Maggie's tear-stained face. She was still in bed, but awake and sitting up. Before anyone spoke, she slid away from us, falling to the floor and spider crawling backwards into the corner of her room. Her beautiful blue eyes jumped from one to the other of us, then cast furtive glances to the left and right as if she were a small animal trapped by a predator, searching for some place to hide from the reality she knew was coming. Then she dropped her head between her knees, took a deep breath and started screaming, wailing so hard and continuously that finally, she wasn't able to breathe and passed out.

Maggie slid onto the floor with her, wrapped her in an embrace, and pulled her onto her lap, rocking her like a small child as the moans settled into soft whimpers. She looked up at me forlornly and I pantomimed a call, silently asking if we should call a doctor. She shook her head and motioned us from the room as Angela buried her head in her sister's hair and started screaming again. Much as I wanted to help, there was nothing to do but go downstairs and leave the two of them to their grief.

Before I had reached the bottom of the steps, Rita had gone to her room and slammed her door. I sat on the couch, feeling useless and wondering what to do next when Rosa came in. She already knew and shared a hug, then started cooking. Living people needed food she said. I went outside and called Jasmine Thatcher first, then dialed Susan Foster.

"I wanted you to know that Frank Jeffries hung himself this morning."

"Local police just notified me. Did Maggie call you?"

"I came over to run with her. Eddy and I found him. Same stall where Davey was hanging."

"Did he leave a note, a confession? One fake suicide is enough. I have people going there to make sure all the forensics work out."

"He used three of his own belts. Nobody else wanting to hang him would go to that much trouble. I think he really cared about Maria and couldn't live with what he thought he had done to her. This one's on you, I'm afraid."

"Maybe so, but I can live with it. I don't know if the end justifies the means, but he wasn't a good guy, Slater. He was anything but that. He didn't kill Davey, but he helped set it up to cover his own ass. Davey thought he was going to meet someone who wanted to get more girls out. You were right about the list. A person with a lot to lose was sure some of those girls knew who he was and he got very nervous when he found out they were being brought back to the states. He's connected to a lot of people in power and it would ruin things for him if our government knew he was involved in this kind of shit. He killed Davey because of his part in bringing the girls back to the US where they might identify him. I don't know if Frank realized they were going to kill Davey, but once they did, he and two thugs took the body back to the horse-barn to make it look like a suicide."

"Have a name?" I tried to sound casual.

Susy chuckled into the phone. "Not for you, Slater. You already crossed too many lines. It's not someone I can prosecute, not right now. But trust me, I'll find some way to get the bastard, legal or not. Look, we shut down the talent agency at least, that made a lot of kids safer. Someday we'll get the chance to even the score for Davey and Sam, I promise you that."

"I hope you'll let me in on that, Susy. Next time we work together, let's try to keep each other honest, alright?"

"Next time? I thought you were going into construction."

"Part time. But something tells me you haven't heard the last of me, or Maggie."

"Well, thanks for the warning. Actually, I'm kind of looking forward to it. Tell Maggie I'm sorry about her dad. Does she know anything about her uncle?"

"She knows he died a few years ago in a plane crash. What else is there?"

"Good answer, Slater. Take care of yourself."

***

The last of the mourners had found their way out of the big house, and Jasmine and I had finished piling dishes in the dishwasher. I had no idea if I should stick around and try to be supportive, or clear out and let the family have some time alone. I wasn't sure that alone time was what either Maggie or her sister needed.

Rita Jeffries breezed into the kitchen and gave me a quick hug. "Eric, thank you so much for helping out. Jasmine, you must be exhausted. Thank you for being here for Maggie, but can I ask you to give us some time alone? We've all grown very fond of you, dear, but Maggie needs to be with her sister right now. She's always the one that knows what to do with Angie."

"Alright. I know I'm not Angela's favorite person." Jasmine wrapped her arms around Rita and held her awkwardly for a minute. "I'll talk to Maggie and have her call me if any of you need something. I'm really sorry about your loss, Mrs. Jeffries."

"Thank you, Jasmine. The truth is Frank was never here enough for me to miss him and we weren't close for a lot of years. Angela is struggling, but Angela always struggles. Maggie is saying goodbye to the last of her dad's friends. Eric, if you wouldn't mind, can you go up and check in on Angie before you go? She refused to come down for the service. I think she's alright, but she may do something rash. The last thing we want is for her to take too many pills again. Maybe she'll talk to you. She hasn't spoken a word to me all day."

It was the most I had ever heard Rita Jeffries say at one time. She didn't seem devastated, or even unhappy.

I knocked softly on Angela's door and she asked who it was, then told me to come in. She had a loveseat in her room, and she was curled up on it. A bottle of Crown Royal and a glass sat on a table within her reach. I saw her put the glass down just as I walked in. Her eyes teared when she saw me, and she dropped her bare feet to the floor and patted the cushion next to her. I sat down and without a word she climbed into my lap, buried her face against my shoulder, and started sobbing.

I held onto her, trying to whisper the right thing, anything that would help in that moment. She moaned a little and suddenly turned her face up to mine and started kissing me. It wasn't warm or sexual, it was desperation and raw emotion that needed a direction to go. As I eased her away and slid her off my lap, all I could think about was the fact that she wasn't wearing much, a bra and underwear with some sort of tiny wrap that passed for half a housecoat. It didn't excite me, it made me uneasy. I stood up and took a couple steps away as she reached out a hand.

"I'm sorry, Eric, I didn't mean it that way. I just really needed to feel close to someone, if only for a moment."

The door swung open and Maggie stepped into the room, looking tired and visibly angry. She glanced at me. "Slater, you have lipstick all over your face."

"He was just holding onto me for a minute, Maggie. You know it's you he likes. You don't have to be jealous."

"I'm not jealous, but this is hardly the time to be sticking your tongue down a guy's throat, Angela. Dad's barely in the ground. Fuck!"

"Maggie, it was nothing," I tried.

"It's always nothing with her, Slater, as long as she's the center of attention. She sees that you aren't following her around like a love-sick puppy anymore and it makes her nervous, that's all it is. It's not like she wants a real relationship with anyone. Mom said I should make sure you aren't going to do anything stupid, Angela."

"Why are you being like this? I'm sorry I can't be strong and perfect like you. Have you cried at all? Daddy was no saint, but it wouldn't hurt to show that you cared about him, let it out a little."

"I can't take the time to cry," Maggie snapped. "I have to keep it together and be the normal one while you pull your tortured Angela act again and hide up here in your room like you're the victim. Mom's pretending to be strong, but really, she just doesn't give a shit. And you don't care how I feel. You're too self-centered to let another person's pain affect you. You're too stuck in your own head to have any real feelings for anyone else. Do you really care that he's dead, or is it just another reason to feel sorry for yourself?"

Angela lunged to her feet. I expected them to cry, maybe scream, then start hugging. But it got a lot worse. Angela swung quickly, surprising Maggie, and slapped her hard across the face. Then she started yelling again. "You spoiled little bitch. You have no idea what I feel or do, or what I've done for you."

Maggie hit her back, not with a fist fortunately, but with the butt of her palm, hard enough to knock her to the floor. I had seen Maggie in a fight and I wasn't about to let it continue. I got between them. They were both crying now, screaming irrationally, and Angela had a trickle of blood coming from the corner of her mouth. She turned and stared up at her sister, shocked. "What the hell is wrong with you? I'm your sister for God's sake."

Maggie wouldn't let up and when she pushed me aside, I decided to let them have it out. She was hysterical too. "Some sister. Dad is dead, and maybe he was cheating with some girl down south, but he was my father too. What hurts more than anything is that I never even got the chance to know him. I barely knew my own Goddamn father, because of you. You were his special child, the only one in this family that ever mattered to him. You made damn sure you got all of his attention so there wasn't anything left for me."

"Maggie, stop! You don't know what you're talking about," Angela begged. "We're sisters, sisters stick together."

"I'm tired of being your sister, Angela. Since I was ten years old, all I've ever heard is how I have to help you, take care of you, and be sure you're alright because you're so Goddamn fragile. Take your medication, Angela. Stop being a drunk and take care of yourself for one time in your life! You're the big sister, why couldn't you take care of me for once. Just one Goddamn time."

Angela was on her hands and knees sobbing. It broke my heart, but I figured it was time that whatever this was came out. She screamed at the floor, not even lifting her head. "But I did, Maggie, can't you see that? I always took care of you. All those years. I always did!"

Maggie turned cold suddenly. "I can't do this. Take her pills away from her, Slater. I can't do this anymore, I have to go."

She started for the door, but Angela screamed at her again. She was screaming and crying so hard it was difficult to understand what she was saying. "I am your big sister, Maggie, and I did take care of you, always. Always!" She drew a deep breath and continued between sobs. "I kept that son of a bitch off of you for all those years."

Maggie froze, then spun around. "Who? You kept who off me?"

The dread of what Angela was saying hit me, and I knelt down beside her, helping her sit up as Maggie dropped to her knees in front of her. "What are you saying Angie? You kept who off me? Dad? Did that bastard hurt you?"

"All those trips you don't remember when you were little? That's because you never went with us. He didn't want anyone else along. It started when I was twelve, and I couldn't stop it. I couldn't stop him! He was my Daddy, Maggie. Why did he do that to me?" She choked on tears and sobbed again. "I couldn't stop it, or he would have gone after you too, don't you see?"

"You're lying," Maggie said coldly. Angie continued sobbing helplessly, and she relented. "How long? How long did he do that to you?"

"He promised, he wouldn't, touch you, if I kept being with him." She was nearly incoherent, choking out the words. "When you left for college, I finally told Davey. Davey went to him and threatened to shoot him and said he would tell everyone and call the cops. That's why Daddy hated Davey so much. He never knew. He never even knew."

"He never knew what, Angela?" Maggie asked softly, her anger spent as she picked up Angela's hands. "He never knew that Davey was our brother?"

"How?" Angie looked at me quickly, but I shook my head.

Maggie sighed. "I wasn't sure, not until just now. Why wouldn't you tell me about Davey, and all of the rest of it?"

"It broke my heart, but Davey wouldn't let me tell you. He wanted to protect you. I guess because of Daddy." Angela's sobbing slowed and she found her breath. "Davey, he loved you, Maggie. He loved you so much."

"He had your eyes, Angela." Maggie leaned forward and stroked her sister's face, wiping away some of the tears. "Those beautiful, sad fucking eyes of yours. Oh my God, I am so sorry." Angela collapsed into Maggie's arms and they both started sobbing again.

I decided it was time to go home.

***

I went out to the horse barn the next day to say my farewells to Davey Templeton. Going to his grave didn't make any sense to me, because there were no memories there. Life for Davey Templeton had started and ended in the old horse barn, and it seemed like the place to say goodbye to him. I just held onto the old haying rope that was still there after all the years that had passed, thinking about some of the fun we had had as kids, and the fact that his hands had held that rope so many times.

It seemed right somehow that the man Davey had known as his father, the man who had turned away from him for all those years, had finally accepted him, when the monster that had spawned him had turned his back on him at the end. Frank Jeffries undoubtedly thought he was saving Angela when he stepped off that chair and hung himself, but the truth was that it was Davey who had saved her, time and again, holding her and loving her without condition, when an evil, twisted father, and an inexplicably cold mother hadn't.

I didn't know for sure how much Davey knew about the kidnapping of young girls or when he knew it, but I knew in the end he had made the right choices. That was enough for me, and I realized now that I didn't have any right to judge him. It was clear that Davey's life, and Angela's too, had been very different from what I thought, and much more difficult than anything I could have imagined.

As a kid I had missed Davey's need for understanding, or took it for granted because I didn't have the same needs. My mother said she would love me if I was gay, but I had never doubted that she would. Tommy Ackerman hit me with his books, and I got bigger and hit him with my fist. I'd always had the lucky kind of certainty that comes from a life unexamined, and I had expected the same ignorance from the people around me. I couldn't imagine what their lives were like because I was too caught up in my own. It was that total lack of empathy that made me miss the pain my friends were going through.

Sometimes empathy means standing in waist deep water, screaming out Metallica lyrics while you try not to drown, because you know that's what the other person needs in that moment. And sometimes empathy is pushing the neighbor kid's bike home for him, because he ran away, too afraid to face the man who is actually his father. Davey's sisters had managed to understand him in ways I hadn't, and I guess that shouldn't have surprised me.

I untied the thick hemp rope from the crossmember that had held it for as long I could remember, pulled it through the pulley and let it fall to the floor. That was our rope. Unlikely as it was, I didn't want any other kids swinging on it. I kicked it into the corner and closed the barn door behind me.

Davey Templeton had written that I was the lucky one, and he was right, if for the wrong reasons. He and his sisters had showed me what empathy was, and what friendship and love meant. That made me the lucky one.

***

"Hey, Boss man, company." Luis tipped his head toward the street.

We had just finished setting the new picture window in the latest of my remodeling projects. Maggie Jeffries stood leaning against her car, auburn hair blowing off her shoulders as the cool wind hinted at the coming winter. I tossed my gloves down and walked across the lumber-strewn yard, then motioned at the house. "What do you think?"

"It'll make somebody a good first home if you can keep the price down."

"You should buy it. We could be neighbors and run together."

"We can do that anyway. It's not that far to the Point and all you have to do is show up. Looks like you're getting in better shape. You've lost some weight."

"Construction work will do that for you, but thanks for noticing. How are things going over on Point Road? I've been keeping my distance, kind of letting the dust settle. But I'm really glad you stopped by."

"Angie says to tell you hi, and that you're invited for supper any night you want. She might even cook. She's finally taking her medication, so we only fight once in a while. She and Jasmine are even getting along. She stopped drinking twenty-four seven and she's in counseling, so that's a good thing. God knows she needs it, after everything my dad did."

"Surprised you're not on the couch right next to her. And your mom, how's that going?"

"Happier than I've ever seen her. She even called the neighbor lady up a few days ago and asked her to coffee."

"Get out. Edith?"

"Who knew they'd hit it off after all these years? A shared hatred of my father, I guess."

"How about us? My days of mooning over your sister are long gone and the Piper is going to be out of the shop any day now. There's still a thing or two I'd like to teach you."

She eyed me skeptically. "Are we talking about flying?"

"I wasn't."

"You need to meet me at Bayside tonight at eight. And wear a damn jacket so you can get in." She leaned forward suddenly and kissed me, long and hard.

I eased back. "Was that what I think it was?"

"Yeah, Slater, but did you really need a hint at this point? Eight o'clock, and don't be late." She got back in her car and put her seat belt on.

"What's at eight o'clock?" I leaned down and she kissed me again. It went on for a long time. My carpenters started cheering. She pulled back, laughing.

"We have a case, Partner. Lady on the north end got fleeced out of half her inheritance and we have to track the bastard down." She drove away and I walked back to the house where my small crew was taking a break.

"Your girlfriend, she is muy caliente, Mister Slater," Luis said, chuckling.

I stood there grinning and watching the redhead drive away. That much Spanish I knew.

"Not sure I get to call her my girlfriend yet, Luis, but I'm working on it."

End

I hope you enjoyed this "Slater Mystery" and will take just a moment to share your thoughts. Amazon has recently made the review process much easier, and it takes just a few seconds to express your opinion with some stars. Please do. Better yet, a written review tells me what you liked, or didn't, and your opinions are extremely valuable to me.

Sign up for updates at www.tjjonesbooks.com or email me at tjjoneswtr@outlook.com Your email address will never be shared.

Now available: *"The Gypsy: A Romantic Thriller"*

A mass shooting, an FBI coverup, and a wealthy madman with a hitlist and his own private militia. Adam Cain is caught in the middle with only one person to trust, the beautiful and enigmatic woman known as the Gypsy.

All Cain wanted that night was to have a few beers with his best friend, forget about the Army, forget about Afghanistan, and forget that his latest girlfriend had just walked out on him. Then a beautiful woman sat down next to him at the bar, smelling of expensive perfume and talking about second chances. Cain was just starting to think his luck had changed when four men walked into the bar and started killing people."

AND DON'T MISS ANY OF "THE SLATER MYSTERIES"

"My Sister's Detective" Eric Slater partners with his old flames' sister to investigate the death of an old friend. Mystery, Romance, and Murder on the Florida coast.

"My Sister's Fear" The romance takes off, and so do the investigations. Slater and Maggie take on organized crime to stop the trafficking of young girls on the Florida coast.

"Slater's Tempest" A missing heiress, a curious shark, and Slater thinks he's seen a ghost.

"Slater's Vendetta" Slater takes on a street gang and makes a new friend. He's ten.

2022   "Slater's Game" People are dying at Hidden Fairways, and it's not from Covid.

Made in the USA
Middletown, DE
05 September 2023

3028909R00222